A BEST BOOK OF THE YEAR

NEW YORK TIMES

NPR • *WASHINGTON POST*

LOS ANGELES TIMES • *KIRKUS REVIEWS*

NEW YORK PUBLIC LIBRARY

CHICAGO PUBLIC LIBRARY

HARPER'S BAZAAR • *TIME*

BOSTON GLOBE • *ATLANTIC*

BUZZFEED • *VOGUE*

"Electric, alive, and transportive, *Afterparties* is a glimpse of a world rarely seen in literature."
—*New York Times Book Review*, Editors' Choice

"A smart, compassionate take on the push-pull of growing up first-generation Cambodian American."
—Maureen Corrigan, *Fresh Air*, NPR

"Remarkable. . . . [So had] a literary career of extraordinary achievement and immense promise."
—Hua Hsu, *New Yorker*

"Stories that burst with as much compassion as comedy, making us laugh just when we're on the verge of crying."
—*Washington Post*

PRAISE FOR

AFTERPARTIES

"Witty and soulful stories from a writer who was just getting started. . . . So was gregarious, tattooed, queer: a big personality. He radiates in much the same way on the page. . . . [His] stories reimagine and reanimate the Central Valley, in the way that the polyglot stories in Bryan Washington's collection *Lot* reimagined Houston and Ocean Vuong's novel *On Earth We're Briefly Gorgeous* allowed us to see Hartford in a fresh light." —Dwight Garner, *New York Times*

"A wildly energetic, heartfelt, original debut by a young writer of exceptional promise. These stories, powered by So's skill with telling detail, are like beams of wry, affectionate light, falling from different directions on a complicated, struggling, beloved American community."
—George Saunders, author of *Lincoln in the Bardo*

"Marked by sharp wit and overwhelming in the scope of emotions they portray, So's vignettes offer a nuanced and compassionate view of the rich and complex experiences of a group of immigrants who dared to build new lives in an often unforgiving country." —*Time*

"The sheer richness and energy of So's narratives can't be overstated—his characters are full of love, and full of longing, and full of laughter, and full of the possibilities that life offers them and also the ones it hides. It's rare and magical and wild to find queer life, as it's *actually* lived, on the page—or on any pages—with all its multiplicities and creases and paradoxes and curves, and yet So lays it out for us, sparing nothing and giving everything. I was in awe through the entire collection—and you will be, too. *Afterparties* is an actual marvel."
—Bryan Washington, author of *Memorial*

"Luminous. . . . With profane wit and ruthless honesty, the book explores what it is to be young, brown, and queer in a world that so often prefers to see Asians as the model minority, or not at all."
—*Entertainment Weekly* (Critics' Pick)

"A bright and fearless debut, full of heart, joy, and unforgettable characters." —Douglas Stuart, author of *Shuggie Bain*

"Electric. . . . *Afterparties* is a world dappled in patterns of light and dark humor. . . . Rather than stage his characters in easily comprehensible postures, gathering them around the mythic American Dream at self-serious angles, he shows them to us as they loll about in the dream's afterparty."
—*Atlantic*

"A rollicking plunge into sex, drugs, genocide, and wicked wit."
—*San Francisco Chronicle*

"*Afterparties* weaves through a Cambodian American community in the shadow of genocide, following the children of refugees as they grapple with the complexities of masculinity, class, and family. Anthony Veasna So explores the lives of these unforgettable characters with bracing humor and startling tenderness. A stunning collection from an exciting new voice."
—Brit Bennett, author of *The Vanishing Half*

"Even when these stories are funny and hopeful, an inescapable history is always waiting."
—*Kirkus Reviews* (starred review)

"So lovingly documents his community of 'off-brand Asians with dark skin,' investing mundane moments of lived life with an extraordinary magic. While reading, you might have to occasionally pause to admire his talent, his supernatural capacity to map a story that hits every note. As you read his stories, you live them, and at their best, you forget who wrote them and why."
—*Seattle Times*

"Anthony Veasna So is a terrific writer. These wild, complex, and funny stories are brilliant in every way. They also speak in profound ways to this troubled American moment. One of the most exciting debuts of the past decade."
—Dana Spiotta, author of *Innocents and Others*

"These movingly intimate windows into the immigrant experience leave a powerful imprint."
—*Vogue*

"The nine stories here explode like fireworks, flashing between humor, dislocation, and an aura of collective longing that emerges most acutely in the generational push and pull of Stockton's Cambodian American community."
—David L. Ulin, *Alta*

"The mind-frying hilarity of Anthony Veasna So's first book of fiction settles him as the genius of social satire our age needs now more than ever. Few writers can handle firm plot action and wrenching pathos in such elegant prose. This unforgettable new voice is at once poetic and laugh-out-loud funny. These characters kept talking to me long after I closed the book I'm destined to read again and cannot wait to teach. Anthony Veasna So is a shiny new star in literature's firmament and *Afterparties* his first classic." —Mary Karr, author of *Lit: A Memoir*

"A bittersweet triumph. . . . *Afterparties* is a powerful, enduring statement in itself, evidence of how deft So was at revealing the layers of complexity within a single community." —*USA Today*

"Karen Russell, Carmen Maria Machado, Nana Kwame Adjei-Brenyah—you can count on one hand the authors of this century whose debut short-story collections are as prodigious and career-making as *Afterparties*. This lovingly specific, history-haunted comedy of Cambodian American manners should put Anthony Veasna So on smart readers' radar to stay." —Jonathan Dee, author of *The Locals* and *The Privileges*

AFTERPARTIES

AFTERPARTIES

stories

ANTHONY VEASNA SO

An Imprint of HarperCollins*Publishers*

For everyone who underestimated me, including myself.
Oh, and Alex, my love.

An extension of this copyright page appears on page 261.

A hardcover edition of this book was published in 2021 by Ecco, an imprint of HarperCollins Publishers.

FIRST ECCO PAPERBACK EDITION PUBLISHED 2022

Designed by Michelle Crowe

Library of Congress Cataloging-in-Publication Data has been applied for.

ISBN 978-0-06-304989-5 (pbk.)

22 23 24 25 26 LSC 10 9 8 7 6 5 4 3 2 1

CONTENTS

THREE WOMEN OF CHUCK'S DONUTS

The first night the man orders an apple fritter, it is three in the morning, the streetlamp is broken, and California Delta mist obscures the waterfront's run-down buildings, except for Chuck's Donuts, with its cool fluorescent glow. "Isn't it a bit early for an apple fritter?" the owner's twelve-year-old daughter, Kayley, deadpans from behind the counter, and Tevy, four years older, rolls her eyes and says to her sister, "You watch too much TV."

The man ignores them both, sits down at a booth, and proceeds to stare out the window, at the busted potential of this small city's downtown. Kayley studies the man's reflection in the window. He's older but not old, younger than her parents, and his wiry mustache seems misplaced, from a different decade. His face wears an expression full of those mixed-up emotions that only adults must feel, like *plaintive*, say, or *wretched*. His light-gray suit is disheveled, his tie undone.

An hour passes. Kayley whispers to Tevy, "It looks like he's just staring at his own face," to which Tevy says, "I'm trying to study."

The man finally leaves. His apple fritter remains untouched on the table.

"What a trip," Kayley says. "Wonder if he's Cambodian."

"Not every Asian person in this city is Cambodian," Tevy says.

Approaching the empty booth, Kayley examines the apple fritter more closely. "Why would you come in here, sit for an hour, and not eat?"

Tevy stays focused on the open book resting on the laminate countertop.

Their mom walks in from the kitchen, holding a tray of glazed donuts. She is the owner, though she isn't named Chuck—her name is Sothy—and she's never met a Chuck in her life; she simply thought the name was American enough to draw customers. She slides the tray into a cooling rack, then scans the room to make sure her daughters have not let another homeless man inside.

"How can the streetlamp be out?" Sothy exclaims. "Again!" She approaches the windows and tries to look outside but sees mostly her own reflection—stubby limbs sprouting from a grease-stained apron, a plump face topped by a cheap hairnet. This is a needlessly harsh view of herself, but Sothy's perception of the world becomes distorted when she stays in the kitchen too long, kneading dough until time itself seems measured in the number of donuts produced. "We will lose customers if this keeps happening."

"It's fine," Tevy says, not looking up from her book. "A customer just came in."

"Yeah, this weird man sat here for, like, an hour," Kayley says.

"How many donuts did he buy?" Sothy asks.

"Just that," Kayley says, pointing at the apple fritter still sitting on the table.

Sothy sighs. "Tevy, call PG&E."

Tevy looks up from her book. "They aren't gonna answer."

"Leave a message," Sothy says, glaring at her older daughter.

"I bet we can resell this apple fritter," Kayley says. "I swear, he didn't touch it. I watched him the whole time."

"Kayley, don't stare at customers," Sothy says, before returning to the kitchen, where she starts prepping more dough, wondering yet again how practical it is to drag her daughters here every night. Maybe Chuck's Donuts should be open during normal times only, not for twenty-four hours each day, and maybe her daughters should go live with their father, at least some of the time, even if he can hardly be trusted after what he pulled.

She contemplates her hands, the skin discolored and rough, at once wrinkled and sinewy. They are the hands of her mother, who fried homemade cha quai in the markets of Battambang until she grew old and tired and the markets disappeared and her hands went from twisting dough to picking rice in order to serve the Communist ideals of a genocidal regime. How funny, Sothy thinks, that decades after the camps, she lives here in Central California, as a business owner, with her American-born Cambodian daughters who have grown healthy and stubborn, and still, in this new life she has created, her hands have aged into her mother's.

WEEKS AGO, Sothy's only nighttime employee quit. Tired, he said, of her limited kitchen, of his warped sleeping schedule, of how his dreams had slipped into a deranged place. And so a deal was struck for the summer: Sothy would refrain from hiring a new employee until September, and Tevy and Kayley would work alongside their mother, with the money saved going directly into their college funds. Inverting their lives, Tevy and Kayley would sleep during the hot, oppressive days, manning the cash register at night.

Despite some initial indignation, Tevy and Kayley of course agreed. The first two years after it opened—when Kayley was eight, Tevy not yet stricken by teenage resentment, and Sothy still married—Chuck's Donuts seemed blessed with good business. Imagine the downtown streets before the housing crisis, before the city declared bankruptcy and became the foreclosure capital of America. Imagine Chuck's Donuts surrounded by bustling bars and restaurants and a new IMAX movie theater, all filled with people still in denial about their impossible mortgages. Consider Tevy and Kayley at Chuck's Donuts after school each day—how they developed inside jokes with their mother, how they sold donuts so fast they felt like athletes, and how they looked out the store windows and saw a whirl of energy circling them.

Now consider how, in the wake of learning about their father's second family, in the next town over, Tevy and Kayley cling to their memories of Chuck's Donuts. Even with the recession wiping out almost every downtown business, and driving away their nighttime customers, save for the odd worn-out worker from the nearby hospital, consider these summer nights, endless under the fluorescent lights, the family's last pillars of support. Imagine Chuck's Donuts a mausoleum to their glorious past.

THE SECOND NIGHT THE MAN orders an apple fritter, he sits in the same booth. It is one in the morning, though the streetlamp still emits a dark nothing. He stares out the window all the same, and once more leaves his apple fritter untouched. Three days have passed since his first visit. Kayley crouches down, hiding behind the counter, as she watches the man through the donut display case. He wears a medium-gray suit, she notes, instead of the light-gray one, and his hair seems greasier.

"Isn't it weird that his hair is greasier than last time even though it's earlier in the night?" she asks Tevy, to which Tevy, deep in her book, answers, "That's a false causality, to assume that his hair grease is a direct result of time passing."

And Kayley responds, "Well, doesn't *your* hair get greasier throughout the day?"

And Tevy says, "You can't assume that all hair gets greasy. Like, we know *your* hair gets gross in the summer."

And Sothy, walking in, says, "Her hair wouldn't be greasy if she washed it." She wraps her arm around Kayley, pulls her close, and sniffs her head. "You smell bad, oun. How did I raise such a dirty daughter?" she says loudly.

"Like mother, like daughter," Tevy says, and Sothy whacks her head.

"Isn't *that* a false causality?" Kayley asks. "Assuming I'm like Mom just because I'm her daughter." She points at her sister's book. "Whoever wrote that would be ashamed of you."

Tevy closes her book and slams it into Kayley's side, whereupon Kayley digs her ragged nails into Tevy's arm, all of which prompts Sothy to grab them both by their wrists as she dresses them down in Khmer. As her mother's grip tightens around her wrist, Kayley sees, from the corner of her eye, that the man has turned away from the window and is looking directly at them, all three of them "acting like hotheads," as her father used to say. The man's face seems flush with disapproval, and, in this moment, she wishes she were invisible.

Still gripping her daughters' wrists, Sothy starts pulling them toward the kitchen's swinging doors. "Help me glaze the donuts!" she commands. "I'm tired of doing everything!"

"We can't just leave this man in the seating area," Kayley protests, through clenched teeth.

Sothy glances at the man. "He's fine," she says. "He's Khmer."

"You don't need to drag me," Tevy says, breaking free from her mother's grip, but it's too late, and they are in the kitchen, overdosing on the smell of yeast and burning air from the ovens.

Sothy, Tevy, and Kayley gather around the kitchen island. Trays of freshly fried dough, golden and bare, sit next to a bath of glaze. Sothy picks up a naked donut and dips it into the glaze. When she lifts the donut back into the air, trails of white goo trickle off it.

Kayley looks at the kitchen doors. "What if this entire time that man hasn't been staring out the window?" she asks Tevy. "What if he's been watching *us* in the reflection?"

"It's kind of impossible not to do both at the same time," Tevy answers, and she dunks two donuts into the glaze, one in each hand.

"That's just so creepy," Kayley says, an exhilaration blooming within her.

"Get to work," Sothy snaps.

Kayley sighs and picks up a donut.

ANNOYED AS SHE IS by Kayley's whims, Tevy cannot deny being intrigued by the man as well. Who is he, anyway? Is he so rich he can buy apple fritters only to let them sit uneaten? By his fifth visit, his fifth untouched apple fritter, his fifth decision to sit in the same booth, Tevy finds the man worthy of observation, inquiry, and analysis—a subject she might even write about for her philosophy paper.

The summer class she's taking, at the community college

next to the abandoned mall, is called "Knowing." Surely writing about this man, and the questions that arise when confronting him as a philosophical subject, could earn Tevy an A in her class, which would impress college admissions committees next year. Maybe it would even win her a fancy scholarship, allow her to escape this depressed city.

"Knowing" initially caught Tevy's eye because it didn't require any prior math classes; the coursework involved only reading, writing a fifteen-page paper, and attending morning lectures, which she could do before going home to sleep in the afternoon. Tevy doesn't understand most of the texts, but then neither does the professor, she speculates, who looks like a homeless man the community college found on the street. Still, reading Wittgenstein is a compelling enough way to pass the dead hours of the night.

Tevy's philosophical interest in the man was sparked when her mother revealed that she knew, from only a glance, that he was Khmer.

"Like, how can you be sure?" Kayley whispered on the man's third visit, wrinkling her nose in doubt.

Sothy finished arranging the donuts in the display case, then glanced at the man and said, "Of course he is Khmer." And that *of course* compelled Tevy to raise her head from her book. *Of course*, her mother's condescending voice echoed, the words ping-ponging through Tevy's head, as she stared at the man. *Of course, of course.*

Throughout her sixteen years of life, her parents' ability to intuit all aspects of being Khmer, or emphatically *not* being Khmer, has always amazed and frustrated Tevy. She'd do something as simple as drink a glass of ice water, and her father, from across the room, would bellow, "There were no ice cubes in the genocide!" Then he'd lament, "How did my kids become so *not* Khmer?" before bursting into rueful laughter. Other times, she'd eat a piece of dried fish or scratch her scalp or walk with a certain gait, and her father would smile and say, "Now I know you are Khmer."

What does it mean to be Khmer, anyway? How does one know what is and is not Khmer? Have most Khmer people always known, deep down, that they're Khmer? Are there feelings Khmer people experience that others don't?

Variations of these questions used to flash through Tevy's mind whenever her father visited them at Chuck's Donuts, back before the divorce. Carrying a container of papaya salad, he'd step into the middle of the room, and, ignoring any customers, he'd sniff his papaya salad and shout, "Nothing makes me feel more Khmer than the smell of fish sauce and fried dough!"

Being Khmer, as far as Tevy can tell, can't be reduced to the brown skin, black hair, and prominent cheekbones that she shares with her mother and sister. Khmer-ness can manifest as anything, from the color of your cuticles to the particular way your butt goes numb when you sit in a chair too long, and even so, Tevy has recognized nothing she has ever done as being notably Khmer. And now that she's old enough to disavow her lying cheater of a father, Tevy feels completely detached from what she was apparently born as. Unable to imagine what her father felt as he stood in Chuck's Donuts sniffing fish sauce, she can only laugh. Even now, when she can no longer stomach seeing him, she laughs when she thinks about her father.

Tevy carries little guilt about her detachment from her culture. At times, though, she feels overwhelmed, as if her thoughts are coiling through her brain, as if her head will explode. This is what drives her to join Kayley in the pursuit of discovering all there is to know about the man.

ONE NIGHT, Kayley decides that the man is the spitting image of her father. It's unreal, she argues. "Just look at him," she mutters, changing the coffee filters in the industrial brewers. "They have the same chin. Same hair. Same everything."

Sothy, placing fresh donuts in the display case, responds, "Be careful with those machines."

"Dumbass," Tevy hisses, refilling the canisters of cream and sugar. "Don't you think Mom would've *noticed* by now if he looked like Dad?"

By this point, Sothy, Tevy, and Kayley have grown accustomed to the man's presence, aware that on any given night he might appear sometime between midnight and four. The daughters whisper about him, half hoping that where he sits is out of earshot, half hoping he'll overhear them. Kayley speculates about his motives: if he's a police officer on a stakeout, say, or a criminal on the run. She deliberates over whether he's a good man or a bad one. Tevy, on the other hand, theorizes about the man's purpose—if, for example, he feels detached from the world and can center himself only here, in Chuck's Donuts, around other Khmer people. Both sisters wonder about his life: the kind of women he attracts and has dated; the women he has spurned; whether he has siblings, or kids; whether he looks more like his mother or his father.

Sothy ignores them. She is tired of thinking about other people, especially these customers from whom she barely profits.

"Mom, you see what I'm seeing, right?" Kayley says, to no response. "You're not even listening, are you?"

"Why *should* she listen to you?" Tevy snaps.

Kayley throws her arms up. "You're just being mean because you think the man is *hot*," she retorts. "You basically said so yesterday. You're like this gross person who thinks her dad is hot, only now you're taking it out on *me*. And he looks just like Dad, for your information. I brought a picture to prove it." She pulls a photograph from her pocket and holds it up with one hand.

Bright red sears itself onto Tevy's cheeks. "I did *not* say that," she states, and, from across the counter, she tries to snatch the photo from Kayley, only to succeed in knocking an industrial coffee brewer to the ground.

Hearing metal parts clang on the ground and scatter, Sothy finally turns her attention to her daughters. "What did I tell you, Kayley!" she yells, her entire face tense with anger.

"Why are you yelling at *me*? This is *her* fault!" Kayley gestures wildly toward her sister. Tevy, seeing the opportunity, grabs the photo. "Give that back to me," Kayley demands. "You don't even *like* Dad. You never have."

And Tevy says, "Then you're contradicting yourself, aren't you?" Her face still burning, she tries to recapture an even, analytical tone. "So which is it? Am I in love with

Dad or do I, like, hate him? You are so stupid. I wasn't saying the man was hot, anyway. I just pointed out that he's not, like, *ugly*."

"I'm tired of this bullshit," Kayley responds. "You guys treat me like I'm nothing."

Surveying the damage her daughters have caused, Sothy snatches the photograph from Tevy. "Clean this mess up!" she yells, and then walks out of the seating area, exasperated.

In the bathroom, Sothy splashes water on her face. She looks at her reflection in the mirror, noticing the bags under her eyes, the wrinkles fracturing her skin, then she looks down at the photo she's laid next to the faucet. Her ex-husband's youth taunts her with its boyish charm. She cannot imagine the young man in this image—decked out in his tight polo and acid-washed jeans, high on his newfound citizenship—becoming the father who has infected her daughters with so much anxious energy, and who has abandoned her, middle-aged, with obligations she can barely fulfill alone.

Stuffing the photo into the pocket of her apron, Sothy gathers her composure. Had she not left her daughters, she would have seen the man get up from the booth, turn to face the two girls, and walk into the hallway that leads to the bathroom. She would not have opened the bathroom door to find this man towering over her with his silent, sulking presence. And she would never have recognized it, the uncanny resemblance to her ex-husband that her youngest daughter has been raving about all night.

But Sothy does now register the resemblance, along with

a sudden pain in her gut. The man's gaze slams into her, like a punch. It beams a focused chaos, a dim malice, and even though the man merely drifts past her, taking her place in the bathroom, Sothy can't help but think, *They've come for us.*

SINCE HER DIVORCE, Sothy has worked through her days weighed down by the pressure of supporting her daughters without her ex-husband. Exhaustion grinds away at her bones. Her wrists rattle with carpal tunnel syndrome. And rest is not an option. If anything, it consumes more of her energy. A lull in her day, a moment to reflect, and the resentment comes crashing down over her. It isn't the cheating she's mad about, the affair, her daughters' frivolous stepmother who calls her with misguided attempts at reconciliation. Her attraction to her ex-husband, and his to her, dissolved at a steady rate after her first pregnancy. The same cannot be said of their financial contract. That imploded spectacularly.

Her daughters have no idea, but when Sothy opened Chuck's Donuts it was with the help of a generous loan from her ex-husband's distant uncle, an influential business tycoon based in Phnom Penh with a reputation for funding political corruption. She'd heard wild rumors about this uncle, even here in California—that he was responsible for the imprisonment of the prime minister's main political opponent, that he'd gained his riches by joining a criminal organization of ex–Khmer Rouge officials, and that he'd arranged, on behalf of powerful and petty Khmer Rouge sympathizers, the murder of Haing S. Ngor. Sothy didn't know if she wanted to accept the uncle's money, to be indebted to such dark forces, to commit to a life in which she would always be afraid that hit men disguised as Khmer American gangbangers might gun her and her family down and then cover it up as a simple mugging gone wrong. If even Haing S. Ngor, the Oscar-winning movie star of *The Killing Fields*, wasn't safe from this fate, if he couldn't escape the spite of the powerful, how could Sothy think that her own family would be spared? Then again, what else was Sothy supposed to do, with a GED, a husband who worked as a janitor, and two small children? How else could she and her husband stimulate their dire finances? What skills did she have, other than frying dough?

Deep down, Sothy has always understood that it was a bad idea to get into business with her ex-husband's uncle, who, for all she knew, could have bankrolled Pol Pot's coup. And so, now, seeing the man's resemblance to her ex-husband, she wonders if he could be some distant gangster cousin. She fears that her past has finally caught up with her.

FOR SEVERAL DAYS, the man does not visit Chuck's Donuts. But Sothy's worries only deepen. They root themselves into her bones. Her daughters' constant musings about the man only intensify her suspicion that he is a relative of her former uncle-in-law. He has come to take their lives, to torture the money out of them, perhaps to hold her daughters as collateral, investments to sell on the black market.

Still, she can't risk being impulsive, lest she provoke him. And there's the possibility, of course, that he's a complete stranger. Surely he would have harmed them by now. Why this performance of waiting? She keeps herself on guard, tells her daughters to be wary of the man, to call for her if he walks through the door.

Tevy has started writing her philosophy paper, and Kayley is helping her. "On Whether Being Khmer Means You Understand Khmer People," the paper is tentatively titled. Tevy's professor requires students to title their essays in the style of *On Certainty*, as if starting a title with the word *On* makes it philosophical. She decides to structure her paper as a catalog of assumptions made about the man based on the idea that he is Khmer and that the persons making these assumptions—Tevy and Kayley—are also Khmer. Each assumption will be accompanied by a paragraph discussing the validity of the assumption, which will be determined based on the answers provided by the man, to questions that Tevy and Kayley will ask him directly. Both Tevy and Kayley agree to keep the nature of the paper secret from their mother.

The sisters spend several nights refining their list of assumptions about the man. "Maybe he also grew up with parents who never liked each other," Kayley says one night when the downtown appears less bleak, the dust and pollution lending the dark sky a red glow.

"Well, it's not like Khmer people marry for love," Tevy responds.

Kayley looks out the window for anything worth observing but sees only the empty street, a corner of the old downtown motel, the dull orange of the Little Caesars, which her mother hates because the manager won't allow her customers to park in his excessively big lot. "It just seems like he's always looking for someone, you know?" Kayley says. "Maybe he loves someone but that person doesn't love him back."

"Do you remember what Dad said about marriage?" Tevy asks. "He said that, after the camps, people paired up based on their skills. Two people who knew how to cook wouldn't marry, because that would be, like, a waste. If one person in the marriage cooked, then the other person should know how to sell food. He said marriage is like the show *Survivor*, where you make alliances in order to live longer. He thought *Survivor* was actually the most Khmer thing possible, and he would definitely win it, because the genocide was the best training he could've got."

"What were their skills?" Kayley asks. "Mom's and Dad's?"

"The answer to that question is probably the reason they didn't work out," Tevy says.

"What does this have to do with the man?" Kayley asks.

And Tevy responds, "Well, if Khmer people marry for skills, as Dad says, maybe it means it's harder for Khmer people to know how to love. Maybe we're just bad at it—loving, you know—and maybe that's the man's problem."

"Have you ever been in love?" Kayley asks.

"No," Tevy says, and they stop talking. They can hear their mother cooking in the kitchen, the routine clanging of mixers and trays, a string of sounds that just fails to coalesce into melody.

Tevy wonders if her mother has ever loved someone romantically, if her mother is even capable of reaching beyond the realm of survival, if her mother has ever been granted any freedom from worry, and if her mother's present carries the ability to dilate, for even a brief moment, into its own plane of suspended existence, separate from past or future. Kayley, on the other hand, wonders if her mother misses her father, and, if not, whether this means that Kayley's own feelings of gloom, of isolation, of longing, are less valid than she believes. She wonders if the violent chasm between her parents also exists within her own body, because isn't she just a mix of all those antithetical genes?

"Mom should start smoking," Kayley says.

And Tevy asks, "Why?"

"It'd force her to take breaks," Kayley says. "Every time she wanted to smoke, she'd stop working, go outside, and smoke."

"Depends on what would kill her faster," Tevy says. "Smoking or working too much."

Then Kayley asks, softly, "Do you think Dad loves his new wife?"

Tevy answers, "He better."

HERE'S HOW SOTHY AND HER ex-husband were supposed to handle their deal with the uncle: Every month, Sothy would give her then husband 20 percent of Chuck's Donuts' profits. Every month, her then husband would wire that money to his uncle. And every month, they would be one step closer to paying off their loan before anyone with ties to criminal activity could bat an eyelash.

Here's what actually happened: One day, weeks before she discovered that her husband had conceived two sons with another woman while they were married, Sothy received a call at Chuck's Donuts. It was a man speaking in Khmer, his accent thick and pure. At first, Sothy hardly understood what he was saying. His sentences were too fluid, his pronunciation too proper. He didn't truncate his words, the way so many Khmer American immigrants did, and Sothy found herself lulled into a daze by those long-lost syllables. Then she heard what the man's words actually meant. He was the accountant of her husband's uncle. He was asking about their loan, whether they had any intention of paying it back. It had been years, and the uncle hadn't received any payments, the accountant said with menacing regret.

Sothy later found out—from her husband's guilt-stricken mistress, of all people—that her husband had used the profits she'd given him, the money intended to pay off their loan, to support his second family. In the divorce settlement, Sothy agreed not to collect child support, in exchange for sole ownership of Chuck's Donuts, for custody of their daughters, and for her ex-husband's promise to talk to his uncle and to eventually pay off their loan, this time with his own money. He had never intended to cheat his uncle, he proclaimed. He had simply fallen in love with another woman. It was true love. What else could he do? And, of course, he had an obligation to his other children, the sons who bore his name.

Still, he promised to right this wrong. But how can Sothy trust her ex-husband? Will a man sent by the uncle one day appear at her doorstep, or at Chuck's Donuts, or in the alley behind Chuck's Donuts, and right their wrong for them? A promise is a promise, yet, in the end, it is only that.

AN ENTIRE WEEK HAS PASSED since the man's last visit. Sothy's fears have begun to wane. There are too many donuts to make, too many bills to pay. It helped, too, when she called her ex-husband to yell at him.

"You selfish pig of a man," she said. "You better be paying your uncle back. You better not put your daughters in danger. You better not be doing the same things you've always done—thinking only about yourself and what *you* want. I can't even talk to you right now. If your uncle sends someone to collect money from me, I will tell him how disgraceful you are. I will tell him how to find you and then you'll face the consequences of being who you are, who you've always been. Remember, I know you better than anyone."

She hung up before he could respond, and even though this call hasn't gained her any real security, she feels better. She almost wants the man to be a hit man sent by the uncle so that she can direct him straight to her ex-husband. Not that she wants her ex-husband to be killed. But she does want to see him punished.

The night the man returns, Sothy, Tevy, and Kayley are preparing a catering order for the hospital three blocks over. Sothy needs to deliver a hundred donuts to the hospital before eleven thirty. The gig pays good money, more money than Chuck's Donuts has made all month. Sothy would rather not leave her daughters alone, but she cannot send them to deliver the donuts. She'll be gone only an hour. And what can happen? The man never shows up before midnight, anyway.

Just in case, she decides to close the store during her delivery. "Keep this door locked while I'm gone," she tells her daughters after loading her car.

"Why are you so insecure about everything?" Tevy says.

And Kayley says, "We're not babies."

Sothy looks them in the eyes. "Please, be safe."

The door is locked, but the owners' daughters are clearly inside; you can see them through the illuminated windows, sitting at the counter. So the man stands at the glass door and waits. He stares at the daughters until they notice a shadow in a suit hovering outside.

The man waves for them to let him enter, and Kayley says to her sister, "Weird—it looks like he's been in a fight."

And Tevy, noticing the man's messy hair and haunted expression, says, "We need to interview him." She hesitates just a moment before unlocking the door, cracking it open. Inflamed scratches crisscross his neck. Smudges of dirt mottle his wrinkled white shirt.

"I need to get inside," he says gravely. It's the only thing Tevy has heard him say other than "I'll have an apple fritter."

"Our mom told us not to let anyone in," Tevy says.

"I need to get inside," the man repeats, and who is Tevy to ignore the man's sense of purpose?

"Fine," Tevy says, "but you have to let me interview you for a class assignment." She looks him over again, considers his bedraggled appearance. "And you still need to buy something."

The man nods and Tevy opens the door for him. As he crosses the threshold, dread washes over Kayley as she becomes aware of the fact that she and her sister know nothing at all about the man. All their deliberations concerning his presence have gotten them nowhere, really, and right now the only things Kayley truly knows are: she is a child; her sister is not quite an adult; and they are betraying their mother's wishes.

Soon Tevy and Kayley are sitting across from the man in his booth. Scribbled notes and an apple fritter are laid out between them on the table. The man stares out the window, as always, and, as always, the sisters study his face.

"Should we start?" Tevy asks.

The man says nothing.

Tevy tries again. "Can we start?"

"Yes, we can start," the man says, still staring out into the dark night.

THE INTERVIEW BEGINS with the question "You're Khmer, right?" and then a pause, a consideration. Tevy meant this to be a softball question, a warm-up for her groundbreaking points of investigation, but the man's silence unnerves her.

Finally, the man speaks. "I am from Cambodia, but I'm not Cambodian. I'm not Khmer."

And Tevy, feeling sick to her stomach, asks, "Wait, what do you mean?" She looks at her notes, but they aren't any help. She looks at Kayley, but she isn't any help, either. Her sister is as confused as she is.

"My family is Chinese," the man continues. "For several generations, we've married Chinese Cambodians."

"Okay, so you are Chinese *ethnically*, and not Khmer ethnically, but you're still Cambodian, right?" Tevy asks.

"Only I call myself Chinese," the man answers.

"But your family has lived in Cambodia for generations?" Kayley interjects.

"Yes."

"And you and your family survived the Khmer Rouge regime?" Tevy asks.

Again, the man answers, "Yes."

"So do you speak Khmer or Chinese?"

The man answers, "I speak Khmer."

"Do you celebrate Cambodian New Year?"

Again, the man answers, "Yes."

"Do you eat rotten fish?" Kayley asks.

"Prahok?" the man asks. "Yes, I do."

"Do you buy food from the Khmer grocery store or the Chinese one?" Tevy asks.

The man answers, "Khmer."

"What's the difference between a Chinese family living in Cambodia and a Khmer family living in Cambodia?" Tevy asks. "Aren't they both still Cambodian? If they both speak Khmer, if they both survived the same experiences, if they both do the same things, wouldn't that make a Chinese family living in Cambodia somewhat Cambodian?"

The man doesn't look at Tevy or Kayley. Throughout the interview, his eyes have searched for something outside. "My father told me that I am Chinese," the man answers. "He told me that his sons, like all other sons in our family, should marry only Chinese women."

"Well, what about being American?" Tevy asks. "Do you consider yourself American?"

The man answers, "I live in America, and I am Chinese."

"So you don't consider yourself Cambodian at all?" Kayley asks.

He turns his gaze away from the window. For the first time in their conversation, he considers the sisters who are sitting across from him. "You two don't look Khmer," he says. "You look like you have Chinese blood."

"How can you tell?" Tevy asks, startled, her cheeks burning.

The man answers, "It's in the face."

"Well, we are," Tevy says. "Khmer, I mean."

And Kayley says, "Actually, I think Mom said once that her great-grandfather was Chinese."

"Shut up," Tevy says.

And Kayley responds, "God, I was just saying."

The man stops looking at them. "We're done here. I need to focus."

"But I haven't asked my real questions," Tevy protests.

The man says, "One more question."

"Why do you never eat the apple fritters you buy?" Kayley blurts out, before Tevy can even glance at her notes.

"I don't like donuts," the man answers.

The conversation comes to a halt, as Tevy finds this latest answer the most convincing argument the man has made for not being Khmer.

"You can't be serious," Kayley says after a moment. "Then why do you buy so many apple fritters?"

The man doesn't answer. His eyes straining, he leans even closer to the window's surface, almost grazing the glass with his nose.

Tevy looks down at the backs of her hands. She examines the lightness of her brown skin. She remembers how in elementary school she always got so mad at the white kids who misidentified her as Chinese, sometimes even getting into fights with them on the bus. And she remembers her father consoling her in his truck at the bus stop. "I know I joke around a lot," he said once, his hand on her shoulder. "But you are Khmer, through and through. You should know that."

Tevy examines the man's reflection. His vision of the world disappoints her—the idea that people are limited always to what their fathers tell them. Then Tevy notices her sister reeling in discomfort.

"*No*," Kayley says, hitting the table with her fists. "You *have* to have a better answer than that. You can't just come in here almost every night, order an apple fritter, not eat it, and then tell us *you don't like donuts*." Breathing heavily, Kayley leans forward, the edge of the table cutting into her ribs.

"Kayley," Tevy says, concerned. "What's going on with you?"

"Be quiet!" the man yells abruptly, still staring out the window, violently swinging his arm.

Shocked into a frozen silence, the sisters don't know how to respond, and can only watch as the man stands up, clenching his fists, and charges into the center of the seating area. Right then, a woman—probably Khmer, or maybe Chinese Cambodian, or maybe just Chinese—bursts into Chuck's Donuts and starts striking the man with her purse.

"So you're spying on me?" the woman screams.

She is covered in bruises, the sisters see, her left eye nearly swollen shut. They stay in the booth, pressed against the cold glass of the window.

"You beat your own wife, *and* you spy on her," she says, now battering the man, her husband, with slaps. "You're—"

The man tries to push his wife away, but she hurls her body into his, and then they are on the ground, the woman on top of the man, slapping his head over and over again.

"You're scum, you're scum," the woman shrieks, and the sisters have no idea how to stop the violence that is unfolding before them, or whether they should try. They cannot even say whom they feel aligned with—the man, to whose presence they have grown attached, or the bruised woman, whose explosive anger toward the man appears warranted. They remember those punctuated moments of Chuck's Donuts' past, before the recession forced people into paralysis, when the dark energy of their city barreled into the fluorescent seating area. They remember the drive-by gang shootings, the homeless men lying in the alley in heroin-induced comas, the robberies of neighboring businesses, and even of Chuck's Donuts once; they remember how, every now and then, they panicked that their mother wouldn't make it home. They remember the underbelly of their glorious past.

The man is now on top of the woman. He screams, "You've *betrayed* me." He punches her face. The sisters shut their eyes and wish for the man to go away, and the woman, too. They wish this couple had never set foot in Chuck's Donuts, and they keep their eyes closed, holding each other, until suddenly they hear a loud blow, then another, followed by a dull thud.

Their eyes flick open to find their mother helping the woman sit upright. On the ground lies a cast-iron pan, the one that's used when the rare customer orders an egg sandwich, and beside it, unconscious, the man, blood leaking from his head. Brushing hair out of the woman's face, their mother consoles this stranger. Their mother and the woman remain like this for a moment, neither of them acknowledging the man on the ground.

Still seated in the booth with Kayley clutching her, Tevy thinks about the signs, all the signs there have been not to trust this man. She looks down at the ground, at the blood seeping onto the floor, how the color almost matches the red laminate of the countertops. She wonders if the man, in the unconscious layers of his mind, still feels Chinese.

Then Sothy asks the woman, "Are you okay?"

But the woman, struggling to stand up, just looks at her husband.

Again, Sothy asks, "Are you okay?"

"Fuck," the woman says, shaking her head. "Fuck, fuck, *fuck*."

"It's all right," Sothy says, reaching to touch her, but the woman is already rushing out the door.

Emotion drains out of Sothy's face. She is stunned by this latest abandonment, speechless, and so is Tevy, but Kayley calls after the woman, yelling, even though it's too late, "You can't just leave!"

And then Sothy bursts into laughter. She knows that this isn't the appropriate response, that it will leave her daughters more disturbed, just as she knows that there are so many present liabilities—for instance, the fact that she has severely injured one of her own customers, and not even to protect her children from a vicious gangster. But she can't stop laughing. She can't stop thinking of the absurdity of this situation, how if she were in the woman's shoes she also would have fled.

Finally, Sothy calms herself. "Help me clean this up," she says, facing her daughters, giving the slightest of nods toward the man on the ground, as though he were any other mess. "Customers can't see blood so close to the donuts."

BOTH SOTHY AND TEVY AGREE that Kayley is too young to handle blood, so while her mother and sister prop the man up against his booth and begin cleaning the floors, Kayley calls 911 from behind the counter. She tells the operator that the man is unconscious, that he's taken a hit to the head, and then recites the address of Chuck's Donuts.

"You're very close to the hospital," the operator responds. "Can't you take him over yourself?"

Kayley hangs up and says, "We should drive him to the

hospital ourselves." Then, watching her mother and sister, she asks, "Aren't we supposed to not, you know, mess with a crime scene?"

And Sothy answers sternly, "We didn't kill him."

Balancing herself against the donut display case, Kayley watches her mother and sister mop the floor, the man's blood dissolving into pink suds of soap and then into nothing. She thinks about her father. She wants to know whether he ever hit her mother, and if so, whether her mother ever hit him back, and whether that's the reason her mother so naturally came to the woman's defense. As Tevy wipes away the last trails of red, she, too, thinks of their father, but she recognizes that even if their father had been violent with their mother it wouldn't answer, fully, any questions concerning her parents' relationship. What concerns Tevy more is the validity of the idea that every Khmer woman—or just every woman—has to deal with someone like their father, and what the outcome is of this patient, or desperate, dealing. Can the very act of enduring result in wounds that bleed into a person's thoughts, Tevy wonders, distorting how that person experiences the world? Only Sothy's mind stays free of her daughters' father. She considers instead the woman—whether her swollen eye and bruises will heal completely, whether she has anyone to care for her. Sothy pities the woman. Even though she's afraid that the man will now sue her, that the police will not believe her side of the story, she feels grateful that she is not the woman. She understands, more than ever, how lucky she is to have rid her family of her ex-husband's presence.

Sothy drops her mop back into its yellow bucket. "Let's take him to the hospital."

"Everything's gonna be okay, right?" Kayley asks.

And Tevy responds, "Well, we can't just leave him here."

"Stop fighting and help me," Sothy says, walking over to the man. She carefully lifts him up, then wraps his arm around her shoulders. Tevy and Kayley rush to the man's other side and try to do the same.

Outside, the streetlamp is still broken, but they have grown used to the darkness. Struggling to keep the man upright, they lock the door, roll down the steel shutters, whose existence they'd almost forgotten about, for once securing Chuck's Donuts from the world. Then they drag the man's heavy body toward their parked car. The man, barely conscious, begins to groan. The three women of Chuck's Donuts have a variation of the same thought. This man, they realize, didn't mean much at all to them, lent no greater significance to their pain. They can hardly believe they've wasted so much time wondering about him. Yes, they think, we know this man. We've carried him our whole lives.

SUPERKING SON SCORES AGAIN

Superking Son was an artist lost in the politics of normal, assimilated life. Sure, his talents were often sidelined, as the store forced him to worry about importing enough spiky-looking fruits every month. (He recruited way too many of our Mings to carry through customs suitcases filled with jackfruit, bras padded with lychees, and panties stuffed with we-don't-want-to-know.) Sure, he reeked of raw chicken, raw chicken feet, raw cow, raw cow tongue, raw fish, raw squid, raw crab, raw pig, raw pig intestine, and raw—like really raw—pig blood, all jellied, cubed, and stored in buckets before it was thrown into everyone's noodle soup on Sunday mornings. When we walked into the barely air-conditioned store, we pinched our noses to stop from barfing all over aisle six, which would ruin the only aisle with American products, the one with Cokes and Red Bulls and ten-year-old Lunchables no one ate. (Though our Mas would've shoved their shopping carts right through our vomit, without blinking an eye, without even noticing their puking grandchildren—they'd seen much worse.) And, sure, Superking Son wasn't nice. He could be cruel, incredibly so. Kevin won't talk to him anymore, and Kevin was our best smasher last season.

Still, even with this in mind (and up our nostrils), we idolized Superking Son. He was a regular Magic Johnson of badminton, if such a thing could exist; a legend, that is, for the young men of this Cambo hood (a niche fanbase, admittedly). The arcs of his lobs, the gentle drifts of his drops, and the lines of his smashes could be thought of, if rendered visible, as the very edge between known and unknown. He could smash a birdie so hard, make it fly so fast, we swore that when the birdie zipped by it shattered the force field suffocating us, the one composed of our parents' unreasonable expectations, their paranoia that our world could crumble at a moment's notice and send us back to where we started, starving and poor and subject to a genocidal dictator. Word has it that when Superking Son was young, he was an even better player, with a full head of hair.

To us, Superking Son was our badminton coach, our shuttlecock king. That's who he would always be. But what was he for everyone else? Well, it's simple—he was the goddamn grocery-store boy.

WE LOOKED TO SUPERKING SON for guidance—on how to deal with our semiracist teachers, who simultaneously thought we were enterprising hoodlums and math nerds that no speak *Engrish* right, on whether wearing tees big enough to cover our asses was as dope as we hoped. And every time we had exciting news, some game-changing gossip we heard from our Mas, like when Gong Sook went crazy from tending to his crop of reefer before he could sell even one bushel, we headed for Superking Grocery Store. So when Kyle informed us about the new transfer kid—Justin—whom he spotted smashing birdies and doing insane lunges across the court, being all Kobe Bryant at the local open gym, we dropped our skateboards and rushed to find Superking Son.

We ran from our usual spot, the park where our peddling aunts never set up shop, the one next to the middle school that shut down from gang violence, and we ran because we couldn't skate fast. (Our baggy shirts went down to our knees, compromising our mobility, but who cares about mobility when you look as fly as this?) It was February, and as chilly as a rainless California winter ever got, but we worked up a sweat doing all that running. By the time we found Superking Son in his back storeroom, we dripped beads of salty-ass water from head to toe. We were a crew of yellow-brown boys collapsed onto the floor, exhausted from excitement.

Superking Son greeted us by raising his palm against our faces. "You fools need to shut the fuck up so I can concentrate," he said, even though we hadn't uttered a word. He was talking to Cha Quai Factory Son about how many Khmer donuts he wanted to order that week. Superking Son stared intently at a clipboard, as if peering into its soul, his constant pen-chewing the only sound we could hear.

"Come on, man," Cha Quai Factory Son said, "what's taking you so long?" He grabbed the clipboard from Superking Son. "Just go with the usual! Why do this song and dance every week?" He pulled out his own *un*chewed pen, and then signed the invoice before anyone could whine about merchandising fraud. "Stop second-guessing yourself," he added while shaking his head. "God, I've aged ten years waiting for you to make a decision."

"Stop giving me shit for being a good businessman," Superking Son said.

"This guy takes one econ class at comm and now he's the CEO of Cambo grocery stores," Cha Quai Factory Son teased, waving the clipboard around. "Like he's Steve Jobs and those spoiled Chinese sausages are MacBook Airs."

Superking Son crossed his arms over that semipudgy chest—over that layer of fat that had grown at a steady rate since he took over the store. "All right," he said, "everyone out of my storeroom. Y'all are sweaty as fuck and I don't want this asswipe smell sticking to my inventory. I sell food people put in their mouths, damnit."

We urged our coach to wait, each of us frantic for approval. We raved about Justin, how he could replace Kevin as our team's number one player, how Kyle swore he had served the best drop shots he had witnessed in the open gym all year.

"The open gym at Delta College?" Superking Son said, sarcasm stretching his every syllable into one of those diphthongs we learned about in sophomore English. An entire Shakespearean monologue nestled in the gaps between his words. "That's not saying much. At that open gym, I've seen players smack their doubles partners in the face with their rackets."

We only wanted to make the team better, so Superking Son's reaction disheartened us. Yet it wasn't different from what we had grown to expect from him. It wasn't worse than that time a pregnant and morning-sick Ming was found vomiting into the frozen tuna bin, ruining a whole month's worth of fishy profits, which inspired him to assign us two hundred burpees every day for a week. And it was nowhere close to that time his mom, while sweeping, slipped in the produce section and broke her hip, next to the bok choy, of all places. (We're sure this was the moment he started balding. By his fifth medical payment, he looked like Bruce Willis in yellow-brownface.) We told ourselves Superking Son was simply stressed out. Everyone, including our own parents, relied on him to supply their food. He needed to restock his shelves for the upcoming month, or else mayhem would commence, we told ourselves, as if the store didn't need to be restocked every month.

"Bring the kid to conditioning, and we'll see how quickly one of you bastards gets whacked in the head." He stepped over our bodies, grabbed the door, and looked down on us. "I'm serious," he said. "Get out or I'm locking you guys in here." His biceps flexed, that small part of his arm begging to be bigger than it was.

Cha Quai Factory Son started to leave first, but as he approached the door, he slid behind Superking Son. He massaged the shoulders of our coach, digging his big, dough-kneading hands into that perpetually tense and sore tissue. We watched as Superking Son's eyebrows furrowed in revolt, even as his mouth was forming silent moans of pleasure. "It's okay," Cha Quai Factory Son said. "Let's give this big boy his alone time so he can think about *business*." Then he patted him on the stomach and jolted out the door.

Superking Son reached out to grab Cha Quai Factory Son, almost falling over in the process. He missed, by more than he would ever admit. And as he leaned forward into the gaping hole of the doorway, watching his vendor flee from his grasp, we could tell he wanted to scream out some last remark. But he didn't. He probably couldn't decide on anything to say.

THERE ARE STORIES OF SUPERKING SON you wouldn't believe. Epic stories, stories that are downright implausible given the laws of physics, gravity, the limitations of the human body. There's the one where Superking Son's doubles partner sprained his ankle during the final match of sectionals. The kid dropped to the ground, right in the middle of the court, and Superking Son fended off the smashes of Edison's two best varsity players by lunging over his partner's injured body. He kept this up for ten minutes, until one of the Edison players also slipped and sprained his ankle, resulting in a historic win for our high school's badminton team. (They later learned the floor had been polished by the janitors, who neglected to tell the badminton coaches. The guys who sprained their ankles sued the school, won a huge settlement, and now both have their own houses in Sacramento. Three bedrooms, two and a half bathrooms, everything you could possibly want.) Then there are the many times he's beaten Cha Quai Factory Son in a singles match, often without letting him score a single point. Once, Superking Son bet Cha Quai Factory Son a hundred dollars he could beat him while eating a Big Mac, one hand gripped around his racket, the other around a juicy burger. Cha Quai Factory Son agreed, but wanted to triple the bet on the stipulation that Superking Son could not spill even a shred of lettuce. Halfway through, Superking Son had played so well, he got his friend to throw him another Big Mac, then a box of ten McNuggets. At the end of the match, the gym floor remained spotless. Cha Quai Factory Son refused to eat at McDonald's for ten years.

We didn't believe the stories at first. We thought, Superking Son's talking out of his ass. He wants to hype himself up to kids over a decade younger than him. That was why he allowed us to practice skating tricks in the parking lot and gave us free Gatorades (albeit the yellow flavor no one bought, never the light blue). Then, after we had entered high school, Superking Son took over as the coach of our badminton team. Just as he'd carried his own peers as a class-ditching player in the nineties, he coached our team through a regional championship. (There weren't opportunities to compete at state or nationals, no D1 recruiters scouting matches with athletic scholarships in their ass pockets. This was badminton, for god's sake.) Superking Son launched us to the very top of the Central Valley standings—the first time we called ourselves number one at anything. But more than that, from the little gestures—the fluid flair of his wrists when demonstrating how to hit, his ability to pick up birdies, with only his racket and foot, and send them flying across the gym to any player he chose, the way he tapped into rallies, making shots with his left hand so as not to annihilate the kid he was coaching—we had realized the stories were true.

JUSTIN WAS NOT IMPRESSED. He was the new kid who showed up to school driving a baller Mustang, and parked it next to Kyle's minivan, which was one of those beat-up machines abandoned at the local car shop and then flipped and sold to Cambo ladies like Kyle's mom, who had prayed and prayed for the miraculous day their eldest children could start chauffeuring around their youngest. (We could tell, from the way Justin spiked his jet-black hair into pointy peaks, that he had the clearest intentions to paint red, yellow, and blue flames on the driver's side of his Mustang.) So no, Justin was not impressed with the abandoned parking lots we hung out in, the mall that did so badly Old Navy closed down, the pop-up restaurants located in Cambo-rented apartments, where we slurped steaming cups of kuy teav in roach-infested kitchens, and he definitely did not see what we saw in Superking Son.

But Justin, despite the pretensions, was a damn good badminton player. Plus, after school let out, he bought us rounds of dollar-menu chicken sandwiches, giving us rides in his Mustang while we inhaled that mystery meat. And we saw where he was coming from, because this year Superking Son was indeed off.

Conditioning was a shitshow. Two weeks of Superking Son showing up late, his clothes stained with sweat (we hoped it was sweat), fish guts and pig intestines all stuck in his hair and stinking up the joint. Two weeks of him miscounting lunges and crunches and not stopping us from planking until we fell to the ground in pain—he was constantly checking his phone instead of keeping track of what we were doing. And he kept forgetting Kyle's name. Kyle, whose dad visited Superking Grocery Store every week to buy lottery tickets and fish oil pills. ("Gotta be healthy for when I'm rich," Kyle's dad often said, kissing both his ticket and his pills for good luck.) Kyle, who Superking Son practically watched grow up, as his own Ma used to babysit Kyle when Kyle was still in diapers. (Babysitting, for her, entailed hours of pushing a naked infant in a shopping cart, up and down every aisle of the store.)

"What's up with your coach, anyway?" Justin asked one day, while driving a couple of us home after practice. "I don't mean to be a hater," he continued, "but I could get better conditioning doing tai chi with the ladies in the park. Like, only the left half of my body is getting a workout, man, like if I kept doing this, my muscles will get all imbalanced and I'll topple over."

Not sure ourselves, we told him there was nothing to worry about, because sometimes Superking Son got caught up with the store. Sometimes our coach was so stressed out he didn't think straight.

"It's amazing that store makes money looking the way it does," Justin said. "It's such a dump. I hope you guys are right, though. My mom's getting on my case about college applications. She wants me to quit badminton and join Model UN, but I keep telling her that the coach is supposed to be this legend and the team can win a bunch of tournaments. Don't get me wrong, I wanna keep playing badminton, but . . . I mean, Model UN does have cute girls . . . girls that wear cute blazers . . . and know stuff about the world . . ."

As Justin trailed off, thinking about all the girls he could woo with his faux diplomacy and political strategy, we saw him slipping away from our world. We saw this college-bound city kid, this Mustang-driving badminton player, how he might be too good for our team, our school, our community of Cambos. Sure, Justin was Cambodian, but he seemed so different. That's what happens when your dad's a pharmacist, we thought. Whenever you wanted, whenever things stopped benefiting you, or whenever you simply got bored, you could just whip out something else, like a skill set in Model UN.

WE HAD THE MIND TO THROW an intervention for Superking Son. We needed to do something to keep Justin around. Every day for a week, we met during lunch as a team—sans Justin and sans Superking Son, obviously—to discuss intervention strategies, our evidence and counterarguments, who would say each point and in what order and where each of us would stand to demonstrate the appropriate amount of solidarity. We even made contingency plans, which detailed an escape route if Superking Son were to freak out and start chucking produce at our heads (it happened more often than not). But when we got to the store, ready for a confrontation, we found Superking Son in the back room surrounded by what came across as a militia, minus the rifles and bulletproof vests. We saw our Hennessy-drenched uncles, the older half siblings no one dared to talk about, and those cousins who attended our school but never seemed to be present at roll call.

Hiding behind the stacked crates, we spied on them. Superking Son was in the center of the circle, staring intently at the floor. His hand seemed stuck to his chin. Some ghostly vision played out in front of his eyes, and it shocked the color out of his face. Cha Quai Factory Son was there, too, his hands on Superking Son's shoulders, like he was both consoling him and holding him back from doing something stupid. A wave of money flashed around the circle, stopping only to be counted and recounted, probably to make sure no one had slipped any bills into his pocket. We spied on these men, each of us brainstorming reasons for this meeting that were innocent and harmless, not doomed by the laws of faux-Buddhist, karmic retribution. If we're being honest with ourselves, none of us figured out a reason worth a damn.

BADMINTON PRACTICE ONLY WORSENED. Superking Son coached everyone who wasn't Justin, hardly acknowledged his existence, really, not even to reprimand him. Yet when we crowded around a Justin match and cheered as he nailed smash after smash, we swore we saw Superking Son in awe of his talent, analyzing Justin's form and failing to find any faults. Sometimes we saw something darker, something seething, within his stares, some envy-fueled plot being calculated in his expression, but then he'd break his gaze from Justin. He'd check his phone, for the thousandth time, and allow anxiety about his father's store to overtake, yet again, his love for badminton.

Justin, for his part, ignored Superking Son's directions and went through practices entirely on his own agenda. That first week, they interacted only through overriding each other's instructions to Justin's hitting partner, Ken, that poor (we mean this literally) and unfortunate schmuck. Every practice, Superking Son told Ken to practice his drop shots, Justin said smashes, Superking Son yelled at Ken for not doing drop shots, Justin still refused to change drills, Superking Son made Ken do laps around the court for undermining his authority, and so on until Ken bailed on practice, hid in the locker room, and smoked a cigarette for his nerves. (He stole packs from his dad, who bought wholesale Marlboro Reds from Costco. His dad handed them out to relatives in Cambodia like candy, in an effort to pretend he was a hotshot tycoon of the American stock market.)

Shit escalated one day when Superking Son was so late that Justin, fed up with waiting, assumed the role of the coach and started practice. We knew that Superking Son would be pissed. We'd seen him fire cashiers for breaking his policy of absolutely no double-bagging, and butchers for using his personal office bathroom. (Of course, he always rehired who he fired, regardless of how much pig blood they got on his toilet and fake granite tile, because his mom would hear from so-and-so's Ming about so-and-so's kids needing food on the table and braces to fix their fucked-up teeth, because they couldn't eat said "food on the table" with overbites or crooked-ass incisors.) At the same time, we were *with* Justin. We felt his exasperation. We looked like a gang of dopey assholes on the floor of the gym, sitting in our butterfly stretches, acting like we were doing substantial exercises, so the janitors would refrain from kicking everyone out to start polishing the floor.

Justin had charisma, so he was able to take charge of us—high schoolers the same age as him, more or less—and not sound like a douche. For once, practice was going smoothly, with nothing jamming the flow of our hitting drills, no kinks or delays or conflicting instructions. We became a well-oiled machine of flying birdies, of perfect wrist technique. Not a single one of us smacked another player in the head with a racket.

"What the hell is going on here?" someone yelled, and we looked over to find Superking Son at the double doors. His phone seemed permanently attached to his hand, he was gripping it so hard. Muffled voices, all sinister and incomprehensible, issued from the speakers.

"You weren't here, so I started everyone on drills," Justin replied, his back facing our coach. He resumed correcting the way Kyle was gripping his racket, while Superking Son stormed across the gym. Soon they were standing within inches of each other. The eyes of Superking Son were fiery. Justin's stayed cold.

"You wanna repeat that, boy?" Superking Son said, sounding like he was competing in a who-can-breathe-more-heavily contest. He straightened his posture, locking his shoulders in place, and we noticed how much taller Justin was than our coach.

"We waited over an hour. You expected us to sit around doing nothing until you got here?" Only a whiff of defiance, of sarcasm, could be heard in Justin's voice, but still, Superking Son puffed up his chest. Still, his face blazed with anger, the red color rushing to his hairless scalp. We braced ourselves for Superking Son to power up into fire-breathing uncle mode, for Justin's even-toned facade to disintegrate in the face of pent-up refugee shit and the frustration of premature balding. We thought this was the last of Justin the effective team captain, the stand-in coach, or at least that their confrontation would make practices even more awkward, and then drive Ken into a full-blown, black-lungs kind of smoking addiction.

Superking Son sucked in a deep breath, and right when we thought he was on the verge of exhaling some grade-A-level-beef insults, hesitation rippled through his expression. Maybe he'd realized it was petty for a business owner, a full-ass adult who paid taxes, to pick fights with a baby-faced high school junior. He could've been the level-headed coach we knew he could be. Superking Son, after all, was one of the good Cambo dudes. He didn't belong to that long legacy of shitty guys who spent their adulthood sleeping on their mom's couch and eating their mom's food. (Kevin's older brother, for instance, had a decent job at the DMV, and still, he lived with his mom, paid her jack shit in rent, and never did chores because he was too busy playing his video games. One day his mom snapped, of course, how could she not? She ended up lighting his PlayStation on fire, just as he was reaching the end of a Call of Duty campaign.) By taking over the grocery store, Superking

Son had done right by his father's life. He had sustained his father's hard work, and made sure that that poor refugee's lifetime of suffering didn't go to waste. We looked up to Superking Son. We wanted to keep it that way.

A dial tone emitted from his phone, and its dull beat gradually subdued Superking Son. "Everyone go back to what you were doing," he yelled, before scrambling his way to the exit. Frantically, he called back the person he was so afraid of snubbing, and as he disappeared into the hallway, we heard him chant, Sorry, sorry, sorry, off into the distance.

THE NEXT WEEK Superking Son posted the roster for our first meet of the season. We crowded around the sheet, ready to be disappointed or excited by our ranking, to see if we had secured a lucrative JV or varsity spot, or whether—god help us, humble Buddha bless us—Superking Son had cast us aside to the exhibition matches, where we would rot away with the freshmen. We knew Justin would be rank 1 for varsity singles—the official team captain. For weeks, we'd been saying that he would destroy the other rank 1 players, to the point of making them all cry, even the smug kid from Edison with the racket that cost a thousand dollars. (Joke was on him, he got scammed into buying a counterfeit Yonex deluxe by Kyle's enterprising cousin.)

"Come on, guys, hurry up," Justin said, standing behind us with his arms crossed. "I wanna score some food from the 7-Eleven." Slowly, each of us turned our heads.

We stared at him. "What's the deal?" he asked. "You know I need my steak-and-cheese taquitos."

It straight up stunned us, the revelation that Justin was not rank 1 for varsity singles, not even rank 2, but a laughable rank 3. Our jaws dropped to the floor; we were speechless. Ken—who was now rank 1, our appointed team captain, and totally unprepared to take on that burden—started breathing so heavily he was almost hyperventilating (the cigarettes didn't help). But Justin only stood there, silent, staring at the roster, though there was so much space between him and that piece of paper, who knew where he was looking?

Maybe Justin was scheming a course of action, a vengeful and ingenious plot, that challenged Superking Son's decision. He could raise hell the way his mom did when Mr. White had the gall to give him a B minus on his Civil War paper. He could also quit, call it a day, and take his taquitos home to eat. Studying his face, we couldn't tell exactly what he was thinking or feeling. What we did see wasn't so much anger as pity. It was sad for Superking Son to stoop this low. Here was one of the good Cambo dudes, fucking over a teenager half his age. Maybe we saw in Justin's expression what we all thought ourselves.

THIS TIME WE CONFRONTED SUPERKING SON, for real. We found him sitting on a footstool, in the aisle at the edge of the building, where customers hardly ever went. Surrounding him were pots and pans, cheap oriental dishes and bowls, and the incense packets for praying that Mas bought to convert their bedrooms into DIY mausoleums for those who had died in the genocide.

We squinted because the store's lights didn't reach this aisle, and we looked down on him because he was basically squatting on the ground. Please, Coach, we pleaded, you have to reconsider the rankings for our team.

"Don't you fools get tired of coming to my shithole?" he asked in a daze, looking straight through us, either at some vision of his life, or at the spilled rice he would be—sooner or later, after harassing his cashiers to do the job—forced to sweep up himself.

We appealed that we were being serious, that it didn't make sense for Justin to be rank 3, not even in terms of stacking our roster against other teams. We would lose all our number 1 and number 2 matches, we argued. Superking Son sighed, not really registering our words. His face beamed the mug-shot look that our Gongs wore when we dragged them to eat unlimited soup, salad, and breadsticks at the Olive Garden—that expression of unresisting contempt.

"Badminton," he said, and sighed again. "My body was made for it, I swear. Never had to think, formulate decisions, be all stressed out when I played a match. I just . . . did it, you know? I used to think, like really I fucking did, that something about Cambos like me, Cambos who grew in the real hood, just made for good badminton. We didn't have it as good as you guys do now. We dealt with a fuckload of bullshit." He spread his arms wide, signaling to us that the store was simply that, a fuckload of bullshit. Or maybe he was referring to us, our problem with his latest decision as a coach, how we always consulted him for guidance, and the pressure of living up to all *our* bullshit.

Superking Son went on talking, and a couple of us peeled off to grab Gatorades and snacks. We needed sustenance to keep listening to his tirade on the generational ethics of badminton. "You motherfuckers will never really get it," he said. "Just like those deadbeats my age, who will never understand the Pol Pot crap."

We began stuffing our mouths with Funyuns wrapped in dry seaweed. We asked him how any of this was related to our team roster, with Justin's ranking, with us.

"How many times do I have to hammer this into your dense skulls?" he said. "Badminton is a balancing act. You need both strength and grace. You need to smash the birdie with just the flick of your wrist. None of that tennis nonsense of swinging with your whole stupid arm. And to master the gentle tap of a drop shot, you gotta use the force of your entire body to lunge across the court. Then you halt your momentum, right before impact, and make the hit. You think your all-star player is good, but I've seen him driving around that tacky-ass Mustang." For a second, we were scared that he would call us out for getting rides from Justin, for buying into his richness. "He's a spoiled dipshit," Superking Son continued. "His dad walks around like that flashy pharmacy makes him better than the rest of us. And his mom, don't get me started—she doesn't even shop here! She considers my store beneath her, can you believe that? You should hear the way his parents talk big and proud to anyone stupid enough to listen. They brag and brag that their son's a genius, that he will go to a real university, that he studies so fucking hard, like he's slaving away by reading SAT books and studying calculus. Man, that dumbass kid doesn't know shit about working hard. Which means he doesn't know shit about badminton, because badminton takes work—real work! You gotta practice until your racket wrist feels like it's on fire. When I was your age, I used to do conditioning workouts while stocking these very shelves. I'd curl boxes of those fucking chips you're eating, with only my wrists!"

Just then, he jerked backward and knocked over a stack of dishes, which prompted half of us to nearly choke on our Funyuns. We had no response to Superking Son, of course, partly because of his crazed logic, but mostly because we didn't agree. It was hard to do well in school, especially as a Cambo. And weren't we supposed to aspire to the status of Justin's family? Weren't we supposed to attend college and become pharmacists? Wasn't that what our parents had been working for? Why our ancestors had freaking died? But we couldn't think of how to express this, how to reason against a guy who carried so much emotional baggage that we almost felt obligated to tip him for his labor.

"Shit," Superking Son said, "badminton was the only thing that made me happy. What a goddamn joke." He dropped his face into his palms. "This place is so fucked."

We looked around the store—at the meat counter lined with blood and guts, at the sacks of long-grain rice piled to the ceiling, and at the oily Khmer donuts supplied by Cha Quai Factory Son, the ones that tasted so good it was difficult not to eat yourself sick. All of a sudden, the building looked sparser, paler, like the walls had caught the flu.

Were the fluorescent lights dying above us and messing with our vision? Had we never seen the store from this aisle? We asked, Why not take a break from coaching, just for a couple of weeks. We urged Superking Son to focus on his father's business, assured him that in the meantime, we could run practices on our own. Justin could watch over our drills and give us pointers, though we didn't mention this last point. We weren't dumbasses. We sensed that the store was off, and we needed him to fix it.

"I can't stay here all day. There's no good reason." We watched him slowly rise to his feet. He prepared himself to face whatever had driven him to the aisle in the first place. "This store . . . disgusts me," he said, mostly to himself. "It always has." He brushed his shirt off, like he saw what was so disgusting crawling over his belly, like the literal essence of Superking Grocery Store had laid claim to his body.

IT WAS QUIET the next few days. Superking Son kept canceling practices, ordering us each time to stay at home and rest. We noticed strange behaviors, and no one would explain them to us, not our loudmouthed Mings and Mas, not Cha Quai Factory Son—why Superking Son had closed the store randomly in the middle of the weekday, why he had failed to appear at Kevin's second cousin's engagement party. Justin, too, was a mystery. He skulked the halls, calculating his next move against Superking Son. At lunch, he ranted that not holding practices, so close to an upcoming meet, was an affront to our manhoods.

The afternoon when practice resumed, Justin bought us bean-and-cheese burritos, and even splurged on a forty-four-ounce mango Slurpee that we all passed around. He didn't mention Superking Son the entire school day. His attitude struck us as weird, but we would never turn down free food. We hadn't received a break since Kyle's half sister's other half brother was promoted to assistant store manager at the nice Walmart. (Every Cambo in the hood had enjoyed the hookup, with a 10 percent discount and extra food samples, until the dude got himself fired for hooking up with his girlfriend in the bathroom.)

Stretching and warm-up went as smooth as ever, in the sense that Superking Son was typically late and not present. Justin offered to lead us through some drills. At first, we were hesitant. "It'll be chill," he said, too eager in his voice to sell us on the "chill" factor. "What's the worst that could happen?"

And, obviously, the worst did happen. Okay, maybe not the worst; regardless, shit went down when Superking Son walked in, looked up from his text messages, and found himself amidst a shuttlecock tornado, before getting whacked in the head, with a racket, by a clueless freshman. "What the fucking shit is going on here?" he yelled, after grabbing the freshman's racket and throwing it to the ground. In response, Justin began cracking up—either hysterically or fake hysterically. He hunched over, his arms wrapped across his stomach. "You wanna start something, don't you?" Superking Son said, pointing at Justin. "You're trying to get me all riled up."

"Good job, Einstein, you totally found me!" Everyone

turned toward Justin. He was walking through the players, stepping on fallen birdies along the way. "I challenge you to a match," he now said, stopping in front of our coach.

Reactions of confusion and doubt ran through the team, while Ken suddenly gasped for air. (Which was probably that smoker's lung he was developing.)

"You're serious?" Superking Son said, imparting to his words as much condescension as possible. Though it hardly mattered, as Justin's posture was completely upright to emphasize his height.

"Yeah, and if I win," Justin said, "you gotta make me rank 1."

Superking Son bellowed an unsettling laugh. "What's gonna happen when you lose?"

"Then I'll quit," Justin said. "As simple as that. You won't have to deal with me undermining your whole I'm-the-coach-and-I-demand-respect routine."

"That's boring," Superking Son scoffed.

"Fine," Justin said, "if I lose, I'll serve as designated birdie collector for every practice and meet." Our own ears perked up at this proposal—cleaning up the mess of white feathering nubs was easily the worst thing about competitive badminton. "And I'll shut the fuck up and stay at rank 3."

Superking Son yanked the racket out of Kyle's hands. "Deal, you stupid shit."

We crowded around the centermost court, the only spot that was well lit by the crappy lights. Superking Son offered Justin the first shot—saying, "Show me what you got," as he handed over the birdie—and right as Justin served, Superking Son charged to the net. He smashed the birdie so hard it ricocheted off the ground and whacked Ken in the face, imprinting a massive red welt. *Damn*s and *Ooooohhhhh*s came from the team as Ken yelled, "My face! My fucking face!"

From the beginning, the two opponents were akin to dance partners. Superking Son lobbed the birdie, but Justin only drove it back, resulting in a grand volleying of net killings, no one scoring for what seemed like forever. Then Justin deployed a series of risky drop shots, with Superking Son, as he trained us to do, always springing forward in a powerful anticipation that Justin, like clockwork, braced himself against using that flawless gripping technique of his. And, of course, it goes without saying, whenever one of them jumped into the air for a smash, the other crouched to the floor and retrieved the thunderous strike, recovering quickly from the bruises piling up on his shins.

The most beautiful and impressive badminton unfolded before our eyes. Their playing fed off their opponent with the intensity of two Mas trash-talking their grandchildren. Feet glided across the court, bouncing, lunging, leaping. Racket strings trembled. Birdies flew impossibly close to the net. Both were so effortless in their technique, so in tune with their own and each other's bodies, they appeared otherworldly, steered by a godlike puppeteer. We exclaimed at every point and unthinkable save. We rooted until all the incredible smashes averaged out into the same perfect shot.

And then our voices crapped out on us. Our tired eyes

found their sheer athleticism routine. The second half of the match turned downright boring. Instead of paying attention, some of us opened our textbooks and studied. Ken lay down on the bleachers with an ice pack attached to his swollen cheek. Others busted out a deck of cards and started a round of big two. (If anything, the big two game became more riveting. Kyle squandered his ace of hearts, lost ten bucks, and completely upended his weekend plans—the bet required the loser to drive the winner's Ma to the temple, the one in the boonies next to the bad Walmart.) Superking Son and Justin were too good. They predicted each other too well. Neither player ever gained more than a two-point lead. There was no drama, no tension or grit, no underdog who could rebound and surprise us. And when Superking Son scored that final winning shot, no one really gave a shit. Even Justin seemed apathetic.

But Superking Son gave tons of shits. He pranced around his side of the court, ran victory laps, and stomped his feet so hard we're pretty sure our half-deaf, half-dead, he-should-retire-but-tenure-is-cushy-and-the-pension-sucks-post-housing-crisis teacher of boring British plays and poems (it was no wonder why kids barely make it to community college) heard him from across campus. He yelled "Fuck yes!" over and over, like outplaying and defeating a high schooler was better than all the sex he'd ever had (which was probably true, given his luck with women). He shifted into the Cambo taunt mode of our elders, donning the same antagonism our moms did whenever we tried to buy new shoes not on sale, our dads whenever we prioritized our homework over the family business, our Mas and Gongs whenever they heard our shameful Khmer accents, and our siblings and cousins whenever we dared to complain about the responsibilities they had previously shouldered, about enduring what could never match what had already happened to everyone we know.

"Who else wants a piece of me?" Superking Son yelled, beating his chest with his racket-free hand. He traversed half the gym to direct his taunts not only at Justin but also at every guy in the room. "None of you have what it takes. None!" He seemed blinded with misguided passion, the bulging veins of his fat neck pumping blood straight to his eyeballs. "Get out of my fucking face!" We felt the spit flying from his slobbering mouth and onto our skin.

Our memories fade around the time Superking Son was challenging *us* to matches, even the poor freshmen on the exhibition team, pointing with his racket at kid after kid and repeating, "Come on! Show me what you got!" like a robot stuck in an infinite loop. What we remember was this: the shock of witnessing Superking Son's inflated ego spurting all over the gym. Our bodies settling into pity. We looked at our beloved coach, an overgrown son prone to anxious, envious tantrums, who was fed up with his place and inheritance, who was perpetually made irritated, disgusted, paranoid, by his own being, and then we looked at each other. Right there in the gym, Superking Son screaming in our faces, we made the collective decision, silently, almost telepathically, that one, Superking Son was an asshole (a tragic one, but still an asshole); two, we had too many assholes in our shitty lives; and three, we didn't have enough asswipes to deal.

LOOK, WHAT CAN WE SAY? We were busy. We had our own responsibilities and expectations we were always on the verge of failing. And sure, there were signs. Tons of them, if we're being honest.

First, our Mas started complaining about the lack of fresh vegetables and fruit. Green papayas as old as their concentration-camp-surviving eyes were decaying on the shelves of the produce section. Then shadowy Cambos started rolling into the store, not to shop for rotting papayas, that was for sure. They rushed through the aisles, sometimes with loads of packages, sometimes in the middle of the afternoon, sometimes at closing, never to be seen exiting the premises. After a while, Superking Son banned us from the back storeroom altogether. That giant bulky guy, the ex-army Cambo (the one took Kevin's sister to prom), guarded the door behind the meat counter. Superking Son hardly ever trekked there himself, not even to play spider solitaire on his ancient HP computer.

We'd seen it happen to Cambo businesses before. We saw it when Angkor Noodles Lady hired a cook who made soggy-ass noodles. (The old cook pulled a classic drunk dad—he went on a bender for a week. When his wife found him, he was passed out at a roulette table in Reno and had gambled away their daughter's college fund.) Angkor Noodles Lady borrowed more and more money from the higher-up Cambos. Each month she promised to pay them back the full amount, plus whatever interest that had accrued, once her business picked up. Business never picked up (the kuy teav was that soggy and gross), and the restaurant floated on Cambo community money until Angkor Noodles Lady finally decided to ditch town. Hiding out in Bakersfield, in the guest room of her nephew's house, she nursed a boxed-wine addiction until she died of liver complications.

Now, Superking Son isn't dead, don't worry. We see him out all the time, usually at the good pho place, usually with Cha Quai Factory Son, who has been ranting about the same bad investment plan for years. (It involves mass-producing in neon party colors those weird suction cups that make Cambo moms look like they're getting abused to people with white savior complexes.) When the store closed and Superking Son had nothing to offer the higher-up Cambos, not even his back room to use as their headquarters, his own mother saved his skin by selling her house and paying off his debts.

We don't know how Superking Son makes a living anymore, but sometimes, if you're lucky, he'll appear at an open gym. He'll play a match or two, give some pointers on form. His lunges and smashes will strike you as impressive for someone his age, someone who probably has knee and wrist pain. Halfway through the session, he'll leave the player queue and perch on the bleachers. He'll watch a crew of younger Cambos play the game that, according to him, was the only thing that made him worthwhile as a person. When open gym is over, you'll drive home, and if you're taking Pershing Avenue to Manchester Street, you'll pass what remains of Superking Grocery Store. And even though the building has been empty for years, gathering dust and gang signs like flies to a pile of bloody meat, even though the community has moved on to bigger and better shit, like college degrees and Costco bulk food, you'll swear, on the graves of all those murdered Cambos, on every cupping bruise your mom self-inflicts to rid her flesh of trauma, we promise you'll swear that the stench of raw fish, and raw everything else, never got the memo to quit and relax. Seriously, you can trust us.

MALY, MALY, MALY

Always they find us inappropriate, but today especially so. Here we are with nowhere to go and nothing to do, sitting in a rusty pickup truck, the one leaking oil, the one with the busted transmission that sounds like the Texas Chainsaw Massacre. Here we are with the engine running for the AC, the doors wide open for our bare legs to spill out. Because this, right here, to survive the heat, this is all we have.

An hour ago we became outcasts. One of us—not me—would not shut the fuck up. And since the grandmas are prepping for the monks and need to focus, we've been banished outside to choke on traces of manure blown in from the asparagus farms surrounding us, our hometown, this shitty place of boring dudes always pissing green stink.

And according to the Mas, everything about us appears at once too masculine and too feminine: our posture—backs arching like the models in the magazines we steal;

our clothes—the rips, studs, and jagged edges—none of it makes sense to them. The two of us are wrong in every direction. Though Maly, the girl cousin, strikes them as less wrong than the boy cousin, me.

"Ma Eng can suck my dick," Maly says, still not shutting the fuck up, her long hair rippling in the gas-tainted breeze of the vents, her blond-orange highlights dancing, or trying to, anyway. "What is up her ass? Seriously, I should have a say in this party's fucking agenda. It's my birthright!"

"At least Ma Eng gives a fuck about you," I say, my chin resting on the steering wheel. Under the truck, the cracked concrete of Ma Eng's driveway seems to be steaming, and I swear the very dust in the air is burning, it's so hard to breathe. We can't even listen to the radio, you know? Can't focus on anything but our own sweaty boredom. I look up at the harsh blue sky, how it crushes the squat duplexes of G Block. I am trying to deprive Maly of my full attention, but her vivid presence, that vortex of cheap highlights, it exhausts my energy. Plus, she's slapping the side of my head.

"Ves, Ves, Ves!" Maly says. "Look at me!"

"Jesus," I whine, batting her hand away. "I thought you 'gave zero fucks' about this party. Why do you care if they're making amok or not?"

"It's what *I* want to eat, okay, and it's *my* dead mom." She violently throws her head sideways, cracking her neck. "I mean, apparently she's not *dead* dead, anymore, but still . . ."

Unsure of what to say, I clench my teeth into a lopsided smile. I can't help but admire her looks, as I always do.

Almost with pride. Maly's got it going on, no matter how disheveled. Even today, on this random August Sunday, as we wait to celebrate the rebirth of her dead mother's spirit in the body of our second cousin's baby, she looks good. Her left leg's thrown up onto the dashboard, and I wouldn't be surprised if she started clipping her toenails. She's in a pair of jean shorts she stole from our other cousin, who was too chunky for them anyway, and a white T-shirt cut into a tank—also stolen—which she's stuffed down her panties so you can notice her thin waist. Hard to say if it's intentional, the way her clothes fit, all these hand-me-downs, which is the effect she uses, I guess, to chew up guys too dumb to realize she will spit them right out.

Through her cheap sunglasses, I see her bug eyes looking at me and past me at the same time, an expression affirming how I feel sometimes, like she's *my* responsibility, like I'm a dead broom reincarnated into a human, my sole purpose to sweep away her messes—whatever Maly happens to shatter next.

"Stop being dramatic," I tell her, my hands tapping the steering wheel. "You know it's all bullshit—the celebration, the monks, our third cousin or whoever the hell she is." I'm not sure I believe what I'm saying or if I'm just trying to make Maly feel better. "It makes zero sense, right?" I add. "Like, I'm no expert, but why would your mom reappear over a decade later?"

Maly shrugs her shoulders, indifferent now, too full of herself to entertain my attempts to console her. It reminds me of our sleepovers. Whenever my dad got stupid drunk, my mom would send me to Ma Eng's. He was never violent in front of me, but who knows what happened between my parents when I was sleeping on Maly's bedroom floor, especially in those years when my dad was jobless—after his restaurant failed and before he started cooking lunch for a rich-kid school—and when it became obvious I wasn't, you know, a normal boy, that I was a girly wimp who despised sports and watched weird movies. I was a precocious freak who came out before puberty, and I was clearly doomed. It's hard enough for people like us, my mom would say. All very cliché, in that gay sob story kind of way, but I can't explain it any better than that. They are my immigrant parents.

Anyway, every night of what my mom called "bonding time with grandma," even though technically Ma Eng's my great-aunt, Maly would nudge me awake with some fake urgent question, like was she actually pretty, or even that funny? For weeks, she obsessed over our eighth grade English teacher, how he claimed she wasn't ready for the high school honors track and then refused to write her a letter of recommendation. Why do teachers always hate me? What if that stupid dirtbag is right? Every night I told her, You're awesome, everyone's a dick, and so on, only to discover that she'd fallen asleep before I even stopped talking.

I was always there for Maly, right where she wanted me, on the floor beside her bed, doling out reassurances until she sank into her dreams. Though maybe she's getting worse these days, needier than usual. Because in less than a week, I'm heading to a four-year university in LA, while Maly's stranded, stuck with Ma Eng for another two years, at least, as she makes do with community college.

Maly has closed the passenger door and is now sticking her head out of the window. She leans her right hip against the door, presses her left foot onto the center console, holding herself in place for a moment, grabbing on to the truck's roof, until she steadies herself into a stillness, like she's posing for a famous photographer. I watch her, skeptically, as she dares to go handless, crams her fingers into her mouth, and whistles a deafening sound.

"Get over here, bitch!" she shouts, and my limbs tense up.

Jogging toward us now is Rithy, his arms bulging around a basketball, baggy gym shorts flopping. He looks like he always does, all brown-kid swagger. He's the kind of guy who recites 50 Cent lyrics and loves *Boyz n the Hood* and *8 Mile* even though he doesn't—I suspect—get their political themes. This summer Rithy and Maly started fucking, which makes sense, as both of them have dead moms and shitty dads, but now I have to remind myself that I've *also* known Rithy forever. That he's not just Maly's personal plaything. Her boy toy, as she calls him.

Maly returns to her seat and tilts her sunglasses down while licking her teeth. Rithy's not even at the truck yet, but there it is: *Lolita*. Neither of us has read the book, and only I've seen the movie, but working at the video store, we both stare at that fading *Lolita* poster. Usually stoned. Stoned enough we get sucked into those heart-shaped glasses, that chick's wild, don't-give-a-fuck look, the crazy bravado of that tagline—HOW DID THEY EVER MAKE A MOVIE OF *LOLITA*?—as we burn illegal DVDs for our dipshit uncle to rent out.

"Aren't you supposed to be, like, setting up a *party*?"

Rithy teases as he leans against the truck's door and stretches out his legs. He's sweating all over, probably from shooting hoops at his cousin's house, and I can almost smell him. Everything Maly says about his body swirls in my head.

"We've been exiled," she tells him flatly. "'Cause every Ma has been a psycho since the genocide. It's like, as long as they don't overthrow a government and, you know, install a communist regime, they aren't being total dicks." Pleased with herself, Maly laughs.

"Your Ma's hella rad, you know it," Rithy responds. "Old lady comes through with the beef sticks." He raises the bottom of his shirt to wipe the sweat off his forehead, flashing that flat stomach of his. I don't even care if it's intentional. "What time's the party again?"

Maly flings both her hands toward the duplex, as though pushing it all away. "Go ask Ma Eng yourself. I'm fucking tired of her bullshit."

"Girl, just tell me," Rithy says, biting his lip.

"Look, we can be late for my dead mom's birthday bash, okay, it's *fine*." She closes the distance between her face and Rithy's. "We're young and beautiful and the concept of time is a fucking buzzkill."

"Six is fine," I chime in.

"Oh, hey, Ves," Rithy says, oblivious to my focus on the veins of his forearms. "Excited for college?"

"You got any weed, Rithy?" Maly interjects, slamming back into her seat.

Rithy twists his face into an even bigger smile. "You know I do."

With barely a nod, Maly tells me she'll be right back,

that if I leave she'll be pissed. She gets out of the truck and walks Rithy to his uncle's duplex, just down the block, as if leading a disoriented puppy home. His hand slides down her back to hover over her ass, which sways just enough with every step. He cocks his head slightly, to witness Maly by his side, before looking forward again. Even from here, I can tell how enraptured he is by her, how much his own dumb luck astounds him, that he should be so blessed this early in his life, all of us only three months into adulthood.

AND HERE'S THE PART WHERE shit gets common, right? Or rather, here's the part that makes outgrown Power Rangers twin sheets feel pretty awesome, allowing the srey to understand how men see her thick eyeliner and her fake nails, letting the proh assert power, for just a moment, over his own dark skin and his addict father with the bad, broken English. Here's the part that seems like a revelation until it's forgotten as life is lived, because nothing's special about an adulthood spent in the asshole of California, which some government official deemed worthy of a bunch of PTSD'd-out refugees, farting out dreams like it's success intolerant.

This is the part just like the thai lakorns, those soap operas from Bangkok dubbed into Khmer and burned onto wholesale discs from Costco. The srey—raggedy and poor, flush with the blood of forgotten royalty, angry from the backstabbing of wills and inheritances—cons her way into the arms of the prince whose family is the very cause of her misfortune. She allows the scheme to redeem her family's name to blind her to the feelings of real love developing beneath the high jinks, the pratfalls, her awkward but whimsical personality. Little does she know, everything will soon feel like a missed opportunity, as the prince enlists in the army to prove his manhood, because every Thai prince in every Thai soap, like every shitty proh in every shitty neighborhood, always craves some higher purpose.

For now, though, the srey basks in the prince's hot breath, the shock of secret touches, the rush of manipulation. And, hey, at least she isn't the sidekick, the faggy best friend. Because there he is, in every episode of every different version of the same dumb story: the kteuy, sidelined to the bleachers, baking in the sun, expected to get off not by his own proh but simply by the idea of the srey he supports getting hers.

Of course, all these depressing thoughts aside, I am relieved, regardless of how demeaning it feels, to have some peace as I wait for Maly and Rithy to finish fucking. I'm even happy for her, that on this nightmare of a day, she can find solace in her boy toy's tight body. Though I'm assuming that's how Maly feels about it. She hardly ever talks about her mom in a serious way.

I look into the windows of the duplex where Ma Eng has lived since the eighties, since before Maly's mom, her niece, committed suicide, and long before she took in Maly when Maly's dad proved just another fuck-off Cambodian man. Ma Eng's pointing antagonistically at the other Mas in her kitchen, instructing them on how to cook certain dishes—not amok—for the party tonight. She's probably still pissed that Maly's shown so little respect for the ceremony's preparations. I wonder how Ma Eng must feel right now, clinging to the desperate wish that her dead sister's dead daughter has another chance at life, that the forces of reincarnation are working their voodoo spells to rebirth lost souls. Especially those who died as pointlessly as Maly's mom, an immigrant woman who just couldn't beat her memories of the genocide, a single mom who looked to the next day, and the day after that, only to see more suffering.

Honestly, if I think about it too hard, I get really mad. I know it's terrible to ask, but why did Maly's mom even *have* a kid? And why does only she get to tap out of living? Well, joke's on her, I guess, because now she has to deal with yet another life, and in G Block, too.

Ma Eng's garage door opens, an uproar of Khmer thundering out of the house. Two Mas I recognize from the video store begin sweeping the concrete floor, where we will pray and eat during the party, on sedge mats that imprint our legs with red, throbbing stripes. Again I turn to face the kitchen windows, but Ma Eng has walked out of my sight. Wrapping my hands around the steering wheel, I think about driving off to college right now, leaving behind my worthless possessions, my secondhand clothes—all of it. I could finally start my life, with a blank slate. Only I can't, not yet anyway, as the Mas helping Ma Eng have parked their cars behind mine, blocking the driveway indefinitely.

I AM ABOUT TO FALL ASLEEP, the cold air from the vent and the oppressive dry heat of the afternoon competing for my skin, when Maly jumps up from under the car window and screams, "Boo!"

"What the fuck is wrong with you?" I say through the coughing fit I've been shocked into, as Maly recovers from laughing hysterically at her own antics.

She throws a joint into my lap. "Say thank you," she tells me, and waves at the Mas in the garage with a fake smile. They only stare at her, clutching their brooms like they're prepared to whack us. "Least now we won't be sober for this shit."

Yet again, like all the times she hid alcohol or lube in my bedroom, offering me a share, Maly looks out for me while remaining, to the very core, self-absorbed. "Well, we can't smoke it here," I say. "Not in front of Ma Eng's henchmen."

We agree to toke up in the closed video store, because we enjoy messing with our uncle's stuff when we're high, so we start walking the quarter mile to get out of G Block, passing duplex after duplex, all of them packed with Cambodian families and guarded by chain-link fences and patches of dirt where grass should be. Halfway to the store, I see the pink duplex my parents rented before we moved, and I remember that G Block used to be called Ghetto Way. I think of how lame and uninspired everything is, these nicknames, this neighborhood.

By the time we reach the video store's strip mall, we're drenched in sweat. The Iranian man who owns the liquor market is smoking a cigarette on the sidewalk. He ignores us, too busy leering at the Vietnamese boys outside the Adalberto's. They are throwing cherry poppers at each other's feet and passing around a Styrofoam cup—probably horchata, that's the big hit at Adalberto's—and I imagine these boys growing up into Rithys and pairing off with their own Malys. The boys now explode into laughter as one of them freaks out over the sparks of those mini firecrackers. The poor kid bolts away and Maly shouts, "Run, Forrest, run!"

Inside the empty store, we light the joint, both take hits, and then I watch Maly shuffle through the art house films our uncle inherited from the previous owner. Usually she goes straight to the back room and sprawls onto the couch, but not today. She's pretending to be a customer, for shits and giggles, and I guess I'm also pretending, by being around her. We usually split an extra-large horchata, too, and if we have enough cash a carne asada burrito—the California kind, stuffed with french fries—but only Maly manages to never gain weight, that asshole. Really, I shouldn't be complaining, even if the weed's making me bloated. I'm okay, body-wise, and the handful of times I cruised in Victory Park I learned that guys aren't picky as long as my mouth is wet and I keep my teeth in check. It was Maly, of course, who taught me how to give a proper blowjob.

I suck in another drag and take in the front room. The tacky sales rack of ten-dollar Angkor Wat shirts. The clueless stupidity of our uncle placing the candy dispensers—which are for kids, obviously—right next to the dirt-red curtain of the porn section. The store's supposed to look like a Blockbuster, but the shelves and bins are spaced out unevenly, with some aisles fitting only one person and others wide enough for jumping jacks. Right now, Maly's in a small aisle and I'm in a big one, the "horror" DVD island separating us.

Our uncle, who's actually the cousin of both my mom and Maly's mom, peaced out to the homeland for the month—probably to play house with his second family—leaving his younger brother in charge and us with the spare keys. With our older uncle gone, our other uncle disappears from lunch till closing on most days. He also refuses to work on the weekends, so the store's not open right now. A week ago, we were told to burn copies of the latest shipment of thai lakorns, to make ourselves *useful* at work, but instead we take turns smoking weed in the alley, and then pig out on candy bananas from the dispensers. We get up from the couch to man the cash register only when the front door jingles. I'm not about to spend my last week at home ripping bootleg soap operas on DVD Shrink with a second-rate laptop. Maybe that's why all the G Block grandmas are so cranky, so filled with contempt, like they're on some karmic warpath of eye rolls. We haven't burned the new thai lakorns, and thus we have cheated them of their one pleasure here in America, thousands of miles away from anything they can actually stand. At least that's what I think to myself, now, stoned as fuck.

"Swear to God," Maly says, still wearing her oversize sunglasses, even here, in this illegitimate video rental business. "These movies are fucking *weird*." In the dark reflection of her lenses, I see Maly draping me in her mom's old dresses as I wobbled on high heels, our lips painted red, eyelids smeared with shadows, before we screened another movie—like *Candyman*, we viewed that one so many times—on the PlayStation 2 my dad bought me, even though he couldn't afford it, hoping I'd be like the normal boys. "Earth to Ves!" she shouts. "The fuck's a Videodrome?"

I snap out of my daze to squint at the DVD she's now holding, by the corner like it's a dirty diaper. "Oh, yeah, I've seen that one," I say, recalling the last time I watched an actual good movie with Maly—*Suspiria*—and how she couldn't stop cracking up. Fucking idiot, Maly said when a character fell into a pit of wire and got her throat slit. "It's about this lame white guy," I explain, "who's obsessed with a TV station called Videodrome." I hit the joint and blow rings of smoke into the air, which Maly studies closely, scrunching up her face. "The station plays, like, snuff porn. You know, people being sex-tortured."

"Why not jack off to actual snuff porn?" Maly asks. "Why even bother with a dull artsy film?"

"It's a metaphor," I answer.

"And the metaphor means . . . what?"

"It's about how we are constantly violated by the media and . . . like . . . TV commercials . . ." I pause to flip through the thai lakorns Ma Eng forced us to watch as kids, which makes me, stupidly, think of my college essay topic: how our Khmer lessons were dubbed Thai shows with confusing plots, shitty camerawork, and female characters who all spoke with the voice of the same voiceover actress. I wrote about that, Maly, my gay sob story. "There's this part of the movie," I continue, "where the white guy's stomach turns into a vagina, you know, and then some other white guy forces a videotape into his vagina-tummy. . . . The rape of our minds, or some shit."

I don't admit that when I first saw this scene, I found it tempting, and hated myself for that. Instead I pass the joint.

"That's fucking idiotic." Maly breathes the smoke into and out of her lungs, leaving the joint hanging from her mouth like a French girl in a Godard film, only brown and poor. "Raped by the media," she says, and kills the rest of the joint. "Would we even *know* English without Judge Judy?"

"Guess it's the only way we survived," I say, still searching, absentmindedly, for a thai lakorn I might recognize, for something that really pulls, or strikes, me. "Like, we had to let ourselves be violated by all those shows we loved as kids . . . *Full House*, *Step by Step*, *Family Matters*—Steve Urkel fucked us in the brains every day after school on ABC Family. 'Did *I* do that?'"

"Ves . . . that's, like, really messed up," Maly replies, and we stare at each other in silence, for a split second, before sliding into laughter.

We stay giggling until a thai lakorn finally catches my eye. "Oh, shit, remember Nang Nak?" I pick up the DVD and hold it over my face, covering my bloodshot eyes with the image of a demented woman, all black hair, pasty skin, and ghostly presence, like the Thai, low-budget version of *The Grudge*. When I lower the DVD, Maly's face looks frozen.

"Holy fuck," she says, removing her sunglasses. Without much body awareness, it seems, she tries to climb over the movie bin, almost in slow motion, as though the air has turned into a thick mud. Somehow she makes it to my aisle, struggling, tumbling onto the floor, kicking the entire Kubrick section, and right after she recovers from that unnecessary stunt, she snatches the DVD from my hands. "I haven't thought about this in years. Is this the whole thing?" She peers over the Khmer words she can't even read. "Wasn't it, like, ten thousand hours long?"

"I mostly remember that crazy shrieking," I say, and start impersonating Nang Nak as a vengeful mother spirit, but Maly doesn't react, so I shut up, mid-haunting screech. Then I examine her expression as she contemplates the faded DVD cover, her puffy eyes locked in a staring contest with Nang Nak's.

An eternity passes before Maly suddenly says, with a strange sincerity, "I've always thought Nang Nak was a badass." She lifts her head, and her eyes, dark orbs in the dim light, cut straight through me. "I'm serious," she says, "like . . . *fuck*, man. She haunted those assholes for years."

Just then I wish Maly could move to LA with me, that we'd keep hanging out until one of us—Maly, obviously—got discovered by some Hollywood hotshot, and then maybe I'd make movies of her, because she'd probably be a great actor, actually, the perfect muse, and what else was she going to do? Though that's also the last thing I want, and besides, I'm not attending film school. I applied and was accepted, but it was too expensive.

"I know it's stupid," Maly adds, almost shaking, "but I want my mom, like, out there, you know? Like . . . shouldn't *she* get to torment everyone, too . . . everyone who wronged her . . ."

"Right," I begin to say, unable to finish my thought. I'm not even sure I understand what she means. I place my hand on her shoulder—a useless move, I know, but it's the only thing I can offer. We hold this position, not talking or making eye contact, until Maly stops trembling. Then she nudges me off and throws the DVD down the other aisle.

She shouts in my face: "You know what we should do right now? We should play a fucking movie! One last time before you, like, leave me *forever*, you dick asshole. And let's make it big this time—epic. Okay? Let's fucking watch a porno! Seriously, stop talking about vagina-tummies and just watch some *porn* with me. See how long it takes for our minds to feel violated by the media, you know?"

I'm not sure how to gauge her enthusiasm, but then Maly dashes for the porn section. "It won't be weird," she says, her voice moving farther and farther from me. "'Cause you're gay and I'm a girl!"

The porno Maly chooses to screen on our uncle's digital projector comes across as standard shit—bright lights flattering to nothing but bouncing breasts and engorged clits and veiny dicks, all stilted dialogue and stilted facial expressions and stilted moans, the porn actors as enviable as they are gross. The whole shebang. Too many POV shots, too many close-ups meant to put the viewer right there. Seeing a sloppy wet penis enter a sloppy wet vagina, from above, going in and out with the practiced tempo of professionals, strikes me as yet another drama for the ages I am meant only to witness, rather than learn from, like the Olympics or presidential debates. My own penis feels faint, nonexistent, and not just because Maly's presence has scared it into hiding but also because I can barely project myself onto the digital projection; what am I, really, but a knockoff version of the woman getting pounded, my dick vestigial and just . . . in the way?

It's beside the point, though, whether I see myself in this porno world—where a mustachioed plumber can unclothe a big-tittied MILF with a devious smirk, an arch of the eyebrow—because, as always, Maly is forcing herself into the center of my perspective, obstructing my view of the giant, high-def vagina.

"Look . . . he's literally fucking my brains out," Maly says, standing in front of the wall we are using as a screen. From where I'm sitting on the couch, the colossal dick appears to thrust in and out of her left ear, across and through her face.

"That's cool," I say, with a half-heartedness I don't try to hide.

"The hell is your problem?" Maly snaps. "That was hilarious," she says, pacing back and forth, as she always does when her high peaks, her attempts to be fun crossing into belligerence. The image of straight sex contorts around her body, wrapping her in fleshy colors.

"Calm down, okay?" I say. "It's *your* porno."

Maly places her hand on her hips and strikes a pose, shooting me an exasperated look, and then sits down.

The porn actors are now fucking more aggressively, and I expect Maly to start heckling them, to crack a joke about the guy's grunting or the woman's moaning. I want her to make a comment that confirms the insanity of this situation. Anything that would align us together as observers of the world, of everyone else but us, outsiders who can see through the bullshit; but instead, she just goes sullen. Lost in thought, she studies the porno. So we sit in silence as the scene nears its climax, as the male actor pulls out of the female actor, as he masturbates vigorously and she writhes in ecstasy, her vagina almost calling out to his penis to unload itself. And unload it sure does, all over her inner thighs, so much so that Maly, jumping from her seat, seems to be exploding herself with some newfound motivation.

"I need to see this baby," Maly says, darting to the door.

Cleaning up so I can run after her, I stop the film and struggle to find the DVD case. Then, before I hit the eject button, the frozen image compels me to pause, and sit there, dumbfounded, stoned. I am entranced by the cum covering the woman's bottom half, though not the vagina itself, and, despite my own preferences, this reminds me of failure, somehow. Failure in its most legit form.

BY THE TIME I CATCH UP with her, Maly's jumping the fence of our second cousin's duplex. Maybe our second cousin wouldn't mind that we're sneaking into her house, but I'm too high and paranoid to deal, and apparently Maly doesn't care about anyone's privacy or taking the extra steps to ask for permission. Anyway, it's too late to calm her down, convince her this may be unwise—breaking into the nursery of a baby who happens to be her dead mother—so I follow her nervously through the back door.

Our second cousin's napping on the couch, and I fight the urge to yell for Maly to abort her mission, to grab her by the shoulders and remind her that none of this matters, that we shouldn't partake in the stupid delusions of old people wishing their lives had gone another way, that we have each other, just as we always have, even if we're about to be separated by three hundred miles, a whole mountain range. Fuck everyone else, I want to say, for burdening the two of us with all their baggage. Let's go back to minding our own business, anything but this. Who cares about our family? What have they ever done but keep us alive only to make us feel like shit?

We find the baby's room without any mishaps, other than my growing sense of unease about following Maly down this fucked-up rabbit hole of hers. Once inside the bedroom, Maly cautiously approaches the sleeping baby. She shakes her head and clutches the rails of the crib. She looms over this tiny and new body of the mother she grew up without.

"It's uglier than I thought it would be," Maly says.

"What did you expect?" I ask from behind her, wondering what she is seeing in the baby's face, whether she recognizes a flicker of her mother's soul, or nothing at all.

"I . . ." She shakes her head again, but quickly this time. "Who do you think my kid will be?"

"You actually believe this?"

"I mean, hypothetically. What if it's Ma Eng? You know, after she dies."

"Now *that* would be serious karma."

"Shit, that'd fucking suck," Maly says. "I have zero interest in facilitating the rebirth of Ma Eng. She'll pop from my vagina reeking of tiger balm, pinching my ears 'cause she's, like . . . already disappointed in me. No way I'm unleashing Ma Eng onto the world all over again."

We laugh until we don't, and endure a silence together, with her back still turned to me.

Finally: "I'd totally have an abortion if I knew—like *really* knew—that Ma Eng was gestating inside of me."

"Even as a dead embryo, or even reincarnated, she'd haunt the fuck out of you."

"Probs," Maly responds, glancing at me from a slant. It's almost like she can't move away from the baby, like something's forcing her to confront it. "Ves . . . is it weird I want my mom reborn as . . . *my* child?"

"I don't think so," I answer. Because what else can I say?

Watching as she redirects her gaze, as she lowers her hand into the crib, I can't help but imagine Maly hurting the baby. I know that doesn't make any sense, but I worry she's about to do something terrible, even as she caresses its head, delicately, with the gentlest touch of her fingers.

"I've changed my mind," Maly says. "She's actually pretty cute."

And this, out of everything, is what chokes me up. The air suddenly stuffy, I feel the cramped dimensions of the room, the dry roof of my mouth, all the words trying to claw their way out of my throat. *Fuck*, I now think, teary-eyed, trespassing not in our second cousin's house but in Maly's world, her one opportunity of peace with this baby. Of course Maly would want to be with her mom, no matter how. Of course she never needed me, not really. Maybe I was the one who was angry, with Maly's mom, with everyone, this entire time. Just me.

Right then, Ma Eng opens the door, presumably to collect our second cousin's baby for the party. Her eyebrows collide. She's surprised to see us, but she only tells us to hurry up, that the food is ready, the monks are at her house, and then orders us to bring the baby. So Maly swoops it up and turns around. Standing before me, her reincarnated mom pressed against her body like armor, Maly looks natural, as if she's been preparing to hold this baby her whole life, her cocky anarchy so easily swept away.

"Let's go," she whispers, following Ma Eng.

It takes me a second to realize Maly is talking to the baby, and I find myself overwhelmed by the quiet of the nursery. For a moment, I am the only person in the neighborhood separate from the celebration, from the grandparents and the parents, including my own, and the babies. From all the generations, old and new, dead and alive, or even reborn. Staying here, in Maly's wake, I understand how truly alone I am.

THIS NIGHT—after the monks bless Maly's reincarnated mom, after everyone toasts the baby and feasts on food the baby can't even eat, after our drunken uncles sing too many karaoke songs, and after Rithy whisks Maly away, for only an hour, to bring her back with nothing but hickeys—I dream I'm in the Videodrome. Around me towers of TVs broadcast the programs meant to brainwash our minds, the conspiracies of our time on every channel, including Maly's lives playing in tandem on hundreds of screens. In every single one, she's a different girl, with different caretakers who express their affection in odd ways, who sacrifice too much to raise her, who abandon her for various reasons. Self-loathing scumbags and narcissistic good guys and corrupt role models of all genders float in and out of her lives, hurting her most of the time, but others, when she's lucky, they push her into something like happiness. Regardless, she eventually has kids, sometimes many, sometimes only one, all of them growing up with forms of entitlement she never understands, all of them loved by her, fiercely, no matter what. And still, every iteration of Maly's life, despite any trace of rebellion, any nitty-gritty details, they all map out to a similar pattern, follow the same arc into the very same ending.

Surrounded by visions of Maly, I regret that I won't remember each of her lives, but I will keep this: standing here in the Videodrome, watching my cousin grow into the same mother across all her reincarnated selves, as I wonder about my kteuy-ness, how it fits into the equation before me, and doesn't.

Then I wake up. I rise out of my twin bed, look around my room, the sunlight from the window exposing the floating dust, like the phantom beam of a projector. And finally, I start packing.

THE SHOP

Dealing with customers, I usually called Dad the owner, or the main smog technician if we needed to sound legit, but as a kid, I had always considered him just another Cambodian mechanic—a stereotype, one who'd pinched enough pennies to open his own car repair shop. The summer after college, I felt like a real dumbass for having thought so little of Dad, but in my defense, that was what Cambo men did. They fixed cars, sold donuts, or got on welfare.

At least according to Doctor Heng's wife, who always, whether her car needed repairs or not, nosed her way into the waiting room of the Shop. Back in our refugee days, when Cambos had just come to California, only *her* husband had stayed in school long enough to do something legitimate with his life, like become a doctor. She spoke about her husband's virtues a ton at the Shop, especially after I'd graduated, failed to get a job with my symbolic systems degree—a concentration meant for coders not smart enough for the hardcore stuff—and moved back to the Central Valley from the Midwest. Her hair done up into a misshapen lump, makeup a shade too light, Doctor Heng's wife would materialize out of nowhere, swinging the sleeves of yet another floral silk blouse, then plop herself in front of the air conditioner and say things like, "My husband, Doctor Heng, he never looks up a thing when he diagnoses a patient. He is so much smarter than other men. He remembers everything."

One day, when I'd just started working at the Shop again, Doctor Heng's wife went on a tirade about how lazy guys were in my generation. "What is wrong with you boys!" she was saying. "Not one Cambodian man since my husband, Doctor Heng, has become a doctor here in America, not even those born with citizenship! My generation came here with nothing. We escaped the Communists. So what are boys like you doing?!"

I was busy handling a customer who was getting impatient about his car. "Let me consult the main smog technician," I said to him, trying my best to communicate through my expression that Doctor Heng's wife was harmless, despite her tone, and despite her aggressive hair.

After the customer went outside to take a phone call, Doctor Heng's wife approached the counter and then whacked me on the head with a rolled-up magazine. "Why did you not become a doctor?"

She tried whacking me again, but I stepped out of her reach. "Ming, please stop," I said. "Violence will not solve our problems, and neither will the model minority myth."

"Useless big words," she scoffed. "That is all you learned going to college." I laughed. It was hard to argue with her.

No one knew why Doctor Heng's wife came around so much, not even Mom and her gossipy friends, but her daily visits had been happening since Dad first opened the Shop. They happened when I was twelve and Brian and I took turns depositing checks at the bank across the street, which dumbasses tried robbing so often it was later replaced by a Church's Chicken. They happened when I was seventeen and studying for the SATs while customers muttered passive-aggressive things to Dad for raising his prices. And they happened when I started hanging around the Shop again, not because Dad paid me—why would I get paid when Dad was already supporting me?—but simply because I had nothing better to do.

Brian thought that Doctor Heng's wife, in her younger days, must have fallen in love with Dad, only to lose all hope after he had proposed to Mom within an instant of their meeting. Following this logic, stopping by the Shop was simply Doctor Heng's wife rubbing it in our faces that her life had turned out amazing, so much better than she had ever imagined when dreaming about Dad—with her Lexus and Omega watches and Louis Vuitton bags smelling of fresh leather, all of them so giant I swore they had gained consciousness and could swallow me whole, were I to transgress their master.

Who knows? Maybe Brian was right. Though Dad couldn't have cared less. He barely acknowledged Doctor Heng's wife half the time, nor anyone else who wasn't a customer. Most of his day he spent fixing the mistakes his guys made—a transmission misdiagnosed, an alignment over-rotated, a customer's car interior smudged with oil because one of the guys had forgotten to lay on the seat a clean protector sheet. Dad was a real softie for his fellow Cambo men. He had hired as many friends as he could, way more than the Shop could actually afford, and let them get away with anything. It was a beautiful enterprise, no matter how flawed, the way Dad sustained so many people, a whole ecosystem, both in terms of providing a service to the neighborhood and also providing twelve Cambo men with jobs. He even paid some of them under the table so they could qualify for welfare, but only the guys with kids. Dad's epic tolerance for his guys was actually how we got in trouble in the first place. I mean, how we got in trouble when I worked at the Shop full-time, as an adult of sorts. By no means was this the first time the Shop had been in deep shit.

Anyway, at the end of July, Ohm Young left the keys in the ignition of a customer's truck after test-driving its repairs. He'd parked the truck in the strip mall beside to the Shop, where we left the cars that were all done, right in front of the tiny hair salon that also functioned as a massage parlor and full-service mani-pedi spa, not to forget that it was the only decent joint to buy coconut rice wrapped in banana leaves. By the next morning the truck had disappeared. Technically, Ohm Young worked as the assistant manager, though he never really did that much assistant managing.

"Ahhhh, sorry boss," Ohm Young said. "I do not know

what happened." He shrugged, and Dad was shocked into a stupid awe as he tried processing his assistant manager's feat of nonchalance.

"What do you mean you do not know what happened?" cried Doctor Heng's wife, who was present, of course, to witness their exchange. "You lost a car! Not a *piece* of car. An entire *car*!"

"All right, all right, it is going to be okay," Dad said, reassuring everyone in the waiting room, except himself, because he looked a tad bit nauseated, too pale to register as okay. "Toby, go look for the car," he said to me then. "Please, oun, just do it."

It was a near-impossible task, contingent on the idea, I imagined, that some drunken homeless man had stumbled into the truck and taken it for a joyride around the block. Which, in fact, *had* happened once, years before. The homeless man was named Ace, and he returned the car himself, walking right up to the counter and handing Dad the keys like the Shop was a rental company. A younger version of myself would've resisted Dad's request—how many good-natured Aces did he think existed in the world?—but I couldn't hold it against him for wanting to try, for hanging on to a shred of hope that everything might turn out fine, that the worst parts of his life were over, so nothing happening now could be that bad.

"Okay, I'll go," I said, and he forced a smile, tried his best to seem optimistic. Dad was one of those guys who smiled and laughed constantly, but never without a sad look in his eyes. I'd realized this about him shortly after graduating. One of Dad's other guys, Ohm Luo, a smog technician who didn't do much smog checking, had cracked a joke about always finding himself in oppressive regimes—first under Pol Pot, then under his wife, and now Ohm Young had driven their whole neighborhood mad practicing the electric keyboard during block parties—which made Dad laugh and laugh, and when he stopped laughing, and his eyes caught mine, I saw it, that look of faint, enduring grief.

Realizations I should have had as a kid were, I guess, what kept me mopping the floors of the Shop. Really, I needed to apply for jobs in the Bay Area, jobs with equity and benefits, not just free lunches with Dad and his fake best friend, Ohm Sothuy, who owned a rival car repair shop on the other side of the Costco. I knew I was supposed to find a legitimate job, but at this point in my life, dumb epiphanies about home seemed so precious, urgent, fleeting.

"I will come, too," Doctor Heng's wife said to Dad, clutching her Louis Vuitton bag as if prepared for battle. "I need to talk to this guy over here, anyway," she added, gesturing toward me.

Doctor Heng's wife and I climbed into my Honda Accord, which was twenty years old but would never die, no matter how much it wanted to, as Dad kept fixing our cars to run forever. There was a comfort to driving this car, which had been passed from Mom to Brian and then back to Mom and finally to me, but it did have subpar air-conditioning.

"My hot flashes are bad, bad, bad," Doctor Heng's wife said, fanning herself with my expired registration sheet. "When you marry a girl, make sure her mother is not having a bad menopause. It is genetic, you know. Everything is genetic. Everything gets handed down."

"I'm gay," I told her, turning onto Swain Road, one of the residential streets by the Shop. I drove as slowly as possible so we could check the cars parked on the street. "We're looking for a 2005 Toyota Tundra truck," I added. "It's like a muddy gold."

"Yes, I know," she responded, though she for sure *hadn't* known. She was now fanning herself with a Louis Vuitton wallet that matched her Louis Vuitton bag. "You can still marry a girl," she said, and I half expected her to start speculating about the genetics of gayness in my bloodline.

"I am well aware of that," I said, "the fact that I am allowed, legally, to marry a woman."

Then Doctor Heng's wife pinched my cheek and jumped into a monologue: "Stupid! Listen to me. I am being serious, like I am always being. I do not joke, and do not assume anything I say is a joking matter. I only have the best and smartest intentions for you and everyone your age. Why are boys so dense? Gay boys should be less dense than other boys, no? So how come you are not? Marry a girl because that is what you should do. I am not saying you cannot be gay. How hard is it to be normal and gay? This is the plan. You will marry a girl from Cambodia, a nice girl, a girl from a good family, a rich family, a princess from a rich family, and her parents will pay you fifty thousand, fifty thousand at least, to marry their daughter and get her a green card, and you and this girl will have children, because that is what you should do, have children. And after five years, when the girl succeeds the citizenship test, you can divorce her and get joint custody of the children. Then you will invest your fifty thousand in the stock market. Your life will be established. You can be as gay as you want after your life is established. That is the plan."

Her monologue waned as we merged onto a busier street, as Doctor Heng's wife now listed the companies CNBC had marked as optimal investments. We passed six fast-food chains and three parking lots. Then, at El Dorado Street, Doctor Heng's wife yelled at me to pull into the lot of Angkor Pharmacy. I parked, and as Doctor Heng's wife was leaping out of my car and charging into the building, I considered her plan for my life. The whole premise was hilarious to me. It transformed my future into a slapstick comedy, similar to *The Wedding Banquet*, but this time starring off-brand Asians with dark skin.

Looking around the strip mall, I saw the Dollar Tree where I would buy my school supplies and the record store where I would shoplift from because the sheet music for my piano lessons had been, like the lessons themselves, stupid expensive. There was also the cheap sushi restaurant with amazing fatty tuna and terrible imitation crab—a combination that never made sense to me—where I had told my high school girlfriend, and prom date, that I was gay, and finally, at the edge of the lot, there was the Cambo grocery store that Mom still visited sometimes, but only when she was pissed off at the owners of the better Cambo store. A group of dark Asian kids in baggy clothes, reminding me of my childhood friends, were rushing toward the Cambo store with dollars in their hands—though I probably imagined the cash part—their limbs awkward, lanky, spastic, and as I watched them move with such speedy motion, I remembered being younger and how I so desperately wanted to rush away from the valley where my parents had been dumped, gripping whatever promise I had in my fists. Real Possibility, I had convinced myself, existed in the big cities on TV, metropolitan areas where Real Life unfolded, where I could be as gay as I needed to be. Wishing my car's air-conditioning wasn't faulty, I wiped the sweat off my forehead, before thinking, *I can't believe I am sitting in this beat-up Honda, a college graduate, and entertaining the prospect of marrying a Cambodian princess for money.* Even so, it was such a heartfelt idea, to think an arrangement like that, the stuff of farce, could actually bridge worlds.

Inside Angkor Pharmacy, Doctor Heng's wife was leaning against the counter, engaged in a conversation with the owner, who was just then rummaging through a pile of papers and nodding his head at such a steady rate he definitely wasn't listening at all. When she got back in the car, I asked, "Did you get your prescription?" but she only looked at me confused, like my question was so dumb she could hardly process it.

"Prescription?—What are you talking about?" she responded. "I came to propose a new business plan for Angkor Pharmacy. They need to start selling more than just medicine. Look at how well Walgreens is doing!" And when I started laughing at that, she shot me an angry glance and said, "What did I tell you? Do not laugh at me. I am *not* a funny woman."

But I couldn't help it. Hands gripping the steering wheel, I just couldn't stop laughing. "So there are other 'dense boys' you give advice?" I said, choking on my corny joke as I exited the parking lot.

"You are not my only concern," she said.

We drove through a few more neighborhoods after that, searching for the lost truck, listening to a CD of old Khmer songs, the same CD that had been stuck in the stereo since the Honda had belonged to Mom. I barely understood the lyrics, aside from a few phrases in the choruses, but I knew the melodies, the voices, the weird mix of mournful, psychedelic tones. When I tried articulating my feelings about home, my mind inevitably returned to these songs, the way the incomprehensible intertwined with what made me feel so comfortable. I'd lived with misunderstanding for so long, I'd stopped even viewing it as bad. It was just there, embedded in everything I loved.

Back at the Shop, the owner of the lost truck was screaming at Dad, about suing us, about rallying the neighborhood to take its business elsewhere. Dad responded by explaining that the police were currently investigating the truck's location, that he'd sent his own son to search for it, that he would take responsibility for the financial burden of buying a new car. Ohm Young and I listened from the garage. Standing there, I could already imagine Dad leaving the waiting room, masking his panic with blankness, only for Ohm Young to shrug off his blundering self, for an encore of that astounding nonchalance, and say, "Sorry, boss, I do not know what happened."

Business went into a slump after that. The truck was never found. Some regulars stopped being regulars. When he came over for family dinners, Brian started conversations about Dad selling the Shop, ridding himself of all that business overhead, and investing instead in rental properties, which he'd wanted Dad to do for a while. At the time, Brian was a real estate agent and sold houses on the side of town with fancy gated communities, so he knew about this stuff.

"Look, this is all I'm saying," Brian said one night, "the housing market's as down as it'll ever go, so now's the time to buy. Prices are gonna jolt back up, like very soon, and I don't want us to be kicking ourselves stupid. I'm telling you, the loans will pay themselves off in *no* time."

Dad sighed, as though his oldest son had yet to learn the single, most important lesson he'd been trying to teach for years. "Why do you think the housing crisis was hitting everyone in the first place? You need live carefully. You cannot be trusting banks just like that."

"Property is the only stable investment!" Brian cried, his mouth full of ginger pork. "When the government blows up, and society erupts into chaos, the only thing left will be *land*, and I for one—"

"Dude," I said, "swallow your food before yelling apocalyptic nonsense at Ba."

"I'm not yelling!" Brian yelled, punching me in the arm. "I'm just saying—*I'm* the one trying to be careful here. Ba can't fix cars for the rest of his life!"

Brian and Dad continued to argue, with Brian launching into a crackpot theory that a newfound innovation was on the verge of making cars obsolete, Dad repeating to Brian to mind his own business, and so on. Occasionally, I stepped in as their referee, calling Brian out for getting too heated, as he often did, or interrupting Dad to say Brian had actually made a decent point, despite sounding like he believed the Singularity was bound to destroy us. Mom, who'd spent the entire dinner scrolling through her iPad, tuned this conversation out, interjecting only to scold Brian for moving into his own apartment and wasting money on rent, to which Brian responded, "Mom, no girl's gonna date a twenty-six-year-old guy still living at home!"

Mom rolled her eyes at Brian. "Is it so wrong to want both my sons under my roof?" she said, before returning to her iPad because she hated talking about the Shop. As far as she was concerned, she'd exhausted enough of her life force begging Dad to fire those of his guys—Ohm Young, in particular—she deemed useless. Throughout my childhood, she would balance the Shop's books late into the night, her neck craning over greasy, smudgy invoices, with those steady hands running through her hair as if money might tumble from her scalp. By my high school years, after tolerating Dad's joking, for the thousandth time, that his guys had wives and kids and gambling addictions to support, Mom had renounced her mission of boosting the Shop's profit margin and began working overtime shifts at the Social Security office. Now, instead of balancing the books, she binged trashy and corny gong-siams dubbed into Khmer on YouTube. She stopped talking about money, and started daydreaming about retirement and traveling to Thailand to learn how to cook authentic Thai dishes, as she had already mastered every Khmer recipe, even the ones of meals she didn't like. "Thai food is just bad Khmer food," she once said, "but it's better than other kinds of food. What am I gonna do? Learn to cook pasta?"

Her future plans never referenced Dad, though sometimes she talked about a time when she'd live among Brian, me, and the grandkids she expected. "I want two kids from you, and four kids from Brian," she'd say, and I never understood why she wanted fewer kids from me than my older brother. The fact is, I didn't want any number of kids, really. I was content with myself as a gay man, and I knew gay men could have kids, of course, but it didn't seem worth jumping through all the hoops—the surrogates, or the adoption, all the paperwork. The only time I took the idea of kids seriously was when I thought about everyone who had died, two million points of connection reincarnated into the abyss, how young Cambos like me should repopulate the world with more Cambos, especially those with fancy college degrees, whose kids could be legacy admits.

Soon it was only other Cambos coming to the Shop. That was how you knew business was bad: if white or Black or Hispanic people or even mainstream East Asians weren't walking through the doors. Our hometown had a lot of Cambos, sure, but not enough for a robust customer base. No one needed to fix their cars *that* often. Plus, these Cambos were usually relatives or relatives of relatives, or friends or friends of friends, so Dad gave them so many discounts, we barely turned a profit. Dad's guys started playing card games in the back of the garage, where posters of naked Thai women competed for their attention with a

Chinese zodiac calendar. Without a continual flow of customers in the waiting room, I organized old invoices and scraped crusted oil off every surface. I even tried learning how to balance the books, but Dad got frustrated trying to explain all the expenses. The waiting room was the cleanest it'd been since the Shop opened. It made me sad to think that the better the Shop looked, the worse it was doing. This seemed, in some cosmic way, unfair.

When there was no more crusted oil to scrape, I skimmed through job postings on my phone, refreshing the alumni career website over and over again. Doctor Heng's wife lectured me about going back to school and studying pre-pharmacy. I didn't apply for any jobs, feeling burned from all the career fairs and interviews I'd bombed in college. Still, it seemed productive to scroll through my hypothetical futures—data analyst, technical writer, user interface engineer. Though, the harder I thought about it, the less I could imagine taking any of these jobs. Dressing up in slacks and button-downs. Making small talk with coworkers about the weather and their favorite hiking trails.

Eventually, the days grew shorter, summer crawling into fall, and some nights, after working at the Shop, I hooked up with one of Brian's old friends. We had run into each other at Costco. Mobil 5W-30 oil was on sale, but you could buy only three boxes at a time. There was some local law that limited the amount of a flammable substance that a customer could have at once. So Dad sent me to Costco every few hours to stock up, and there I was in the checkout line, hoping the cashier wouldn't recognize me from earlier that morning, when Paul strolled over from the food court, projecting that casual angst peculiar to guys who never left our hometown, who stayed committed to a dusty California free of ambition or beaches. He asked me how I was doing, so I roped him into buying three boxes of oil for me. When I thanked him, he said, with a low-key smirk, that he was sure I'd make it up to him. After that, we fell back into old patterns of driving onto the secluded parts of the Delta's levee. It was the safest place to have car sex, especially if blowjobs struck you as boring.

Paul was half Mexican, half Italian, and his girlfriend was Filipina. He worked as the manager of an AT&T store. Made good money, actually, if you included his commissions. He was handsome, in an unassuming way, with a constant stubble that made me go crazy when dragged across my back or stomach. His nose was huge but well proportioned. Sometimes I closed my eyes and used his nose to apply pressure to my closed eye sockets. It was weird but satisfying, like my eyeballs were getting massaged. If Paul wasn't into it, he never said anything to stop me. During one of my winter breaks in college, I'd messaged him on Grindr, after recognizing his Mars Volta T-shirt in the headless torso serving as his profile pic, and we'd hooked up here and there in the years leading up to my graduation, always in his red Sienna minivan, which used to be the minivan his older sister had driven to drop off Paul, Brian, and me at our K–8 school. That car had been infamous in our teenage mythology. High schoolers had called it the party van, because during lunch periods, Paul's older sister drove as many friends as possible to eat at the Costco food court. Then, when Paul started high school and inherited the van, he assumed the role of shuttling fellow teenagers to cheap food. Ten years later, you could still find Paul at Costco, in the middle of the week, eating $1.50 hot dogs.

One night, after Paul finished in me, we were in the back seat of his minivan, my back still glued to his torso with sweat, lube, and cum. We stayed like this for a while, Paul burrowing his chin into my shoulder, as I watched the windows fog up from the heat of our bodies. Then, out of nowhere, he asked me if it was all right to bring his car to the Shop; he needed an oil change. Not unless he convinced the Mexican, white, and Filipino drivers of the city, I joked, to also bring their cars to the Shop.

"Thing is, I'm too white for the Mexicans and too Mexican for the whites," Paul said, running his fingers through my hair. "And I guess I can't get you the Filipinos either, 'cause, you know, I'm cheating around on my girlfriend with *you*."

"Stop being a doofus," I said, "you don't have to ask."

"Just wanted to make sure, you know," he replied. "In case it'd be awkward."

"It's not awkward," I said, remembering a time when I was younger, sitting in the same back seat of this same red minivan, and feeling awkward around Paul, his older sister driving fifty when the speed limit was twenty-five. He was only three years older than me, which felt like nothing now that we were both in our twenties; still, I felt giddy to be having sex with the cooler older guy from my youth, who listened to bands like the Mars Volta. If only my closeted, sex-deprived self from high school could see me now, I sometimes thought, before realizing, yet again, how dumb it was to think that way about Paul—a closeted gay guy too scared to break up with his first girlfriend. Plus, the Mars Volta actually sucks.

"Why are you working at your dad's place, anyway?" Paul asked.

"Why not?" I answered. "I don't have a job. Might as well."

"It just doesn't seem like your *scene*."

"And what would that be?"

"It was just a question. Forget it."

"No, it's not like I'm sensitive about this," I assured him. "I'm genuinely curious."

"Man, I don't know," he started, "you already left for college, so why come back? I thought you'd be living away somewhere with some dope job by now, dating guys who are good guys, you know? Guys who have hella dope jobs, too. Like bankers and doctors and what not."

"I'd never date a banker," I said, bracing myself for Paul to get mopey. This happened sometimes when we got together. He'd get in his own head about cheating on his girlfriend, Meryl, who actually was a nice person. She was a devout Catholic who said "Oh my gosh." She asked about my day, with a sincere intentional of listening to my response, whenever I ran into her. Obviously, I avoided her like the plague. Paul was in love with Meryl, or thought he was, but liked fucking guys too much, and when this overwhelmed him, he said cringeworthy things like "I'm not good enough for you."

This night he was saying, "I just . . . I don't get why you're living at home, I guess."

"Right," I said. "What time is it? We should probably get to bed."

"Naw, I'm serious," he said. "You'd definitely kill it in San Francisco, you know that. Me, I'm gonna be here forever. I can't give up driving places. Parking in the city is fucked."

I didn't know what to say. Truth be told, I could have lived like this forever, too—days at the Shop being lulled by the sounds of rusty machinery, dead bolts being bolted and unbolted, Dad and his guys making fun of American diets for being less effective than the Khmer Rouge diet of boiled grass. All I needed was the occasional hookup, a way to get off that didn't involve my own hands.

"Did you know I went to the gayest college?" I asked.

"Sounds pretty chill," he said, holding me tighter, as if this were the last time we would fuck, though I knew perfectly well it wasn't.

"It was just a ton of gay guys in the middle of nowhere, Ohio," I said, moving away from him so I could collect my clothes. "A bunch of theater majors and aspiring musicians and artists. I actually lost my virginity to a triple major in theater, music, and art, though I think he's in a coding boot camp now. Anyway, I had so much bad sex those first two years, my dick and ass were, like, constantly sore. I couldn't even sit through lectures right. I had to lean onto a single butt cheek at a time."

Paul laughed. "Why are you telling me this?"

"It was fun," I continued. "I'm not saying it wasn't. But, you know, when I think back to college, that's all it really was, you know?"

"I'm not getting you," he said.

"I feel happy—that's all—just being here." I maneuvered back into my pants, leaned over, and kissed him, then gathered the cum on his stomach and slathered his face with my sticky hand.

"God*damn* it," he said, wiping the cum away, and we both started laughing.

Later, as Paul drove me home, I watched the other cars in the street. Headlights streaked through the night in flashes of yellow and white. It was too dark to see clearly, but still I looked for the lost truck. I wanted so badly for one of the passing blurs to be that golden Toyota Tundra.

A few days rolled by without us having car sex, and then Paul brought his red minivan into the Shop. Brian accompanied him. They walked in through the glass door, Brian leading the way in his best suit, the navy one he wore to close major sales. It accentuated his amiable confidence, the air of being fully able to force you into a headlock and somehow make it seem good natured, like *you* were the one asking to be restrained in the first place. Brian had never moved away, because he excelled in this city. It was reassuring to know that something about home allowed guys like my brother to thrive.

"I'm here to block Ba from giving this dumbass a discount," Brian said, as he leaned toward us, across the counter, pointing at Paul discreetly with his thumb as if he ever spoke a single word that softly. "But seriously, Paul has a job. He can pay for his own oil change."

Paul pulled out his wallet. "Hit me with the full charge, Mr. Chey."

"Don't worry about it," Dad said. "Just by making sure these guys are never killing each other, you are doing me a favor." He patted my head with a paternal amusement, a joking condescension, the grease from broken cars getting into my hair.

"That's not the reason he likes you," I said to Paul. "He still talks about your ability to eat durian."

"Christ," Brian said, pushing off the counter to pace around the room while stretching his arms, as if limbering himself up to jump on new opportunities. "Can we not talk about durian right now? You're making me nauseous."

"You guys are so not Cambodian," Dad said as he waved his hand. "You are not even Cambodian American! Durian is real, true Khmer food."

"Hey," I said, "I *like* durian. I don't even think it smells bad. It just reminds me of gasoline, which, if you haven't noticed, I've spent half my life marinating in the smell of . . ."

"Which one's durian?" Paul asked.

Brian stopped stretching, grabbed Paul's shoulders, and playfully shook him. He yelled: "It's just the only food that Andrew Zimmern has refused to eat on *Bizarre Foods*! Think about that for a second! The badass dude eats fried grasshoppers and even *he* thinks durian is gross. You know the fruit is protected by a giant spiky shell, right? They're so crazy and lethal they fall from trees and strike elephants on the head and, like, kill 'em! How is that not a sign we shouldn't mess with that shit?"

"Oh yeah," Paul said, squinting. "I think I do like durian."

Dad threw a pen at Brian and snorted. "My kids are

spoiled!" he said. "Anything you can eat, you should be eating. You think every meal we had during Khmer Rouge was *smelling* right?"

I laughed, enjoying this banter, the kind I'd missed every day of college. "Ba, you gotta stop using the genocide to win arguments," I said, but before he could reply, or even chuckle, Doctor Heng's wife was bursting into the waiting room.

"Bong, I checked with the monks!" she said, after she had nearly crashed into Paul. "I know what you need to do!"

Dad raised his eyebrows and sighed. Skeptical defeat was his go-to response for just about anything this familiar woman happened to be saying. Oblivious to his expression, Doctor Heng's wife dug into her Louis Vuitton purse—which appeared bigger than ever that day—and pulled out a golden statue of Buddha, slamming its base on the counter with a loud thud. "We need to boost your karma," she continued, and rotated the Buddha so that his cocky smirk was facing me and Dad. "This is the key to your success." Then she slipped into a breakneck Khmer that made me dizzy to try to understand, though I gathered she was explaining the details of some grandiose agenda. Dad only nodded in silence. After a while of this, Brian signaled for me to meet him outside. I attached an empty invoice to a clipboard, handed it to Paul, along with a pen, and left to join my brother on the sidewalk.

Brian was peering into the waiting room. "How's Ba today?" he asked, his eyes serious and arms crossed.

"I don't know," I answered while also looking through the glass door. Doctor Heng's wife was placing the Buddha around the room, testing different locations, I assumed, for the best usage of its spiritual effect. "He seems fine to me."

"Are you not paying attention at *all*?" Brian now asked. "His business is failing, and everyone knows."

"It's a slump," I shrugged. "The Shop got, like, one bad Yelp review 'cause of the stolen car. We've been through worse."

"Dumbfuck," Brian said, shaking his head. "Just look at the guy!"

So I did, but he seemed totally normal—tired but amused. "Guess I should check in with him," I said, wondering if I'd gotten used to seeing Dad as defeated, if I could no longer tell the difference.

Brian's face settled into a slight irritation. "Yeah, do that," he said. "Stop being a dumbfuck."

I motioned to confirm that I would, indeed, stop being a dumbfuck, and then found myself staring at Paul, who glanced up from the clipboard and locked eyes with me. He smiled and risked a wink. It was corny, so damn corny, and again I felt like a kid gushing over his older crush, but this time I felt exposed, with Brian, Dad, and Doctor Heng's wife, of all people, standing that close.

The next couple of weeks, Cambos rolled in and out of the Shop. Some brought their cars for actual repairs, but everyone brought statues of Buddha, of all sizes and colors, to decorate the waiting room, even one that was painted an alarming hot pink. Doctor Heng's wife orchestrated the whole affair, having informed the community of the Shop's urgent need for better karma. Mas and Gongs, Mings and Pous—all the older Cambos I'd ever met in my life—tried helping Dad the best they knew how. We put Buddhas anywhere it made sense: a crowd of medium Buddhas on top of the mini fridge, an army of tiny Buddhas lining the edge of the desk, a giant Buddha hanging out with the bamboo plant in the corner, with a few Buddhas stuffed between the desk and the wall, just to ensure we had our bases covered.

When people ran out of actual Buddhas, they started coming with insignias scribbled onto scraps of paper. We taped dozens of them over the walls, alongside the smog-check certificates and the framed photo of my youth baseball team, which the Shop had sponsored. I stopped a half-blind Gong from taping an insignia in the center of the computer screen; we settled on the lower-right corner.

Every time a Cambo waltzed into the waiting room with another Buddhist emblem, Dad looked more disgruntled, more disappointed to hear the door swing open, the sound of a potential new customer, only to realize it was just another guy who'd picked rice with him, for twelve hours a day, in the concentration camps. Each point of good karma the Shop accrued seemed pilfered straight from his soul. All the same, Dad always entertained these Cambos. They had only good intentions, and Dad asked them about their kids, their siblings, their relatives back in Cambodia. Witnessing the Shop bloat with spiritualism, you had to appreciate the middling optimism keeping our community afloat, those teachings all but promising that our lives, and our reincarnated lives thereafter, would remain, at best, tolerable.

I stopped scrolling through job postings, as I spent most

of the day trying to cheer Dad up. Even non-Cambodian customers, I told him, might find these superstitions amusing. As they waited for their cars to be fixed, they could play visual counting games, like the kind found in magazines for toddlers. "How many ink blotches and fat Buddhas can you spot here at March Lane Brake and Tune?" I asked, and Dad laughed until he didn't.

For lunches, Dad started packing recycled containers from Baskin-Robbins with leftover plain rice. He clutched invoices so close to his face I sometimes thought he might suffocate. I couldn't remember if Dad had always been this stressed, if he had always held invoices that way. When I was a kid, he would avoid doctors, never wanting to spring for the copays, let alone an optometrist for something as basic as his ability to see. Yet even that hardly explained his behavior.

During the Shop's karmic makeover, Paul and I hooked up almost every night. Our sex became rougher, quicker, as if we had recently met off Grindr. I forgot lube a couple of times, and Paul never carried any around—because what if Meryl found it?—so we just used spit. The pain and the chafing and the hemorrhoids weren't great, but my need for relief only grew as the days marched into winter, as I got more and more worried about the Shop.

"Way to make a guy feel special," Paul joked one night, after I came only five minutes into our hookup, and pushed him out of my sore asshole.

"Sorry," I replied. "Yeah, uhm, lemme give you a hand."

A few moments later, I was putting on my clothes, my

head and arm stuck in my T-shirt, when Paul said, "Wait a minute, Meryl's doing church shit, so I'm free all night. Also I have something to tell you." He helped me escape my shirt and pulled me down. I collapsed into his embrace, landing on his torso so hard it hurt, or maybe my hemorrhoids had made me sensitive all over. "I think I'm finally ready to come out," he said, and then, unsure of how to respond, I shuffled my body to look at his face. His expression was genuine, calm, wearing a gentle smirk like the Buddhas protecting the Shop. "I think it's unfair to Meryl," he added, "if I don't, you know, come out."

"No shit," I blurted, but he remained unfazed, and kept grinning. "What prompted this?"

"I guess I finally worked up the courage," he said. "You were my motivation, to be honest. You're so comfortable and chill, even here, in front of your dad and everything."

He squeezed my chest, and I asked myself, Does he expect me to be his new Meryl? Then I thought, Maybe that would be nice. I imagined our lives together, our buying a house close to my parents, shopping at a Cambo grocery store every week. We would be an openly gay couple in the community, a radical symbol of love for the youth, for anyone who ever thought they had to quit their home, their family, their lives, just to be themselves.

"Why did you never move away?" I asked. "Like, seriously, I'm not special. I just had the opportunity to leave."

He made a face, as though this were the hardest question he'd received in years. "It never made much sense," he said. "What would I even do?"

"You know AT&T stores are everywhere?" I joked.

"I'm being serious, you dick," he said, then ruffled my hair while tickling my side.

"Okay, okay," I laughed, elbowing him to stop. "So when's the official confession?"

"We'll see," he answered, and I didn't know how much *I* factored into his *we*, whether I wanted to be a part of it or not.

The following week Dad seemed on the verge of snapping. He yelled at me for using blue paper towels to clean the windows, and not old newspapers. He even threatened to send his guys home, indefinitely and without pay, after Ohm Young had teased that he wasn't being a good boss by ordering everyone lunch.

"You are lucky I am standing to see your face!" Dad yelled at Ohm Young, who laughed in response until he realized Dad wasn't joking.

In the afternoon, a new customer finally appeared, the first one we had since the beginning of the week. She was elderly and white, dressed in a white grandma cardigan. Dad was so excited that he opened a new box of pens so she could write her contact information on the invoice with ease. He promised that the *owner* and the *main smog technician* would be handling her repairs, trying his best to speak with zero trace of his slight accent. I thought the customer was about to die, right there in the waiting room, she spoke that languidly, and this, combined with Dad's straining to avoid stressing the last syllable of his words—like the older Cambos usually do—lent the entire interaction a slow motion quality.

Apparently, I realized, Dad could no longer trust his guys to do even the simplest of tasks. He did the customer's preliminary diagnostic himself, which wasn't actually necessary, as all the car needed was an oil change. In the waiting room, the customer asked if the supermarket across the street was open, and I told her, "Yes, Ma'am," even though I'd never called anyone that in my life. As she left to go shopping, I considered whether I should say that the supermarket carried mostly expired canned foods, but I didn't want to disrupt the shaky equilibrium of her patronage.

Ohm Young came into the waiting room shortly after the customer left. He was holding a small stack of papers. "You know how to read songs still?" he asked.

"Let me see," I said, remembering how as a teenager I'd labeled all the notes of Ohm Young's sheet music, even going so far as to writing down which finger should play what key on the piano. He would hover over my shoulder as I transcribed rock classics from the eighties, from when everyone first immigrated. The sheet music he handed me now was for the song "Every Breath You Take."

"It's good you are here for your dad," he said, rubbing the top of my head. "Because you can do *this* for me!"

"Yeah, yeah," I said. "What's this for anyway?"

"When the monks come, I will ask them if my band can play at Cambodian New Year. The monks love Sting."

"Wait, the monks are coming?"

"You do not know? They come tomorrow."

"That's bad, right?" I said, and glanced to my left, through the open door to the garage. Just then, Dad was ducking his head under the hood of the customer's car. I could only catch his butt sticking up in the air.

"Monks coming—that happens when you fail." Ohm Young sighed. "They come when you first open business, to bless everything, but after that, they are not supposed to come. No, we are not supposed to need them . . . Hey! Please keep on doing the music, okay? My band is my plan B. I cannot be the assistant manager my whole life. It is too stressful."

"Oh. Right," I said, staring at the endless bars of melody. "That makes sense."

Dad had finished working on the customer's car by the time she returned with a plastic bag full of canned garbanzo beans. He completed her invoice with a painstaking attention to detail, marking down the $29.99 charge and taking careful notes of all the labor he had done. Then, as the customer paid and took back her keys, as satisfied with our services as one could be, really, I suddenly heard the voice Doctor Heng's wife in my head. It was that lecture she delivered in my Honda, the one of about marrying a Cambodian girl who wanted a green card. How many oil changes, I found myself wondering, would add up to fifty thousand dollars? And just how long would it take to get there?

At home that night, Mom was prepping egg rolls in the kitchen while Dad napped on the couch, the TV blaring out a football game. I asked Mom if I could help, and she responded, "So today you have time for me?" She scooped minced meat out of a bowl and onto a wrapper. "How lucky of me! My own son will not abandon me like he does every other night."

"This for the monks tomorrow?" I asked, and she rolled her eyes.

"If anyone ever listened to me, we wouldn't need this. You think I have time to cook a hundred naem chien on a workday?"

"What can I do? Want me to help wrap?"

"No, you're too clumsy." She shook her head. "Go mix the fish sauce for dipping."

"How do I do that?" I asked. "I . . . forgot."

Mom threw her hands, both covered in raw meat, over her head, pretended to mess up her hair out of frustration. She wanted me to know how dumb I was, for my failure to remember her recipes, and honestly I agreed with her. Then she walked over to the cabinets and pulled out an empty plastic cylinder, one of those cheap containers that restaurants provide for leftovers. Along the side, she had stuck three pieces of blue painter's tape, all spaced out unevenly. She pointed at each, saying, "Warm water to here, fish sauce to here, vinegar to here. Sugar and roasted peanuts to taste."

"What happens when we lose this container?" I joked, taking it from her hands. "How will we make dipping sauce without you?"

"You better not lose my stuff when I die," she replied, and scooped more meat. "So when are we meeting him?"

"Meeting who?" I answered.

"The boy you're seeing," she said.

"Where did you hear that from?" I asked as I heated the water.

"Don't tell me you go out every night and aren't with a boy. Don't lie to me. I'm your mother." She raised the new egg roll to our eye level. "Here, you see?" she said. "*This* is perfect." And it was.

Avoiding her question about Paul, I finished mixing the ingredients, and then held the takeout container now filled with clear bronze liquid. I felt its weight shift from my left hand to my right. Of course, based off Mom's method, it was easy to record the exact ratios that her dipping sauce required. Yet at that moment, for whatever reason, the future appeared so precarious, the way a tradition like this could depend on a flimsy plastic.

"I'm not seeing anyone, really, I'm not," I finally told Mom, still thinking about our culture, how Cambos like us retained our Camboness mostly through our food. Egg rolls stirring up portals back to the homeland, but just in your mouth, until they disintegrated into saliva and vanished down your throat. Mom looked at me, skeptically, and rolled another egg roll.

After Mom and I had cleaned the kitchen, I sat on my bed and texted Paul that I didn't feel well, but that we'd definitely hook up the next day. I put my phone away and fell asleep. The following morning, I could smell Mom deep-frying egg rolls in the backyard, before heading off to work. I read the texts Paul had sent the previous night. Awwww, ain't a thing but some blue balls. Then, I think tonight's the night it happens. Gonna tell Meryl. Then, nothing.

I thought of responding, *How'd it go*, feeling more excited than I cared to admit, if also unsettled, as though a simple text might cement something into our relationship I wasn't ready for yet. I ended up sending nothing.

Later that morning at the Shop, hours before the divine assault was scheduled, Dad and I mopped up the residual grease from the garage floor, shined the Buddhas in the waiting room to have a pristine glimmering, and took down the many posters of naked Thai women. We set up a folded table, placed a clean sheet over it, and arranged Mom's egg rolls next to the other dishes all prepared by the wives of Dad's guys—lemongrass beef sticks, glass noodles stir-fried with bean curd and ground pork, red-hot papaya salad drenched in fish sauce, and also, of course, the requisite and huge pot of steaming white rice. The entire time Dad had looked especially grave, as if the Communists were pulling off another coup d'état. I wanted to cheer him up, to assert that no one thought any less of him, but I couldn't think of anything to say.

Around noon, five monks came marching behind Doctor Heng's wife, all of them sporting the same burnt orange robes and sandy beige Crocs, armed with packets and packets of incense. Dad and I bowed to each monk in a row, our hands clasped together. Then the monks walked around the Shop, examining the corners and crevices, sprinkling blessed water over the grease stained walls. When they finished the inspection, the monks lit their incense in every room, even the storage room, with those cases of flammable Mobil 5W-30 oil. The aroma of burning flowers, I guessed, was supposed to create a force field that would thwart evil spirits while attracting customers.

After the Shop had been suffused with a light haze, Doctor Heng's wife spread a few woven mats over the garage floor, then aggressively gestured at Dad, his guys, and me. "Get down!" she shouted through her teeth, as if ten minutes had already passed since her gesturing. "You cannot put yourselves in a position above the monks. They need to sit! What are you doing just standing around?"

We fell to our knees, and the monks followed, sitting down in the center of the mats. They proceeded to chant in low, hushed voices, ones I'd heard since I was a kid but had never bothered to understand. We watched them pray, our hands clasped together again. Fifteen minutes of nonstop droning passed, and maybe I experienced this simply from my numbing thighs and butt cheeks, but the smoke from the incense felt asphyxiating, jammed into my pores and blasted into my nostrils, like it was clogging the very space between my cells. A headache cleaved through my brain, and I remembered the first time Dad had been serious with me about the genocide.

I was ten years old, barely into the double digits, and it was Cambodian New Year. Some older kids had fixated on my shoes or something. Behind the wat and next to the field, where the pop-up stalls were releasing clouds of barbecuing smoke, they pushed me against the rusty chain-link fence. They interrogated me about whether I had Communists for relatives. "Your Gong probably killed people, you faggot," their leader said. "Probably sucked Pol Pot's dick." I didn't fully understand his taunting, but I was still upset, and when I ran back to Dad, sobbing and heaving, he denied any Communist connections to our bloodline but confirmed our history—how half of everyone's relatives had died.

"It was a thing that was done to us, that's all," he said, wiping my tears away. "You better get all this crying out now," he also said. "No use in crying when it already happened." Then he lifted me onto his shoulders, even though I'd grown too big for that, before walking us both inside the wat. A crowd had gathered in front of the monks. We joined them and prayed, for good karma and luck and blessings, for the upcoming year and our future reincarnated lives, and I slipped into a total hopelessness. What had we done to deserve such violence? How terrible it must have been, our country and culture's past karma.

These concerns came rushing back to me as I kneeled on the Shop's oily floor, on the same style of woven mats from that fateful Cambodian New Year. I felt a gloom only deepened by the thrumming of unintelligible chanting. I couldn't bear watching Dad resort to these half-broken beliefs.

So I thought about Paul. He was a decent guy with a decent job, someone I liked enough to bring into my real, established life, the one I hadn't even started to build. And he would become even more decent, if he *had* come out, and stopped lying to his girlfriend. I could take a chance on Paul, I thought. I could settle down and commit to working with Dad. I could be the second dutiful and mature son my parents would rely on for support. I didn't know what I had to offer, really, other than cleaning as the Shop's janitor and transcribing music for Ohm Young. Even so, the prospect of my moving away, for yet another time, struck me as incredibly selfish.

"Ba," I whispered, and he either didn't hear or was ignoring me. Regardless, I kept muttering, "Ba . . . Ba . . . *Ba*."

"You need to be focusing," Dad answered, though I had no clear idea of what I needed to focus on.

"Ba, don't worry," I continued, my legs shaking from the numbness. "I'm gonna help you. I don't know how, but I'm gonna help the Shop."

"Oun," Dad said gruffly, "can you just be worrying about yourself?" He sighed and angled his face at me. "The Shop is providing for you, that's why we have the Shop."

And it hit me—once more that look of grief. But this time no one spared me its full force. The past year flashed across my eyes. The days I'd spent at the Shop doing nothing, my inability to apply for legitimate jobs. What had everyone thought of me, I wondered, of Dad? His son jobless, a college degree going to waste. I began to realize the extent I had been a complete child, one that was chaining my father down to a failing business. Dad's attention returned to the monks all trying to fix the Shop, and I couldn't breathe. I couldn't believe myself.

Then Paul came to my thoughts again, how we were supposed to hang out that night. What I'd just envisioned, committing to a life here, it appeared so stupid, even as the sentiment retained a sort of comfort. I took my phone out of my pocket, secretly checking my notifications as it lay on the ground. Several texts from Paul were popping up, but before I could open any of them, the monks stopped chanting and everyone stopped praying.

Doctor Heng's wife placed empty bowls in front of the monks, and then handed the rest of us, the representatives of the Shop, our own bowls she had filled with warm rice. Still crouched on our knees, we formed a line. We shuffled in a procession, crawling on the mats, scooping rice into the bowls of each of the monks. When the ritual was done, the monks started eating their feast, and I stood next to the waiting room's door, one hand stuffed into my pocket, the other gripping my phone. With my motivation to read my texts waning, I took in the garage of the Shop. It felt smaller now. Machines that had once seemed gigantic only reached my shoulders.

Listening from outside the waiting room, I heard Doctor Heng's wife talking to Dad, so I peeked through the doorway. "Bong, you need to make a donation," she was saying at the counter. "Write the check before the monks get full. Do it quickly, Bong."

"Okay, okay, okay," Dad said, as though chanting his own kind of prayer, and as he wrote out the check, I found myself trying to understand the creases of his disgruntled, defeated brow. They were spelling something out for me, some dispatch sent from across the universe, by the accumulation of our reincarnated lives, from every different past we'd ever experienced. "If this day is harnessing as much karma as possible," his wrinkles read, "more spiritual power than this community has ever seen, maybe the Shop will have good business. And when that happens, hopefully, fingers crossed, we will soon break even from the cost of our donation."

As I stood between the waiting room and the garage, I watched Dad finish signing the check. Watched him hand that flimsy paper to Doctor Heng's wife, who stuffed it into her giant purse. All that money, probably a whole month's earnings, was now swimming among loose pocket change, and I stopped caring about those texts from Paul, the smallness of the Shop, the monks stuffing their mouths with Mom's egg rolls. Nothing behind me seemed to matter. Everything receded into the smoky blur of the incense, the shadows of all those Buddhas.

I wished for only one thing—to send a response to Dad's message, etched onto my own forehead, a beacon I'd shoot out into the ether. "But what," I was ready to ask, for every life Dad and I had lived and lost, "will we do after?"

THE MONKS

Two days at the wat and all I've done is count shit. The dots on the ceiling. How long it takes for a stick of incense to crumble into ashes. The number of steps to the kitchen, where the grandmas are always talking smack about everyone, even about each other to their own faces. What goes down at the temple was supposed to be more spiritual, and eye-opening, and informative, like how preachers in the movies holler out prayers. How they push regular guys to see themselves differently. Instead, I count the white stitches on my orange robes. Then the stitches on the robes of the monks praying next to me.

My crew would bust my balls if they found out my temple life consists of counting. And if they found out I sleep in a tiny, funky-smelling room. It's not a *bad* funky, but more like a couple-banged-in-a-pile-of-ash funky. We told you the wat's hella fake, my boys would say. Sad dopes with no jobs, no place to live, they become monks. And Maly, she'd be pissed. She didn't want me to shave my head for the bon, told me I looked like an aborted alien fetus after the initial ceremonies, before I came to the temple to ensure Dad's spirit, or whatever he is now, passes gently into its next life. "Come back when your scalp stops feeling like a giant dick," she said, kicking me off her bed. "I can't believe you're wasting a week on that sick fuck you called a dad," she also said.

After Dad's funeral was the last time I got off. Just a quickie with Maly, who wouldn't kiss me because of my bald head. I still appreciated her. Nothing since then, not even a good bate session. Counting relaxes me though. It's something to pass the time. If I could, I would count how many hours I've been alive, or seconds, or how much longer I have until I'm shipped off to basic combat training, but I don't have the patience for all that. I'm not a whiz kid. I'm not living a Cambo version of *Stand and Deliver.* I fucked up my classes, and none of my teachers cared enough to warn me. They were too busy putting on *Stand and Deliver* so they could avoid teaching the real stuff.

Maybe if I score a calculator from the Cha's office, I can take my counting to the next level. But he would just tell me to chill. He'd rant about the universe being like this and how karma being like that, and before I know it, I'd be scrubbing off the silly string that's been stuck to the pavement since last Cambodian New Year. It's all for that nirvana, he'd say, laughing his ass off from the porch. Boy, you better build up your karma if you're going off to war, he'd say.

BEFORE LUNCH

Push-ups, 45 (5 more than Pou does in the morning)

Sit-ups, 60 (10 more than Pou does in the morning)

Times I thought about Maly's body, lost count, maybe the whole time?

The other day, when I first got here, the Cha handed me a notepad. We stood in the center of the big prayer room, and the giant and fake-gold Buddha stared us down from the stage. I swear the stage has been overdue for a collapse since I was in middle school. Khmer music played in the background. Being there without a crowd of kneeling grandparents, I felt strange, and naked. I imagined a sea of old Cambos surrounding us, their wrinkly heads bobbing up and down to pray. "Am I supposed to write Buddhist stuff in here?" I asked.

"You write your feelings down, Rithy," the Cha said roughly. His white polo drowned him in shirt. I could tell the polo was a knockoff because the horse logo was twice the size it should've been. It was also placed exactly where a guy's right nipple goes. "I saw it on TV," the Cha added. "This talk show lady interviewed a woman who wrote every day for a year. It helped her forget her dead husband."

"You mean it helped her forget her sadness?" I asked, staring at his logo-nipple. I couldn't figure out if the fabric was just that lumpy, or if the Cha's nipples poked through shirts weirdly.

"You know what I mean," the Cha said, waving like he

was fed up. "Take it and write." He placed his hands over mine and pushed the notepad closer to me.

"Got it, I think," I said. "Anything else I should know or do?"

"Tomorrow you'll start doing chores," he answered. "We all earn our keep. There are robes in your room. Don't mess them up, we're not made of money." He pointed at the hallway to the left of him. "It's the second door. Don't be an idiot and get lost."

I started to ask him if there was a schedule of monk things for the day, or a list of Buddhist objectives I'm supposed to meet for my dad's bon, but the Cha interrupted me.

"Tell your uncle I said hello," he said, like my temple week had already ended. "I'm gonna whip his ass at poker night," he also said. Then he flew across the prayer mats, straight into his office.

In my room, I turned the notepad over and found hella grease stains, plus the words SPEEDY TRANSMISSIONS MANUFACTURER printed in bubble letters, above a cartoon car with big round eyes. The Cha doesn't realize that hundreds of these dirty notepads live in Pou's house. And since I live with my uncle, too, and have for years because Dad was no help, the Cha's gift felt empty. He basically re-regifted me something my uncle had regifted to him. I waited in my room for the rest of the afternoon, for a monk to come for me, or the Cha, whose literal job is to be a mediator between the monks and normal guys like me, but no one did. When I finally left to hunt for food, the monks seemed surprised to see me. They forgot why I was here.

Now I'm at the wat for five more days, and not much

has happened since the Cha gave me the notepad. I don't have many feelings worth writing down, so I jot down lists of what I count. When the Cha sees me writing, he doesn't ask me to do random shit for the monks. He thinks I'm processing my sadness and leaves me alone. I wouldn't mind doing things for the monks if those things mattered, if they did something for Dad's spirit, but the Cha makes it seem like they're just chores.

Sometimes when I'm writing, I think about my uncle, how he's probably doing his same-old self at the house. Every night Pou comes back from fixing cars and he counts how much money he made. He adds up his paychecks, bills, and expenses, along with the number of push-ups he did that morning, all in his dirty notepads. When I try to throw out his old notepads, Pou hurls empty beer cans at my head. I guess breathing in those stacked-up notepads is another way for him to keep track of how much he's gained.

STEPS FROM MY ROOM

to the prayer room, where I keep falling asleep while praying, 25

to the kitchen, where the grandmas slip me extra food, 58

to the fountain, which is pretty peaceful, 115

It's not that I don't like the monks. Some are chill. Two of them split cigs with me in the mornings, after our prayer sessions and before our chores. I call them Monk B and Monk C because we don't talk or share facts about ourselves, like our names. We smoke out by the fountain, away from all the statues of Buddha in the garden. I think the monks are trying to hide their smoking habits from all the Buddhas.

But Monk A doesn't like me. He's always yelling at me for sweeping wrong or messing up the incense trays. He thinks I'm a fuckup for enlisting, according to the Cha. I probably am, so I don't blame him or anything. What did the Cha say? Oh yeah, he said, "War's not the best conversation starter, for any of us. Don't you know shit about the Khmer Rouge?" I should keep that in mind from now on.

Here is what I know about the monks: Monk A is skinny and Monk C is not, which I don't get because there's not much food here, unless there's a funeral or a wedding or it's Cambodian New Year. Monk B, though, is jacked, with black tattoos that wrap around his arms. The other day I asked Monk B how he got so jacked, if he did some monk training regimen. He shrugged and just kept smoking. Then he offered me another cig. He must do push-ups, maybe even pull-ups. Maybe his room has ceiling pipes he can hang from. I should've brushed up on Khmer. I would've been able to communicate with the monks. At least thank them for the cigs without sounding like a jackass.

Monk B and C treat me well, but that's because I'm a guest, not an actual monk. They also feel sorry, probably. No one expected me to follow tradition. Even Pou was surprised. "I don't get why you wanna stay at the wat," he said. "Everyone knows your dad was a dipshit," he also said. I told him I feel like someone should do right by him. He had no one at the end of it all.

There's a new monk, too. Monk D's my age, roughly my height and size, and speaks decent English compared to the other monks. He doesn't smoke out by the fountain. He spends his time following Monk A because he's in monk training. I bet he still feels out of place. I actually overheard Monk D's real name from the Cha. No one calls him by it, so I'm not sure if it's still his name. I wonder if the older monks say their old names in their heads. Do they think of themselves as only monks? Maybe when I leave for the army that will happen to me. I'll stop thinking of myself as one thing, and as part of another. I wonder if that will make me a better or worse person.

BEFORE SLEEP

Push-ups, 88

Sit-ups, 125

Squats, 55

Burpees, 50

My third night at the wat, I went outside to jog laps around the backyard. Monk D was sitting on the ground, facing one of the Buddhas in the garden. He barely glanced at me when I sat down next to him. We did say hi to each other though. I mentioned that it seemed like neither of us thought those temple mats were comfy, not enough to sleep well, and he nodded. He looked like he didn't want to talk, but I stayed. I wasn't gonna end the conversation myself. He was still a monk, and you can't be rude to monks.

"You see how this one is strange?" Monk D asked. I scoped out the other Buddhas in the garden. It was true, this Buddha was different from the rest. The colored paint was chipping and faded and the guy who'd made him added a ton of muscles that bulged out of the Buddha's robes. I guess the statue maker was tired of Buddha being a fat guy people laugh at while shopping for chopsticks. I gave the Buddha a closer look and realized he was cross-eyed. He looked like a dumb jock, flexing until his pupils went all fucked up.

"Why is that?" I asked. I actually didn't expect Monk D to know why, or to keep speaking, but he told me about the Buddha. According to what Monk A told Monk D, the statue was gifted to the temple by this guy who donates money every year. Monk A didn't want to offend the guy because of his donations, so he put the Buddha in the garden, with the other statues that come directly from Cambodia. The guy used to be a legit statue maker. Then he lost a couple of fingers, an eye, and most of his family in the genocide. Now he works as a janitor for a school. He still makes statues but they always turn out looking weird.

Staring at the Buddha, I thought about the statue maker, how he doesn't have a family to distract him from the talent he lost. Some little kids he could support and use as an excuse for not making statues.

"Do you have a girlfriend?" Monk D asked, breaking our silence. I told him I did have a girlfriend. "Why you staying here if you have a girlfriend?" he responded.

"Because I'm supposed to be here," I said. "Isn't that why you're here?"

"No," he said, shaking his head. "I'm here because I want to be here." He stood up and brushed the dirt off his robes. Then he went back inside the temple.

I jogged around the backyard after Monk D left. I counted my laps by having the cross-eyed Buddha work as my marker. It was probably the jogging that wiped me out, but every time I counted a lap, I swore passing the Buddha by was draining my energy. Like it was haunted and a ghost was sapping the life from me. It would've made more sense if the statue guy had never added extra muscles, if the Buddha was just a regular fat Buddha.

Times Pou calls my dad a shit, around 5 a day

Times Pou talks about mom, hardly ever but sometimes

Times Pou calls my dad a shit while drinking low-calorie beer, too many to count

Times I agree with Pou, usually I think

When I woke up, the Cha said to meet him in his office after lunch. I found myself rushing through my chores. I think I swept even more dust into the smaller prayer rooms. I hoped the Cha would finally teach me some ritual I needed to complete. Something that would help Dad's spirit not be restless. Something that would guarantee him a peaceful new life, anything nicer than the shitshow that was his last one.

The Cha's office was smaller than I'd expected, the size of a supply closet. I couldn't imagine how the Cha had gotten his desk through the doorway. Monk A and the Cha sat on the same side, on mismatched folding chairs. They crammed against each other so closely their arms touched. There was no chair for me. I think Monk A had taken the chair that was supposed to be on my side of the desk. I felt awkward there in front of them.

"Rithy, how are you doing?" the Cha asked, and Monk A nodded.

"I'm fine," I said. For a second I considered squatting to their level. I wasn't sure how to position myself. Now I'm pretty sure that looking down at a monk counts as being disrespectful.

"We want to check on you," the Cha said. He shuffled through a stack of papers. On his desk were a bunch of Pou's dirty notepads. "Make sure you're doing good." This time Monk A didn't nod.

"That's it?" I blurted, and both Monk A's nostrils got wider.

"Boy, you better watch your tone," the Cha said, lifting his head from his papers. "You have something you wanna say?" he asked while squinting at me .

"I mean . . . I've been here for three days and all I do is clean."

"And?" he asked.

"Aren't there more *important tasks* I need to complete?" I answered.

"Being here is fine," he replied. "Don't worry about it."

"I thought I'm *supposed* to be worrying?" I said. "Isn't that the point, to worry about my dad's spirit?" My voice rose and I stressed my words by waving my arms. It just happened. I couldn't help it.

Then Monk A scolded me in Khmer. He told me to calm down in a hard, intimidating way, but I was on a roll.

"Why am I here if it's not directly helping my dad?" I

continued. "How is me just *being* at the wat helping anyone, except you guys, who get to do less chores for a week?" My hands pointed in the direction of Monk A, and this made him mad. He yelled at me in Khmer for a long time, louder than I'd ever known him to speak. Louder than when he addresses an audience at weddings and funerals. He spoke so fast his words blurred together and my head hurt because I couldn't translate at his pace.

"Please," I said, interrupting Monk A. "I need some air." Without waiting for a response, I left the Cha's office and went outside, knowing I'd come across as rude. I paced back and forth. I was tired of Monk A and the Cha acting like they were helping. And I was tired of feeling fuzzy, about the temple, about everything I did.

The other monks stared from across the courtyard, smoking in silence. It was like they had never moved from those spots. Like they did nothing but kill themselves with cigs.

Rooms I've swept at the temple so far, 5

Total push-ups I've done at the temple so far, at least 300

Hours I work a week, 60

Total cigs I've smoked with the monks so far, at least a whole pack

Little cousins I drive to and pick up from school, 4

How much I owe people outside the temple, too much to think about

The Cha told my uncle about our interaction. He called me into his office again and it reminded me of that time I got sent to the vice-principal's in high school. I'd missed too much class and some other shit. I got tagged in the records as truant. He didn't know that sometimes I skipped sixth and seventh period to make money and help Pou pay his doctor bills. That was a rough time, when Pou's spine got fucked and he took a break from fixing cars ten hours a day.

Monk A wasn't in the room, only the Cha, but the spare chair had stayed on the Cha's side of the desk. I figured that was intentional on his part. After a moment, the Cha pointed at the phone lying sideways on his desk. I had to lean forward because it was old school, with a cord and everything, and right when I lifted its speaker to my ear, Pou screaming "What kind of crap are you pulling?" nearly knocked me over.

"Jesus," I said, then felt weird for saying *Jesus* in the temple. "Pou, why are you so mad? I'm just trying to complete a good bon."

Pou snorted. "I don't give a damn about your father's bon."

I looked at the Cha's blank expression. I wondered if he also didn't give a damn.

Pou went on: "But you wanted to do the wat, so you need do it right. Don't make me look bad. If a monk wants to lecture you, hell, if he wants to slap the stupid out your skull, you better stay put and take it."

"I *am* trying to do the wat right," I said. "All I want is some guidance."

"Look, traditions don't gotta be logical," Pou said, sounding more exhausted than mad but still pretty mad. "What do you expect? We aren't home, so why the hell would anything make sense. Now stop doing all this thinking and do what you're told." I wanted to ask how I could do what I'm told when no one was telling me shit, but then Pou added, "Don't forget, you have to help with the roof. You better not forget when you get back." That was the last comment he said before hanging up. Later, Monk A doubled my daily chores for the rest of my week here.

So now I am sweeping the whole building. I am supposed to be learning a lesson, which is not to ignore a yelling monk, I guess. Honestly, I thought about leaving the wat, calling Maly to pick me up, but I can't face Pou, not without patching things up with Monk A and the Cha.

Monk D approaches me while I'm cleaning the big prayer room. He puts his hand on my shoulder. It almost seems like he wants to hug me. But he only points at the speakers. "You hear that?" he asks.

"Yeah," I answer, "it's some praying song."

"Focus," he says, raising his finger a little higher.

I close my eyes to catch the music. I listen for a bit, following the beat. Then it hits me. "It's a cover of 'Hey Jude,'" I say before laughing.

Monk D nods, smiles at me, and walks away.

Doing the rest of my chores, I think about what Pou told me, about us not being home. If I had to choose, I guess anywhere Maly's living would be my home. Though we'll probably break up when I leave for the army. She's not the type to wait around for a guy, and I don't need her to be. I didn't enlist because I want more pressure. That's the opposite of what I want. Funny, I've lived here, in this city, my entire life, but I wouldn't really call it my home.

Years Maly and I have been together, since we were 18, so 2

Times Maly broke up with me, 4

Times I broke up with Maly, 2

How often Maly goes down on me, usually but never after I work out

How often I go down on Maly, sometimes but maybe not enough

How long our sex lasts, an entire episode of *The Simpsons*, so 22 minutes

How often we have sex while high, we never have sex not high

The monk's early bedtime really isn't going well for me. Even though I was exhausted from the double amount of chores, I couldn't fall asleep that fourth night. I found the joint I hid in my room and twirled it in my fingers. For a good hour I considered lighting it up, right on my mat.

I'd tucked the joint into my shoe before coming here. It's what I used to do in school, because sometimes I toked up during fifth period, behind the boys' locker room. Sometimes I got stressed. It's pretty gross to hit a joint that has touched my feet. But it gets the job done. Smoking weed would've knocked me out. But I'm trying to kick the habit. Can't depend on grass to sleep in the future. Plus, I'm saving the joint for my last night, when Dad's bon is complete.

I figured staying at the wat would help me get away from weed, at least for a bit. My crew didn't understand. Because I have some time before leaving, before my basic combat training, they told me I should be as high as possible, all day every day. "The shit isn't addictive," they said. "What's the problem?" They think I enlisted to make myself miserable.

For a while, I saw Dad only when he scored weed from me. He called using a different number every time we set up a deal, and I never told anyone about seeing him. Pou would flip his shit, even now that Dad is dead. Pou always swore he'd kick Dad's ass for bailing after Mom died. But I have to give him one thing, really. Dad kept my cell number memorized, all through those last few years.

We usually met at the donut shop not owned by Cambos, as Dad always wanted to be discreet. He'd try to make the whole deal seem like a regular family breakfast. He'd buy me coffee and whatnot, make a point of remembering I like crullers. He'd ask me questions about my life. We never talked about his stuff. I knew neither of us cared to hash that out sitting in Happy Donuts. I half think he wasn't that into weed. I mean, the guy was shooting up every weekend. But maybe he needed the extra motivation to talk to me while sober. I bet he sometimes just wanted to feel normal for twenty minutes, or thought he did at least. He'd forget who he was sometimes, I bet, and then convince himself to see his son and eat donuts. And then, afterward, when he remembered himself again, he'd smoke weed on top of the junk, because maybe his normal felt that bad? If his normal hadn't been terrible, why else did he end up the way he did?

Once I almost brought Maly to meet him. It was Dad's idea. He said he'd make sure Maly, as the old Cambos say, wasn't a woman who carried a basket with holes. I was about to text Maly about it and everything. I wanted Dad to see me with a girlfriend, because he would actually understand that. It wouldn't register as nothing, like everything else I told him. But I knew Maly might try to defend me, start yelling at him for not being around. I didn't want that. He'd been through so much, I still feel like I owe him. The guy had endured genocide to get me here. The guy had lost his wife. He deserved a break, even from being my dad.

THINGS I WILL MISS WHEN I'M SHIPPED OFF

Having sex with Maly

Maly, in general

Smoking weed with the crew

Watching kung fu movies

Cambodian food

Being able to decide things for myself

Today Monk D and I ate dinner together. Then, when it got dark, we walked into the field behind the temple. Empty Coke cans and plastic bags crinkled under our steps. Trash litters the dead grass, practically the whole field, even though New Year's was in April and now it's winter.

"You know," I said, "I used to think it was cool the monks lived outside the city. Like it made them gangster or something." I lit a cig from a pack Monk B had given me.

"But now I think it's sad. I guess the city decided there's no space for the wat."

"Everything's sad. That's how it goes," Monk D said. He put a cig in his mouth, but then the lighter didn't work because of the wind. He signaled for me to help. Our faces leaned into each other. Our cigs touched and lit up.

"That's messed up," I said, stepping back and looking around. The last time I'd stood in the middle of the field, I talked to an army recruiter. It wasn't the first time recruiters tabled at Cambodian New Year, but it was the first time I saw an Asian guy doing it. I recognized him as some Hmong dude who'd been a few years ahead of me in school. He was smiling in his uniform, ignoring the mean-mugging looks from the Cambo grandpas, who hate Hmong people for no legit reason. We started talking and he asked me how life had been. I didn't tell him I was working two shit jobs, that I'd dropped out of my first semester of community college. I shrugged, and then said, "Eh." He told me he "got it," before handing me a stack of army literature. A week later, I flipped through the pamphlets. I liked how organized the headings and subheadings and bullet points were. They could detail every second of a guy's future, I thought.

"Do you have a picture of your girlfriend?" Monk D asked me out of nowhere.

"I don't carry pictures of my girlfriend in my monk robes," I answered.

"Explain her to me then," Monk D said.

"Lemme finish this smoke." I glanced at the temple. All the lights were turned off, so it looked like a giant black blob. It seemed weird that people went there for answers, peace, or anything really. I thought about Maly's body. My hands cupping her breasts as she got on top of me, the way she always did. Feeling myself inside of her, and herself surrounding me. How warm that made me feel. Breathing in her smell. I could feel a hard-on growing under my robes. I didn't feel embarrassed though. It was dark out. And I felt comfortable around Monk D, like he wouldn't mind.

I finished my cig and threw the butt into a patch of dirt. I described Maly to him. Basic stuff. How tall she was, the color of her hair. Monk D told me to stop. "No, no, explain how she is in the world," he said, waving his hand so that his cig made spirals in the air.

I started explaining Maly, which parts stick out to me, the things I will never understand yet will always appreciate. His eyes were closed and his cig started to burn out. He looked happy. It feels good I had something to do with this.

HOW I EXPLAIN MALY

Knows exactly how to say something to make it funny

Walks like she knows exactly where she's going all the time, even when she has no idea

Laughs a lot, like she sees something you don't see, not in a mean way, more like she wants you to be in on it, too

Super protective over people she loves, like her cousins

Sounds smart and like she's from around here at the same time

My second-to-last day at the temple started normal enough. I woke up and did push-ups, then did some chores. I don't know why, but I was turned on the entire morning, almost hard. Definitely had a chub the entire time I polished the relics in the prayer room.

I was gonna find a place to bate in the afternoon, but at lunchtime, the Cha told everyone to gather in the garden. By the biggest statue of Buddha, the one lying on the ground like he's chilling in bed and listening to music. We chugged the rest of our cold porridge and walked outside. Monk A was already there, standing by the Buddha's giant feet. He had lit incense and stuck the little sticks straight into the ground. There was haze floating all around him. It made him look pretty cool and badass, to be honest, like a superhuman.

When everyone crowded around Monk A, he called for me to stand next to him. Then the other monks sat down in the dirt. They assumed their usual prayer positions, where you tuck your legs under your ass and it feels like doing core exercises. Like planking for an hour straight, or until you start shaking. Monk A chanted a prayer and the other monks joined. I stood there like a dope with nothing to do. I looked at Monk D and he smirked at me, which made me feel better.

When Monk A finished chanting, he placed his hands on both my shoulders. The other monks all looked at me, too. Monk A started speaking about me, how my time here had almost ended, how my dad would be proud to see me honoring his life. Then he touched the Buddha statue's feet and gave a long speech on the original temple the Buddha's based on. People in Cambodia used to climb a mountain to visit this wat. They'd wash the great Buddha's feet to bring themselves good luck. To center themselves in a correct place.

Before I knew it the Cha was handing me a bowl of water, telling me to wash the giant feet. "Come on, do it," he said. "This is what you asked for." When I didn't budge, he pushed me closer to the statue. He pointed at the wet rag inside the bowl, then at the feet. I lowered myself to the ground and made dark wet circles on the stone. I looked behind me and the monks' heads were down. They chanted another prayer. I had an audience cheering me on, but I was still just doing chores.

THINGS I WON'T MISS

Doing the dishes and Pou's laundry

Pou talking at me about the future

Pou talking at me about the past

Thinking about my dad, seeing him around town

Interacting with Monk A

Getting random texts from fools I don't know looking for weed

Being forced to decide things for myself

After I was sure the monks were asleep, I went outside again. I wanted to get high. I walked back to the giant Buddha and stared at his feet while I smoked my joint. I waited for a weed vision to come to me. I'd cleaned the Buddha's feet to the chanting of a bunch of monks, and now the feet were supposed to become my spirit guides, unlock the secrets of the world for me, tell me about myself and Dad, grant me some out-of-body experience. Lead me someplace better, anywhere. But the feet stayed the same, and so did I. Just a big old rock and me, a regular dope getting high.

Monk D came up to my side. "You've been holding out on me," he said, taking the joint.

I thought of asking him to explain the feet-washing ritual, but then I realized Monk A had already explained it. "It's getting cold," I said instead. "Let's go to my room." I continued to stare at the Buddha's feet as I waited for Monk D to kill the joint. I remember thinking that the feet's true power might be unleashed if a real monk was high. But still, nothing happened.

In my room we sat on my sleeping mat, high as fuck, our backs against the wall. I showed Monk D a photo of Maly, which had been in the jeans I'd worn coming to the temple. It was printed on regular computer paper. Nothing special. Maly was smiling and sitting on the beach in a bikini, the happiest she's been, I like to think. It was the only time we got out of town together. Monk D was in awe of the photo. He held it close to his face. "Stop hogging my girlfriend," I said, laughing, pushing his hands so we could both see her. I left my hand on top of his. I felt nice touching his skin.

It was a damn good photo of Maly. Seeing its effect on Monk D reminded me of that, made me feel content about myself. Like I'd accomplished something real in having Maly as a girlfriend. My hand made its way to Monk D's upper thigh. His hand rested on my knee, still holding the photo. Our eyes both fixed on Maly, but I think we saw each other, too, and ourselves. My other hand reached under my robes, started stroking. He did the same. Neither of us were rushing. Finishing didn't seem like the point.

"We shouldn't make a mess," I said. "The Mas won't appreciate cleaning cum off our robes." Monk D nodded in agreement, head moving up and down, at the same pace as his wrist. I looked around the room. There was only the sleeping mat, my normal clothes, and another Buddha statue.

"We could do it on Buddha," I joked.

"You wanna get me kicked out?" he said.

"Do monks ever get fired from their jobs?" I asked.

Monk D slowed down his stroking. "I'm not trying to find out."

"I guess this is the best place to do it," I said, pointing at the photo.

"Are you sure?" he asked.

I considered what it would mean if we came onto a photo of Maly. Then I wondered if I was spending too much time worrying about a piece of paper. I rose to my knees and took the photo from him. "Let's do it on the back side," I said, turning it over. He got up, too, and faced me in the same position, like we were reflections. For balance he grabbed my shoulder. I let go of myself. He unloaded himself. And I felt transported.

THINGS I'M LOOKING FORWARD TO

Not sure yet but I'm sure something will come up

something has before

By the time Pou picks me up it's already dark. The winter days are short, his shifts are long. I spent most of the day with Monk D. We did our chores, ate lunch in the field, said bye. We didn't talk about the previous night. But we shared something between us, and that felt good, like how I used to feel when I'd get donuts with Dad.

"I'll see you," Monk D said when it was time for me to go. He punched my side. "At some wedding when you get back, I'll be doing the blessing, and you'll have to serve me food."

"Yeah, for sure," I said, punching him back.

In Pou's truck I watch the wat shrink in the side mirror. It's a black blob again, a shadow. You can't see the temple's details, none of the monks walking around. None of the fake gold lamps. Not the peeling orange, yellow, and blue paint. The rusty old parking signs in Khmer, darkness covers them completely. The way you can tell it's the temple is by the outline. I wonder if that's all you can know about someone, their outline. I wonder what will end up as mine.

We turn left and the wat leaves my sight. "The Cha's obsessed with Khmer covers of the Beatles," I say.

Pou laughs. "Well, Khmer folk played the songs better." He kept his eyes on the road. "It's 'cause America stole sounds from us in the first place. They stole our sounds and they dropped bombs on us and now you wanna go fight for them, you stupid shit."

He grabs my shoulder and gives me a nudge. "Just kidding," Pou adds. "Look, I know the Cha's giving you a hard time. He's only joking. I was looking it up, and there are a lot of benefits you get from enlisting. You can go to college. You'll always have a job. I get worried about you, that you'll become like your dad, like a dipshit. But this is a smart move. Logical." He continues talking about the reasons my decision makes sense. He counts off all the financial benefits I would have. I nod, and keep nodding.

The streets outside slowly become more city-like as we get farther from the wat. Fewer abandoned barns and more empty parking lots. More buses and less dirt. As Pou talks, I realize I never asked Monk D why he came to the temple. I can see his reasons though, a shitload of them. I can see the expectations crowding his old life, both his own and the ones hurled at him, how they probably stopped running together right, how adding them up to total one person, it'd result in a Frankenstein-looking giant. Its proportions all fucked up, it'd limp around, yell out noises that weren't words, and try to be understood. And I can see that in becoming a monk, he could shed these expectations, replace them with something else. Something with a clear outline. But if I tell Monk D this, I bet he'd blow smoke in my face and laugh, pass me his cig and urge me to chill. Somethings can't be explained to death, he'd say. Guess they don't need to be, I'd say. That's how shit goes, we'd say.

WE WOULD'VE BEEN PRINCES!

I.

ENOUGH HENNESSY FOR AN AFTERPARTY

Thank god, Buddha, the monks, and the CHA, who didn't get as drunk as usual, who piloted the prayers and ceremonies with aplomb, and don't forget those other party animals who trashed the banquet room—whom the cousins called Mings and Pous because, sure, everyone at the reception was related, anyone over the age of forty was definitely someone's auntie or uncle—bless them all, the WEDDING was done. And the cousins of the BRIDE could at last liberate themselves from their duties; from the itchy traditional outfits that were rentals, so nobody knew if they'd ever, really, been washed; from the praying in one-hundred-degree weather, chanting words that meant nothing to the BRIDE and GROOM, getting palm flowers chucked at their faces by tipsy guests; and, most tedious of all, from being subjected, whether as witness or participant, to the never-ending photo ops, with the BRIDAL PARTY arranged in the middle of a golf course, next to a man-made lake, during the golden hour of sunrise, and then again, twelve hours later, backlit by the sunset, with the GROOM shaking the hands of his groomsmen, individually and then all at once, like they were playing the human knot, and then, of course, a candid shot of the BRIDE and her bridesmaids having their makeup repainted, then the BRIDE posing with her parents, then with her siblings, then with her half siblings, then with her cousins, second cousins, third cousins twice removed, then with the in-laws, then with the family that owns Chuck's Donuts and the other family that owns Angkor Pharmacy, and finally these same poses all over again, but in the white, American dress.

So let the real drinking commence! Their new location was still undetermined, but it hardly mattered—anyplace but Dragon Palace Restaurant, which had been packed to the gills with three hundred California Valley Cambos. No more stuck-up Pous pretending they have royal blood, that this city was the Hollywood of celebrity ex-refugees, that the sidewalk off El Dorado Street was one giant red carpet for them to strut down. No more downplaying how much they drank in front of their Gongs and Mas. The younger crowd knew better than to get sloshed in front of their seventy-year-old devout Buddhist grandparents who had survived not just genocide, but the AUTO-GENOCIDE. Especially not after the BRIDE's fifth-favorite cousin, Marlon—straddling the edge of blackout drunk like a true recovering drug addict—danced with too much verve next to the FAMOUS SINGER, who had been flown out from Phnom Penh by their resident RICH MING. But now the grown-ups were gone! The BRIDE and GROOM were already on their way to Vegas for honeymoon gambling! Even Marlon's younger brother, Bond, the BRIDE's eighth-favorite cousin, had loosened the tie looped around his neck.

The FAMOUS SINGER was asking for a ride to RICH MING's vacant rental home, which was both the headquarters for the BRIDAL PARTY, and also guest lodgings for the FAMOUS SINGER. Her voice coarse from singing for hours on end, the FAMOUS SINGER needed a hot lemon water to soothe her throat, she claimed, and drank tea brewed only with Evian mineral water.

"Here I am to save the day!" Marlon screamed, launching himself into the air, landing on a chair before the FAMOUS SINGER. Holding two unopened bottles of Hennessy cognac, he jumped down and fell to one knee, as if offering booze in exchange for her hand in marriage. "I'll even drive you!"

"You are drunk, boy," the FAMOUS SINGER whispered, unwilling to raise her voice now that she was no longer, technically, on the clock.

"Then my beautiful brother will drive us!" Marlon sang. He pointed a bottle to the right, though Bond stood to his left. "But you gottta bring everyone home for an afterparty." He swung his bottles around to indicate that he meant the twenty- and thirty-year-olds scattered about the empty dinner tables, all the cousins of the BRIDE.

The FAMOUS SINGER aimed her symmetrical face at Bond. "How much did you drink?" she asked, her fake eyelashes batting a mini hurricane.

"We need more time in your presence!" Marlon slurred.

"It's okay, I can drive," Bond said, eyes glued to the FAMOUS SINGER's six-inch heels.

"So what do you say?" Marlon asked, standing up and grinning. Something about his unabashed drunkenness, his gleeful childlike pronouncements, complemented his broad shoulders. "Party with us?"

Was it blood that zoomed to the FAMOUS SINGER's cheeks or just maternal pity? Being handsome and pathetic was Marlon's selling point. Mothers adored that poor fellow brimming with wasted possibility. "Fine, but I need to drink my lemon water," the FAMOUS SINGER said, and the crowd of cousins cheered. Everyone snatched a bottle of leftover Hennessy, a takeout box of lobster scraps and fried rice drenched in lobster juice, and then rallied to RICH MING's rental home.

II.

A RUNDOWN OF THE OBJECTIVE, AS MARLON'S TOO DRUNK TO REMEMBER

Bond knew he should have stopped Marlon from the beginning. All night he'd wanted to yank the Heinekens from Marlon's grasp. Wanted to intercept his older brother's swigs of cognac like a basketball player blocking his opponent's every shot. But he was no athlete, not like Marlon. He worked as a paralegal in San Francisco but thought of himself as a struggling painter who lived in Oakland—the word *struggling* feeling more redundant with every passing year, despite his BA in art practice from UC Berkeley.

Driving their dad's new Lexus SUV, Bond glanced into the rearview mirror and saw Marlon's drunken body sprawled across the back seat, while in the passenger seat the FAMOUS SINGER reapplied her lipstick. It must be hard to look that good, Bond thought, before recalling Marlon in rehab, how his brother had gelled his hair every morning, swept it into a seamless black wave. Bond figured it was the best way Marlon could remember who the hell he was.

Marlon sat up, and in the rearview mirror, his limbs appeared to snap into their rightful place. He leaned forward, bracing himself against the center console. The smell of alcohol and sweat rushed into the front half of the car. "Who the fuck even *is* Visith?"

"He's our parents' second cousin," Bond said in a mock serious, flat voice. "Just closer to our age. He owns the jewelry place on March Lane. You're *so* drunk you forgot your own uncle?"

"No, I get that," Marlon answered. "I want to know why he, like, matters."

Of course he'd already forgotten! Bond gripped the steering wheel harder, the fat premium leather awkward in his hands. He fought the urge to pick at his stress acne. A scene from earlier that night crashed into his thoughts: their mom in tears, pushing away her plate of lobster, ditching their dinner table to sit by herself after she'd tried scolding the tipsy out of Marlon's bloodstream, to which Marlon had joked, "It's not like I'm on meth!" At the center of the table were wide glass cylinders, filled with drowning orchids and topped by candles. How Bond had wished the BRIDE would turn off the ceiling lights; it would've been the craziest, most amazing painting, all those tiny floating flames.

Now the FAMOUS SINGER was glittering the area around her eye sockets, lightly dabbing her skull with two fingers. "Visith is a good Khmer name," she said. "Not like you two, who do not have Khmer names at all."

"Fuck that shit!" Marlon shouted into their ears. "We're named after Marlon Brando and James fucking Bond! Which, in fact—the logic's so Cambodian it hurts: name your kids after the first movies you saw after immigrating, and *bam!*" Marlon clapped his hands together, the sound like thunder. "American Dream achieved!" He thrashed his head up and down to the Kanye song playing on the radio.

"Marlon Brando . . . like *STELLA, STELLA!*" the FAMOUS SINGER sang, and Marlon joined her.

"STELLAAAAAAAAAAA!"

His head-banging escalated into a solitary mosh pit.

"Anyway," Bond said, "we gotta find out how much Visith gifted at the wedding." He was referring to the mission they'd agreed on back at the reception, while unloading themselves in adjacent urinals. The drunkenness had temporarily drained out of Marlon, enough for him to realize the extent that he must've bruised their mom's feelings. *It'll calm her down to know*, Bond had told his older brother, as they washed their hands with the restaurant's diluted pink soap. It was the best they could do. "Remember? For Mom?"

"Right," Marlon said, breathing more alcohol yet into the Lexus. "For Mom."

That night, before their mother had stormed off in tears, the BRIDE, the GROOM, and the BRIDAL PARTY, in a customary procession, zigzagged through the dinner tables, collecting ang pavs the bridesmaids had placed on every seat. Subjecting the newlyweds to hazing rituals, the grown-ups stood on their chairs and forced the BRIDE to grab their red gift envelopes, all stuffed with cash, from high above her head, with only her teeth, while they also cheered for the GROOM to plant wet kisses on the lips of Mings and Mas and one wasted Gong.

At their table, Marlon and Bond's dad, a strict proponent of tradition who loved to outclass his peers, had initially filled their family's collective envelopes with six thousand dollars. Which induced their mom to plead, desperately, for the family to spend less money, in case something horrible happened, such as—though it was left unsaid—Marlon's pill addiction resurfacing and his returning to rehab. Then Marlon spotted Visith heading for the bathroom, right as the bridal procession was approaching his table. "Woah, is Visith trying to swerve his gifting duties?" Marlon casually asked, igniting a frenzy of outraged speculations from their mom, who would now—Bond knew—not be able to sleep at all. Her righteous indignation, when piqued, was known to rev up her chronic insomnia.

"I swear, on Buddha himself," Marlon said, resprawling his limbs across the back seat, "Visith fucking slipped his ang pav right into his pocket so he could ignore it."

The FAMOUS SINGER shook her head. "That is not

okay," she said. "He is of the age to be giving back. The BRIDE and the GROOM need that money to build new lives."

"Yeah, and our parents are hella petty," Marlon added. "They're, like, dying for an excuse to give jack shit at Visith's own stupid wedding, you know, especially if he ain't paying his dues. Our mom can't stand him. She doesn't wanna attend his wedding next month—it's basically a green card marriage for this rando chick from Battambang whose parents are buying Visith a new goddamn house—but our pops is making her go. She's hated the motherfucker ever since the guy sold her fake-ass diamonds."

"Which she got refunded," Bond said.

"Only after hounding him for weeks," Marlon said. "And he gave some bullshit explanation about inventory errors."

"So Visith is not respectable," the FAMOUS SINGER said, retouching her face with blush. "Shame—he has a Rolex, too, like a hard worker."

Marlon made an ugly sound around his tongue.

"He wears Rolexes as marketing for his jewelry store," Bond explained, and Marlon contributed an even more obnoxious noise. "Still," Bond continued, rolling his eyes, "Visith has decent business, so it's hard to see why he wouldn't shell out some money. It's not like *everyo*ne in the family needs to give more than, like, a hundred bucks." He turned the car left, onto the street that was lined with the rental properties owned by RICH MING—the lady had practically bought up the whole neighborhood. He slowed down and squinted to see the address numbers on the dark houses.

"Yeah, well," Marlon said, "motherfucker never tips at Ming Lee's noodle shop either."

"You're fucking drunk," Bond said. "We need, like, actual proof. If not for Mom, then for Dad to agree with Mom."

"You cannot inquire with the BRIDE?" the FAMOUS SINGER asked.

"Oh my god, have you *met* her?" Marlon sprang back into an upright position. "Let's just get him, like, seriously messed up," he said, reaching into the pocket of his younger brother's suit jacket, which caused Bond to jerk the car into a whiplashing stop, the tires screeching against the asphalt.

"Jesus Christ!" Bond yelled, elbowing his brother. "Can you just—*not*?"

Marlon backed off and grinned. He held up a joint. "I knew you had one!" he said. "Now we can lure him into a confession—people always spill when they're high."

"Getting him cross-faded isn't gonna do shit," Bond said, snatching his joint back from his brother. "That's not our plan."

"You have a better idea?" Marlon asked, and Bond grimaced.

"Okay. Fine," Bond said. "That's the plan until we figure out a *better* plan." He almost blurted, Please don't get more wasted yourself, but then found himself thinking, Well, at least he's not doing meth.

"That is a dumb idea," the FAMOUS SINGER scoffed. "What is wrong with asking the BRIDE?"

"Her mom's best friends with Visith's older sister, for one thing," Bond said, stepping on the gas pedal. "And both have big mouths. Our parents don't want anyone to know they're thinking of snubbing Visith. They hate gossip."

"Nah," Marlon said, "they hate gossip when it's about *them*."

It was past midnight when Bond parked in front of their destination. The house sat at the foot of the Delta's levee—one of those ritzy waterfront pads—its beaming windows the sole light on the block. The FAMOUS SINGER unbuckled her seat belt, making even that look elegant. "Without gossip," she said, "how do you know not to respect a man with a Rolex?"

"Preach, baby!" Marlon howled, and jumped out of the car. Then, alongside the FAMOUS SINGER, he shimmied his way to the house, totally forgetting about the wide-open door of the Lexus, because, whatever, his younger brother would take care of anything that required handling, right?

In the stillness Marlon left behind, Bond inhaled and closed his eyes. He saw himself rendered in geometric brushstrokes, sitting in his dad's overpriced SUV and framed by the driver's window. A mixture of deep blues, fluorescent glows, and natural light from the moon. The background: the house atop a grassy mound, a beacon of bright yellow windows, and two figures ascending the lawn—one, the FAMOUS SINGER, a silhouette of long hair, a modern Apsara, and the other, a bulkier version of himself, a burst of energy drifting away.

III.

THE BRIDESMAIDS GET THE PARTY STARTED WITH SOME MARIAH CAREY

He was buzzed. Not incapacitated, not "off the wagon," and everyone—especially his mom, and definitely his younger brother—needed to chill the hell out. Marlon stood in the center of the living room and swayed. He double-fisted swigs of cognac and the neon green of a Gatorade he found in the fridge, which no one seemed to notice because no one appreciated that he knew how to handle his goddamn shit.

"Why is there no music playing?" he yelled. "I need to dance if I'm gonna enjoy my electrolytes!"

He threw his Gatorade into the air and caught it, then thanked Buddha that he had remembered to twist the bottle shut. He'd been thanking Buddha, as a joke, for all his fortunes, since doing a monthlong stint at the dingy rehab of their hometown, which required each group therapy monologue to begin with "I thank god I am alive."

"Do I have to do fucking everything!" screamed Monica, the LOCAL ACCOUNTANT, who did everyone's taxes pro bono, and who was also the BRIDE's maid of honor and first-favorite cousin, according to the number of Instagram posts of them posing at the club.

Behind the kitchen island, Monica rummaged through a never-ending procession of overfilled plastic bags from the reception. Her fellow bridesmaids kept walking in through the front door with more junk to organize, catalog, recycle, dismantle, and return for a refund because the BRIDE's parents hated being ripped off, despite their flair for decadence, so amply manifested in the course of this three-day wedding. And now, to top it off, apparently she had to make a hot lemon water for the FAMOUS SINGER, who was, as far as Monica could tell, a forty-year-old-fake-eyelash-wearing-uppity-motherfucking-diva.

"Woah," Marlon said, still swaying, "Guess I won't be applying for a spot in the BRIDE TRIBE." He pointed at Monica's tank top, the words splayed across her chest in purple glitter. He faltered a bit, so Bond put his hand on Marlon's shoulder, tried to anchor him firmly to the ground. "I'm fine, I'm *fine*," Marlon said. "It's called *dancing*."

Bond shrugged and walked over to the kitchen to help Monica.

"Come on!" Marlon called after Bond. "Don't get sucked into her schtick! I mean, does this really need to be done right *now* and not, like, tomorrow? This is an afterparty! When's the next time everyone's gonna visit home again? Let's have fun before the weekend's dead, before it's just me, stuck in this fake city, without my Cambos. Me with nothing to do but go on bad Tinder dates to Chipotle!"

Someone yanked Marlon by his shirtsleeves and he collapsed into the sectional couch. "So that's what you think of your uncle!" Visith said. "I'm not enough for you? This why I never see you around?" Visith grabbed and constrained his nephew the way Pous did when Marlon was young, when Marlon would be minding his goddamn business as he played with hand-me-down Hot Wheels, only to get yanked into some goading argument among the grown-ups to serve as a rhetorical pawn in their dialogue about morality or honor or whether King Sihanouk was worse than Pol Pot or whether *The Killing Fields* was actually a bad movie or why some Cambos listened to hip-hop-good-for-nothing-trash-music and others became model students who studied nursing or dentistry or even accounting.

This dude definitely gifted squat, Marlon thought, wishing Bond had a telepathic connection straight to his brain. "If you're our uncle," he said, "it's, like, *barely*."

"Yeah, shut the fuck up Visith!" Monica yelled. "Marlon's right, for once. Punch me in the face the day I start calling you *Pou*." She handed over to Bond a bag of fake-Buddhist wedding favors, tiny silver goblets all filled with chocolates.

"What am I supposed to do with these?" Bond asked.

"Get 'em out of my face," Monica answered.

Just then, the rest of the bridesmaids and groomsmen and miscellaneous cousins—second cousins, third cousins, other Cambos unrelated to the BRIDE but whose families had escaped the regime with the BRIDE's family through a forest of minefields—charged into the living room and kitchen in an overwhelming surge of rowdy drunken shouting. The bag of favors vanished from Bond's grasp, and he felt the sensation he often experienced when visiting home, that his parents had conceived him to work on a conveyor belt of nonsensical family issues. How else could he explain the tasks that continued to jam up the flow of his free time? Like attending debrief sessions with Marlon's rehab counselor because their mom could barely deal and their dad ignored any and all problems involving these sons of his who would never understand the horrors, the nightmares, the endless grief, that came with the AUTO-GENOCIDE.

Bond observed the open room. The FAMOUS SINGER had reemerged from her bedroom, looking better than she did at the wedding. A bridesmaid was holding the decorated money box from the reception, but she promptly disappeared into the hallway. Maybe they didn't need to bother with Visith, Bond thought, considering all those signed and sealed envelopes. Then he saw Visith acting chummy with a fuming Marlon. Bond hoped his brother wouldn't say something stupid, that he would refrain from accusing a sober Visith, outright, if he had snubbed the BRIDE, because then Visith would get offended and stories would spread about Marlon's offense and then their parents' reputations would run the gauntlet of the Cambo rumor cycle. Which was the last thing anyone needed. He scanned the room again. Among the crowd of cousins, the bag of wedding favors was nowhere to be found.

A shot glass appeared in Bond's hands, as two bridesmaids bounced across the room handing servings of Hennessy to everyone except Monica, who was given a whole bottle to alleviate her suffering as the maid of honor. The bridesmaids found a speaker and plugged its aux cable into a phone. "Can you really be a drunk Cambo without blasting Mariah Carey?" one of them shouted.

"All I Want for Christmas Is You" blared from the speaker, and Visith said, "It's *July*, dumbasses."

"So what? It's the best Mariah song!" Marlon said, inciting *Fuck yeahs* from the two bridesmaids. He broke free from Visith and started dancing in the middle of the living room, elbows bent close to his torso, shoulders bopping up and down. He waved at his younger brother and yelled, "Drink!"

Bond sighed, twisted his face, and downed his shot of cognac.

The afterparty had officially started, and Marlon felt relieved. The entire night he had yearned to ache into that warm nothingness. Hollow pangs of muscle memory throbbed in his thighs, his shoulders, the places where he had felt the most heat. Cravings pulsed through his whole body. But he would survive this night. If everyone had fun—if his younger brother managed to chill out—he could do it. He wanted to forget the damage he had done to his life, to dance and drink and pretend, at least for one night, that everything would be okay, that he could fill the emptiness inside with these Cambos he loved. Grooving to Mariah Carey, Marlon looked straight into the kitchen's fluorescent lights. A stream of white seared his vision, flushed out his brain. He gulped down another swig.

IV.

THE DRUNKEN MONOLOGUES CAMBOS DELIVER AT 1:15 A.M.

"Someone take a picture of me in this 'Bride Tribe' tank so I can post it on Instagram, tag the BRIDE to make her happy, and change into my normal clothes," Monica said.

"Or, I don't know, kill myself—whatever's easier with this giant-ass hair!"

Four drinks deep, Monica had grown simultaneously angrier and more dutiful toward the BRIDE. By now the afterparty had spilled out into the garage and the hallway, where Bond was helping Monica, for no reason he could readily discern, stuff bags into a closet.

"How did you get your dress off and the tank on in the first place?" Bond asked, genuinely curious. Monica's tightly wound locks fed a mess of frozen curls sitting on her head like an alien leech controlling her mind.

"I don't even know," she said. "The dress was so tight on me, I went into a blind rage tearing it off."

Maybe that's where the ang pavs went, Bond thought, peering into the closet. If so, he could see if there was a red envelope signed by Visith. "Is the money box safe?" he said, feeling clumsy for asking.

"Why, you gonna steal it or some shit?"

"What?—no—Jesus." His phone buzzed, and to seem less flustered, Bond pulled it out to check his messages. A photo of Visith shotgunning a beer popped up, accompanied by a text from Marlon saying, Too late! The garage party be bumpin and I'm the GAME MASTER. A response to Bond's earlier text saying, Hold off on the plan, I think I found a better way.

"You *should* steal it," Monica said, her face engulfed in a red glow. "Steal her money and then redistribute it to everyone as, like, reparations. She got, what, fifty grand for getting married? Why are we rewarding her? Anybody can get married. *I* can get married tomorrow. Old white guys fill out online forms and brides are Fedex-ed to them!"

She brought the bottle to her mouth, whiffed the alcohol, and mimed a hurling face. "I can't drink anymore or I'll die."

Monica threw the bottle into Bond's hands. He thought of another painting, a gaudy portrait of Monica—hideous hair, grotesque makeup, with the BRIDE TRIBE tank rendered in a dramatic chiaroscuro—then shook off the notion. "I don't know," he said, collecting his more decent thoughts. "These weddings are kinda nice. I mean, when's the next time someone's gonna pay the FAMOUS SINGER to perform for us?"

"Don't get me started on her!" Monica yelled. "All weekend she'd ordered me to make hot lemons. Once I had to do it three fucking times before it was 'right.' How can you be picky about *that*?" Monica took out the bag she had, only a second ago, stuffed into the closet, and started digging through it.

"Look, what needs to be done?" Bond said, and then remembered pairing with Monica as lab partners in AP chemistry, how she would micromanage their experiments to death, doubling the work necessary to receive a good grade. He snatched the bag from her. "*I'll* do it."

"You wouldn't do it right," she said, grabbing it back, and Bond felt like pulling out his hair, or maybe hers.

"It's the money," she continued. "Being rich has fucked with people's heads. Forty years ago our parents survived Pol Pot, and *now*, what the holy fuck are we even doing? Obsessing over wedding favors? Wasting hundreds of dollars on getting our hair done? Do you know what the TRADITIONAL CLOTHING LADY said to me? She said,

It's good we hired her to do the wedding outfits because most Cambodians here used to be low *country* people, and no one but *her* carries the expensive styles from Phnom Penh. Can you believe that? Apparently once you have money, you develop fake problems! You should *hear* the shit people tell me when I do their taxes." Monica stopped going through the bag and considered Bond, her eyes lighting up. "Marlon's a perfect example!" she said. "He was making *hella* money, and then he got anxiety and depressed or whatever, and then he got addicted to drugs. It's the money, I swear. Like, do you think our parents had 'anxieties' when they lived through the genocide? No, they worried about fucking surviving."

Bond took a drink and clenched his jaw. Sure, Marlon drove him crazy—you had to be a selfish dumbass to get roaring-ass drunk in front of your mother when she was forever paranoid about your history with substance abuse—but when had Monica become an expert on his family? And where was Monica when his family had *no* money? Where was anyone?

"You really have no idea what you're talking about," Bond said.

"What? Are you offended?" Monica taunted. "You don't need to be defensive. I'm not your mom."

"Marlon's really messed up. He's always been."

"We're *all* messed up!" Monica shouted. "Do you think any of us aren't? But when you have money, you start focusing on every little way you've been fucked over. And meanwhile, the rest of us *deal*! I can't imagine what I'd do with the money this wedding cost. With the money the

BRIDE's parents have, or, fuck, *your* parents!" She whacked her head repeatedly, to satisfy an elusive itch buried somewhere beneath her frozen hair. "Like, oh my god, you know the BRIDE made us store her money box so she could keep it as a memory. She kept texting to remind me not to throw it away! And don't get me started on how she, like, *needed* us to put the ang pavs in her car before she left the reception. Like she couldn't trust her cousins? It's not like she doesn't know where we all live! I bet she was texting me while counting all her stupid fucking money."

Bond clenched his jaw harder. He had spent an hour following Monica around, listening to her rant about the wedding. He watched in complicity as she tried proving just how much smarter, how much more responsible, she was than the BRIDE—than Marlon, than him, than everyone—because what? Because when she got drunk she completed random unnecessary tasks? And now he'd found out the money box was empty!

Fucking shit, Bond thought. And fuck Monica. He swore the sneer across her face communicated everyone's exact thoughts on him and his brother. Those poor parents, he imagined all of them thinking. Look at their disgraceful kids, tarnishing their parents' reputations with drug addictions and frivolous artistic delusions. Why had those parents worked so hard for a future like this?

If only the cousin understood how much he toiled away for his family. The countless times, while growing up, he had cleaned the entire apartment, walked a mile to buy groceries, and cooked the family meals because his dad was working night shifts or cramming for engineering school, because Marlon was out with his friends being angry in the world, because his mom cycled through depressive episodes, leaving her so crippled that her sons—twelve and sixteen during the worst of it—had to beg her just to get out of bed, to eat, to live. For god's sake, here he was, scheming to find proof of his uncle gifting nothing at his cousin's wedding. All for his mom.

Suddenly, he found everything unbearable—the sight of Monica, the thumping vocal runs of Mariah Carey, the *whoops* and *damns* coming from what sounded like a dance battle in the garage. He pushed past Monica to enter a bedroom, knocking the bag from her grasp. Dozens of used, damp candles from the reception spilled onto the ground. "I was *counting* those!" Bond heard Monica yell from behind the door.

V.

THE GAME MASTER HATCHES A NEW PLAN TO EXPOSE VISITH

The rules of the drinking game eluded the drunken cousins, but that stopped no one from trash-talking their opponents like they got paid six-figure salaries to administer verbal beatdowns to their own flesh and blood. Marlon—the self-appointed GAME MASTER—had concocted for the garage crowd an amalgamation of beer pong, dice but without actual dice, an aerobics workout, truth or dare, and darts, with crumpled paper instead of actual darts. And people were *engrossed*, even the FAMOUS SINGER. Recovering drug addict or not, Marlon was the FUN COUSIN.

The final round had started, and Visith, competing against a bridesmaid for the championship title, was getting booed out of the dance circle for refusing to pop and lock. "This is dumb!" Visith said. "Let's go back to throwing balls in cups."

"You are too scared to dance in front of us?" the FAMOUS SINGER asked, her proper tone more belittling than regular trash talk.

"Wait—we can pivot," Marlon said, proud to have used the word *pivot* in a context not involving his online coding classes, which he was taking for the tech boot camp his parents were paying for because he'd ruined his career in finance by sinking into an Adderall-induced psychosis, right in front of his old boss. A brilliant idea had sparked in his head, and Marlon wanted to capitalize on it before his eventual comedown, before he felt the sensation, like he often did after midnight, that the whole world was stomping on his chest. He quickly looked around, then started gathering supplies from the cabinets. This new plan would expose Visith once and for all, Marlon thought, fighting his drunken spins by throwing himself into meaningful action.

On the table in the center of the garage, Marlon unloaded an armful of supplies and proceeded to tear paper into a pile of scraps. He secretly marked a piece, and then passed them out to everyone, along with several pens. "Write down the amount you gifted the newlyweds," Marlon said, earning looks of skepticism. He handed Visith and the bridesmaid a scrap of paper each, making sure to give his uncle the one he'd marked. "Don't worry, it's anonymous."

When everyone was done, Marlon collected the scraps in a tin can. "Listen up!" he said, standing in between the final two competitors. "This, here, is the last game: Whoever draws the higher number is declared best cousin!"

"That's lame!" yelled one of the Mariah Carey–loving bridesmaids. "I wanna see some dancing!"

"Guys, don't be fooled by how basic this game seems!" Marlon said, punctuating his words with his free hand, his heartbeat sprinting into a belligerent thumping. "The winner we deserve shouldn't be decided by dancing or skill. Trust me. Choosing one of these numbers is a test of fate, of what the universe thinks we deserve, who it deems our winner. This is about Buddha! About karma! Are we destined for greatness? Or failure? Some people are born winners, am I right? And others, unfortunately, are born losers. This is what we're testing!"

"Just pick a number so this drunk will shut the fuck up," someone said to Visith and the last bridesmaid standing.

Red in the face and covered in cognac-infused sweat, Visith stepped forward and rolled up his shirtsleeve. "I got this in the bag," he said. "I mean, I was born a prince. If Pol Pot didn't ruin Cambodia, I would've been the oldest son of the richest family in the province. It's in my blood!"

Marlon couldn't help but notice the Rolex strapped to his uncle's wrist, the multiple diamond rings circling his fingers, as Visith fished a number out of the can. Did he think he deserved more than this, Marlon wondered, and the thought unleashed an exhaustion that had been creeping on him all night, the feeling that nothing would ever be enough, that his entire existence had started with some chemical deficiency. He wanted another drink, a hit.

"Seven hundred!" Visith shouted, holding his number high in the air.

Then the bridesmaid stuck her hand into the can. When she pulled out her scrap, Marlon saw that it was the marked one he'd given to Visith. "Five hundred," she said, disappointed.

Visith whooped in celebration. He punched the air. "Say hello to the best cousin!" he hollered in a cry of triumph.

"This is bullshit," the bridesmaid said. "I would've totally won a dance-off." She pointed antagonistically at Visith. "But you just had to be a baby!"

The crowd roared in agreement.

"He doesn't deserve the win!" someone shouted.

"Make him dance!" someone else shouted, and the rowdy cousins started chanting: "Dance! Dance! Dance!"

"Fuck you all!" Visith slurred. "Bunch of sore losers."

Marlon stepped away from Visith, aligning himself with the crowd. *Motherfucker has to be lying*, he thought, there was no way he gifted that much money.

"Let me tell you the difference between winning and losing," Visith now said, clearing the floor with a grand flailing of his arms, and also the slobber he spit on everyone. "It's shame! Losers have shame and winners *don't.* You think you're gonna make me feel bad about changing the game?" Visith scoffed an aggressive laugh, loud enough that the cousins went silent. "Fuck *that*," he continued.

"That's exactly how you win! How do you think our family became rich? How some of us stayed rich while others sat on their asses doing jack shit? It's time for a lesson, straight from my mouth to your ignorant brains!"

Visith wiped the sweat off his forehead, prepared himself to take down the crowd, to assert himself as the ELDEST COUSIN, while Marlon suddenly understood how dumb his plan had been, how easy it would've been to jot down any old number onto that scrap of paper, how maybe everyone was right to see him as the PRIVILEGED FAILURE whose parents kept bailing him out.

"Our family," Visith started, "we used to jump on any advantage we could. Great-great-Gong came from China, stepped onto a piece of land in Battambang, and he decided, 'This shit is mine.' He didn't care that villagers already lived there. The baller just started building his rice factory, then convinced the villagers it would benefit them to work for *him*. Why worry about land when you can clock in hours and get paid salaries? Did he tell them how much money he would make versus them? Hell no, he wasn't a goddamn loser. He made business decisions without shame, took whatever he fucking wanted." Chest puffed up, nostrils flared out, Visith walked the invisible perimeter between him and the cousins. "*That's* why I'm successful and you dumbasses aren't: *I* remember how we became rich. I don't let anything set me back, see?—I don't give a fuck."

Visith stopped when he reached Marlon and the FAMOUS SINGER. He was staring Marlon down, snickering and heaving like a madman, with bloodshot eyes and an assault of body odor. "You know what I'm talking about," Visith said, petting Marlon's head. And then, as if to prove his larger point, Visith turned toward the FAMOUS SINGER, grabbed her by the waist, and forced a kiss on her mouth.

The cousins in the garage flinched, at the sight of their uncle's sloppy moves, a couple of the bridesmaids even gasping, and Marlon watched in disbelief as the FAMOUS SINGER shoved Visith off, as she whacked him several times—hard enough to make it clear that a line had been seriously crossed, but light enough to avoid a real scene. He found himself thinking, Someone should punch this fucker in the face, and as soon as he'd completed the thought, Marlon's right fist was colliding into his uncle's nose, forcing a howl of pain from his throat, so that of course Visith retaliated by punching his aggressor in the ribs, cracking one or two, Marlon swore, groaning, crouching from the pain, and then lunging at his uncle, both of them falling to the ground, hammering blows into guts and maneuvering skulls into headlocks and limbs into half nelsons, until neither could maintain a steady breath at all, really, their panting and slobbering the music of pure, childish violence, and until Monica burst into the garage, ordering all the dumbstruck bystanders to pull the idiot man-babies *off* each other.

From across the room, Marlon stared at the blood dripping from those nostrils as the lunatic, held back by two boy cousins, continued to scream at him. His thoughts mushrooming into a dense fog, Marlon felt the alcohol draining from his aching, bruised body. He considered bailing on this party, just walking out the door and going anywhere, like all those times he had joined another sports team, started another extracurricular activity, hung out in another empty parking lot downing cough syrup with his friends, just so he could avoid dealing with his dad, his mom, even his younger brother. Of course this party had ended with blood everywhere. He was born in the midst of chaos, so how the hell could he ever prevent it?

VI.

THE FAMOUS SINGER TEACHES EVERYONE THE TRADITIONAL BUTT-GRABBING GAME OF MATRIMONY

Marlon made it as far as the living room before the guilt stopped him. Leaving Bond to finish their mission alone simply wasn't an option. And where would he even go? He wasn't in high school anymore. There were no friends to hit up. There was nothing for him outside of this house, this party, his family. All he had now was Bond.

He stumbled his way back up the hallway, bursting through each door to see if his younger brother stood behind it. After walking right into a closet and then a bathroom, where a bridesmaid was just then vomiting into the toilet, he found Bond smoking weed in a bedroom. The sight of his brother immediately lulled Marlon into a calm. "Hey, it's a *you* painting," he said, sitting next to Bond at the foot of the bed.

"Ming bought it at my first show," Bond said, giving Marlon the joint. "What the hell was that in the garage? Sounded like a zoo out there."

"Nothing. Visith's nose might be broken. My fault, I guess."

Bond shot Marlon a knowing glance.

"Don't look at me like that," Marlon said. "He totally deserved it. Probably."

"So he didn't gift any money?"

"He *claims* he did."

Bond seized the joint from Marlon. He took a hit, then blew smoke in his brother's face. "You don't deserve this, and also shouldn't have it."

"Come on," Marlon said. "I'm super sober now, after Visith beat the fuck out of me. One of my ribs might be, like, really broken."

"Yeah, that's not how alcohol works."

"Man . . . you know you wanna get high with your older bro."

"Fine, here." Bond lifted the joint to his brother's mouth, and Marlon inhaled its smoke deeply, only to immediately start coughing.

"For a recovering drug addict, you really can't handle your shit," Bond said, and they both laughed. Then the brothers studied the painting in front of them: their mom with a riotous perm, standing in a field of rose bushes, donning the kind of bright patterns found in the eighties.

"I've always liked this one."

"Yeah? So why'd you get so fucked up at my show?"

"The real question is why weren't *you* fucked up," Marlon said, grinning. He passed the joint back to his brother. "I mean, for a starving hipster artist and all, you've gotten pretty uptight."

Bond sighed. "I used to be so cool," he half joked.

He remembered the night of his first show, how he'd known instantly Marlon was relapsing, maybe with a handful of painkillers, a dash of Adderall for sure, to get through his twelve-hour workday. He sensed it from Marlon's clammy hands, his dilated, searching pupils, the way his greasy hair kept falling into his face. Why had he then allowed his brother to drink an entire bottle of wine, before passing out in the corner, triggering yet another spell of their mother's killer depressions? He looked at Marlon. It was hard not to admire the way his brother's features seemed a perfect mingling of their parents'.

"My bullshit probably sucked the coolness right out of you." Marlon stared intently ahead, his expression dead serious. "I'm sorry, you know? For being, like, the worst older brother."

"Don't worry about it," Bond said brusquely, feeling a dull pang in his chest. "If you weren't, Dad would be, like, way more pissed over the loans I have from majoring in art." Through his stoned eyes, the painting had started to bleed into the wall, roses proliferating across his frame of view. He wondered if Marlon could see the same vision he did, before realizing how stupid a thought that was, before he noticed a familiar tinge of anguish in his brother's slight grin. He knew Marlon was waiting for him to say something else. Perhaps his joke about their dad hadn't been enough to alleviate the pressure, the guilt, the crazy whirlwind of thoughts, his older brother was always feeling. But he couldn't bring himself to utter a word, not even to mention what he'd been obsessing over all night—the mission, Marlon's drinking, their mom.

The door swung open, and Bond and Marlon looked over to find the FAMOUS SINGER. "Fuck," Bond said, ash dropping onto his pants, "this is the room you're staying in?"

The FAMOUS SINGER raised one eyebrow, gleamed a patronizing look, and waved over at the piles and piles of her luggage in the corner. Then she sat down and accepted the joint from Bond—a peace offering.

"In Cambodia, we put this on pizza," she said, exhaling smoke, "and call it happy pizza."

"You should write a song about that," Marlon said.

"I am writing a song about it," the FAMOUS SINGER said, to Marlon's surprise. She sucked in another hit, killing the last of the weed. "You think I am making a joke. No, I am serious. Cambodians, we never let ourselves enjoy life. It is always thinking on the past, worrying for the future."

"That's no good," Bond responded.

"Did you find out how much money Visith gifted, or do you need to inquire with the BRIDE, like I said?"

"Not entirely confirmed," Marlon said.

"I expect little from that child," the FAMOUS SINGER said, standing up and smoothing over the creases in her dress. "Come with me. I have an idea, a good one."

Both in a daze, Marlon and Bond followed the FAMOUS

SINGER into the living room, where Mariah Carey's voice still blasted from the speaker. The cousins were milling about, some too drunk to change the playlist, others already too hungover to care. Visith sat on the sectional couch, stripped down to his undershirt. Surrounded by her fellow bridesmaids, Monica stood by the kitchen island, furiously discussing the bottomless stupidity of every boy cousin at the party. Someone had made cognac-Gatorade margaritas, and half-empty cups of bright green littered all the hard surfaces, and even some of the softer, rounder ones—like the couch cushions—these cups precarious in their positioning.

The FAMOUS SINGER instructed Marlon and Bond to line up five chairs in a row, in front of the sectional and everyone else in the room. When the formation was finished, she stood up on a chair, drawing the room's attention with her expert stage presence. "A little bird told me," the FAMOUS SINGER said, "that Visith will also be married soon, to a woman living in Cambodia."

"Yeah," Visith said, "that's true." He glared at Marlon as if he were about to tackle him to the ground.

"Well, if you want to marry a woman from Cambodia, you must obey tradition," the FAMOUS SINGER said. "So I will teach everyone a ceremony to perform at Visith's wedding." The FAMOUS SINGER gestured at Visith. "Here, take my place and turn your back to your audience." Then she pointed for Bond, Marlon, and two other boy cousins to join Visith on the remaining chairs. "I will act as Visith's bride for this demonstration," the FAMOUS SINGER continued. "In this game, the bride will be blindfolded, and she must touch all the men's behinds and guess, just from touching, which behind belongs to her husband."

"This *cannot* be real," Monica said, scowling with disgust and delight, to which the FAMOUS SINGER beamed a sternness that convinced all the cousins of the ceremony's deep legitimacy.

"Now, let me start the demonstration."

With rapt attention, the room watched the FAMOUS SINGER pretend to pat the thighs and glutes of the standing men. The palpable awkwardness of the situation made everyone smile, and when the mere proximity of the FAMOUS SINGER and her alarming beauty almost caused Visith to slip and fall to the floor, everyone burst into laughter. For a brief moment, the cousins, even the ones elevated on the chairs, were again a bunch of kids, a brand new generation in a strange country, still learning what it means to be Cambodian.

After the demonstration was over, the cousins returned to their conversations and their half-empty drinks. The five men descended from their positions. On his way back to the sectional, Visith rammed into Marlon with a forceful shove of his shoulder, but before anyone could react, Bond took hold of Marlon's arm and pulled him down, so that the brothers were now just slumping into those chairs. "Yeah, I don't think you wanna start another fight," Bond said. "Not after the ass-grabbing wedding game of our ancestors."

Soon the FAMOUS SINGER was sitting down next to them. She covertly handed Bond a leather object, nodding with a stiff and steady motion to keep her hair in place. "It belongs to Visith," she said, winking to signal that she'd picked their uncle's pocket. Quickly shifting to block Visith's view, Bond looked down, turning the stolen wallet over in his hands, feeling its bulky heft.

"What're you waiting for?" Marlon asked.

"All right," Bond said, "calm your shit." He pried the wallet open, and there, inside, nestled between a wad of bills, was a red envelope. "How did you know this would be here?" he asked the FAMOUS SINGER, who shrugged and said, "I assumed having his possessions would help. It is simple logic."

"What does this mean?" Marlon asked.

"Well," Bond answered, "it really does look like Visith was hiding his ang pav, you know, from everyone else."

"Wow," Marlon said. "So I was actually right?"

"Yeah, motherfucker definitely gave squat," Bond replied, and tossed the wallet under his chair.

"Dad will have his proof now," Marlon said.

"And Mom will be happy," Bond said. "Well, happier."

And with that, the brothers sighed in mutual relief. They both—yes, Bond as well, to Marlon's delight—grinned at one another with juvenile giddiness. For the moment, they could do nothing else.

VII.

THE DRUNKEN CONVERSATIONS CAMBOS HAVE AT 3:42 A.M.

"Sometimes I forget we grew up with the same stuff, you know?" Marlon said, before taking a drink from a dwindling bottle of Hennessy. They were sitting outside on the front lawn, their asses chilled by the morning dew. "Like, do you remember when we were kids and Dad would be working at the power plant? So it would be us two trying to make Mom feel better, cooking her, like, the worst food ever, like those grilled cheeses we microwaved?"

"Yeah, and then I was the one who dealt with Mom," Bond said, taking the bottle from Marlon. "In high school, you were always *busy*." He poured cognac into his mouth, and then stared out into the dark sky. "The other day I had this realization, you know, that I actually started making art because it was the easiest way to pass time. Mom would lie in bed, staring off into space, talking about her dead siblings, and I'd draw on the floor of her room."

Marlon considered his brother's profile. He thought about all the times he'd raged too hard in his life, how often he'd taken his parents too seriously, as an influence so immense he needed to uphold their expectations and also transgress against them, because to have just one reaction would never suffice. "That was dumb of me."

"I'll drink to that," Bond said, bringing the bottle back to his lips.

"It's weird," Marlon said. "I've been back at home, you know, and everything's reversed from when we grew up. Dad makes tons of money now. Mom's healthy and she's hella extra about making sure I don't relapse. She cooks, like, every day. She does my laundry, and I keep telling her *I* can do it—hell, I used to do *her* laundry."

"So, like, what're you trying to say?"

"I don't know, man. Don't you find that a little weird?"

Bond peered down the hill, across the lawn, at the Lexus SUV parked on the street. Sure, he had noticed all that, he'd lived it—how he and his brother were raised in a one-bedroom apartment and then, out of nowhere, well into his own adolescence, his parents upgraded to a four-bedroom house in a gated community. But what was there to say? The whiplash he felt about their lives seemed inexpressible, at least in words. Maybe this was the curse of being a painter. His exact thoughts and feelings solidified in oils, only coming to him slowly, latently, after summoning mental images that might translate into scenes, once brush was applied to canvas.

"Oh," Marlon said, "I forgot." He sifted through his pockets, removed a handful of wedding favors, and piled them on the lawn. "Scored some candy."

Bond grabbed a favor and examined it. He scoffed.

"What's wrong?"

"I just realized how hungry I am."

"The BRIDE was fucking stingy about the food, am I right?" Marlon said. "What was up with those portions?"

"Give a bunch of Cambos money," Bond answered, "and they're still gonna believe a coup d'état's coming for us."

"And that, my beautiful brother," Marlon said, "is what makes the Cambo world go round."

Bond unwrapped the wedding favor. He popped the stale chocolate into his mouth. "I do find it strange, though, that we ended up where we, like, ended up."

"Yeah, it really is," Marlon said. "Glad you also think it." He threw an empty favor into the street, and Bond, without even thinking, elbowed Marlon's side for him to stop.

Bond took a deep breath. He felt calm, but his hands were shaky. Dizzy from the alcohol, he could feel a headache coming. He focused on his shoes, held tightly on to his bottle, and when the sky stopped spinning, he assembled the words he'd intended to say all night: "I . . . I thought you were doing better."

And Marlon, having expected this, exhaled. "Yeah. I thought so, too."

The brothers faced one another, each giving that look they had been exchanging ever since they could remember. *Even when you're the biggest fool, I got you.*

"I mean," Bond started, "I know it's just alcohol and weed, but Mom—"

"You know how many jobs I've tried applying for?" Marlon asked.

Bond shook his head. "I didn't know you were doing that already."

"Yeah, well, I can't keep track anymore," Marlon said. "And it's not like I don't get interviews, but I just . . . I can't formulate thoughts anymore, you know? I get asked these questions over the phone, like 'What are you hoping for in a team' or 'Describe your strengths and weaknesses,' and my brain—my brain's totally *fucked*."

With no words to say, Bond placed his hand on his brother's shoulder.

"Also not helpful we got autogenocided," Marlon said, falling back onto the grass.

"Not at all," Bond responded, "sure as hell isn't." Then he found himself, yet again, breaking into laughter, which in turn made Marlon crack up, and after a moment of more giddiness, of this necessary nonsense, after they finally settled down, they soaked in the silence, let it collect over them.

"When's the next time I'm gonna see you, anyway?"

"Not sure," Bond answered, registering a disappointment that Marlon could barely disguise. "But when I visit, maybe we can actually do something for a change. Like, go bowling or something."

"Now that would be hella fun. Nice, really."

"Right? So let's make it happen."

Before returning to the house, the brothers emptied the rest of the favors, methodically unwrapping the mesh around each, until not one chocolate was left uneaten. And they imagined aloud all the nice things they could do together. They imagined a future severed from their past mistakes, the history they inherited, a world in which—with no questions asked, no hesitation felt—they completed the simple actions they thought, discussed, and dreamed.

HUMAN DEVELOPMENT

I was at a Memorial Day barbecue in the Mission, barely drinking but using my cold beer as an excuse for belligerence, screaming about the math prodigy from our freshman dorm who had been, and probably still was, a white predator of Asian women. "It *needs* to be said!" I shouted, as half of a gay kickball team scowled at me from the beer pong table. The only difference between college and adulthood was that my peers could now afford custom tables built for drinking games.

We were three years out of Stanford, most of us clinging to the Bay Area, and I was the only one not working in tech, and thus the only one without tech money. My life was also pathetically devoid of tech catered lunches, tech laundry services, tech Wi-Fi commuter buses, tech holiday bonuses, tech personalized yoga sessions, tech subsidized gym memberships at Equinox, tech health and dental insurance and unlimited tech PTO, and of course those tech company T-shirts and hoodies that never fit well on anyone, unless the CEO had sprung for a corporate partnership with Lululemon or Patagonia. Not that I felt left out; though I should have, given the state of my bank account. My job was to teach rich kids with fake Adderall prescriptions how to be "socially conscious" at a private high school in Marin. The Frank Chin Endowed Teaching Fellow for Diversity—that was the official title for my two-year-long position, of which I had just finished the first, and the class I taught for the service learning department was called Human Development. To my knowledge, this kind of indoctrination existed exclusively at the most elite of private high schools, the ones whose names started with a capitalized *The* and ended with a capitalized *School*, as if only the wealthy possessed a real capacity to "develop."

Most days I tried to forget that my salary was less than a year's tuition, which many of my students paid for through their trust funds. Summer break had just started, and I wasn't even tutoring, though I needed the extra cash, and probably the social interaction. Still, the concept of high school tuition made me sick.

"Why the fuck would you say something like that?" asked my twin sister's friend, the one who'd invited me to the party, and who was, among other things, a Taiwanese woman working at Google. "Give us a trigger warning next time, Anthony—Jesus."

"Why's the goal of this party to reclaim the culture of closeted frat bros?" I snapped, to make sure she registered my intention of tanking the enterprise of our conversation.

My sister's friend scowled at me. "Why'd you even *come*

tonight?" she asked with contempt. "You look like you haven't slept in days."

Absent an answer, I chugged the rest of my beer. I was in a bad mood.

The entire afternoon I had already wasted trying to overhaul my Human Development class for the upcoming school year. My plan was to abandon the glib lessons on microaggressions, the cringey videos of teenagers role-playing scenes of consent, the PowerPoints that neutered "big" political issues into handy vocabulary terms—everything that was deemed by the social learning department, which was hilariously Caucasian, as "fundamental yet appropriate." After a lacrosse player in my previous class had equated using the N-word to the tone of liberals saying "conservative voter," I decided that high school sophomores would learn more about being decent humans by reading *Moby-Dick*. I felt very serious about this new direction for my pedagogy as the Frank Chin Endowed Teaching Fellow for Diversity, so serious that I was altering the established curriculum without informing my white woman boss. Yet I couldn't bring myself to do the work. I hadn't even started *re*reading *Moby-Dick*.

Five beers later, I was sitting on the couch next to a mob of backend engineers, all of them wasted, lurid in their stated heterosexuality, and deep into a Super Smash Bros. tournament. I texted my sister: this party's in the gay capital of the world and straight incels are playing video games. I waited for a reply until I remembered New York City was three hours ahead. I texted her again: still can't believe you left SF you asshole.

Then I actually got drunk and yelled at a former philosophy classmate. An ex-co-op dude with bleached hair and mediocre stick-and-pokes, he had sold out to become a technical writer for Palantir because his parents had stopped paying his rent. Nobody wanted to hear him talk about Hannah Arendt, I kept asserting, with aggression, to him and his VC consultant girlfriend. I actually loved discussing Arendt—she was the topic of my senior honors thesis—but I was too drunk to recall that. When my former classmate began reciting the first sentence of *The Human Condition*, I muttered something about needing ketamine to disassociate from his very existence, then returned to the couch and scrolled through Grindr, blocking the profiles of every kickball player who was at the party. It was a political statement, not a sexual preference, and regret punched me in the dick when I looked up and realized the guy I'd just blocked was also on his phone, staring directly at me, disappointment slapped across his face. He was hotter in person, too, with broad shoulders, tanned skin from all the kickball, but I got over it. I felt like bottoming. And *didn't* feel like being a hypocrite by letting a white predator colonize my rectum.

It took real intuition and finagling to sift through the preponderance of white-on-white-on-white-on-white profiles—the white muscle daddies and sparkling white twinks, the white otters and white gaymers, the white gym rats trying to sell steroids to doughy white tech bros. What can I say?—I chose six-dollar lattes over the premium fee that empowered gay racists to segregate their sex lives. I messaged ten profiles of color in a row with some combination of "hey," an emoji, and a few nudes so they could see I was decently attractive from more than one angle. One Asian guy replied immediately: hey, I'm also Khmer! Can't believe I found you on this app. You know only .0009 percent of America is a gay Khmer man. Hope we're not cousins cause you're cute as fuck.

Beer rushed up and seared my throat, producing a painful burp. I had forgotten writing "I'm Cambodian" in my profile so that guys would stop asking me what I "am." Forgot because guys never read my profile anyway, and still dragged me into ethnicity guessing games all the time, as though our Grindr messages were a trivia night hosted at a previously hip bar. People of all races, even other Asian men, thought my exact ethnic composition impressed a specific bearing on the way I handled a penis.

I reread the message and cringed, then Instagram-stalked his photos to make sure none of my family members were featured. Ben Lam, he was called, his haircut looking expensive, bone structure chiseled. He was manicured and presentable, wearing tight-fitting clothes in every photo—Christ—even his bedroom selfies. Like many Cambodian people in the Bay Area, he was from my hometown in the valley—*not* Silicon Valley, I should make clear, but the insufferably hot and arid one two hours east. We appeared to have zero blood relation. That was good. Though at forty-five—two decades older than me—he looked young the way older gay men do when they hit the gym twice a day, seven days a week, with monomaniacal drive.

Hoping I wasn't taller than him, that he was at least five ten, I messaged back: can u host?

Thirty minutes later, I was riding the 14 bus down

Mission Street and into Soma, staring out the window and trying to ignore the gay couple in a screaming match. One of them had broken the rules of their open relationship by sleeping with the other's ex. It sucked that my budget had absolutely no leeway for taking Uber pools to my hookups. As the sidewalks transitioned from trendy restaurants to homeless encampments to glassy corporate lobbies, I tried to remember the point in the night when I'd decided to have sex. Mostly I didn't want to mope around my apartment, where I would lie awake doing nothing because my Internet was too slow to stream anything, the Filipino guy who'd moved into my sister's room having crippled the apartment's Wi-Fi with his online gaming. It appalled me that he paid San Francisco rent only to play video games all day and night, every goddamn weekend, and never go outside.

Ben lived in a luxury apartment complex, the kind with amenities, with doormen, a saltwater pool even, according to the billboard outside, and he answered the door in nothing but sharp white briefs. Unsure if he was trying to be sexy, I greeted him with a one-armed side hug. We were the exact same size and height, only *my* muscles had a normal-looking density.

"I'm glad you came," he said. "What's your name? Your profile didn't say."

"Can I get some water?" I asked, dizzy and ignoring his question.

He pointed into a room. "Sure. Just wait for me there. You can sit on the bed."

After hydrating, we kissed until I pushed Ben down,

straddled his body, and asked if he wanted to fuck me. "Sure, of course," he said, so after struggling a bit with the condom wrapper—he insisted on the protection—we covered his dick with latex and lube. Then, as I eased him into my body, I let out a soft, involuntary moan, which startled him into a look of cautious bewilderment, as though he'd just received praise after worrying he'd been doing less than a good job. His apparent inexperience suddenly made me feel inexperienced, too, but our energy was good, intimate even, and we settled into a natural, fumbling rhythm.

I'm not sure if that look ever quit his face, because we ended up in some version of doggy style. He had wanted to do missionary, but seemed oblivious to the differences between heterosexual missionary and—for lack of a better term—gay hookup missionary. When he pulled out and unwrapped his dick, he asked me where I wanted him to finish, and I told him wherever he wanted, except I wasn't in the mood for swallowing. It wasn't long before a jet of lukewarm semen landed across my back, and he collapsed on top of me. For a second, our bodies were like a grilled cheese sandwich glued together with not quite enough cheese.

Rolling off me, he landed in the bed, then caressed my back. I didn't know how to transition into this new dynamic, felt awkward that we weren't still having sex. It seemed bizarre now to launch into conversation, to interact by sharing biographical facts rather than saliva, semen, and touch. He was Cambodian, from the shittier valley. Same as me. What else, really, did I need to know?

"What're you up to tomorrow?" he asked, his right leg

thrown over me, along with an arm. "I'm gonna walk the Golden Gate Bridge with some friends."

"An earthquake can send the bridge right into the bay," I answered, "and I wouldn't care, not at all."

He looked at me with confusion, his silence conveying total uncertainty in how to respond, so I laughed to make sure he knew I was mostly joking. It was a laugh I often forced when dealing with students. This triggered a laugh of relief from him.

"What did the Golden Gate Bridge ever do to you?" he finally asked.

Surprised by his response, that he was invested in my reasoning, I laughed again, genuinely this time. Usually people dismissed my contempt for the biggest tourist attraction of the Bay Area.

"During the school year I commute across it. The sights get old, real quick."

"That would do it."

"Let's do this again," I found myself saying. "My name is Anthony, by the way."

He smiled and kissed me before leaving the bed to take a piss. I took the time to make sure the sheets weren't stained by cum or shit. I wanted to keep things feeling clean.

THE NEXT THREE DAYS I slept at Ben's place. Something about submitting to his body, the permanent newness of his luxury apartment, and the beginning of June, it all knocked me into a kind of productivity. Every morning I walked to my regular coffee shop and read *Moby-Dick*, marking up passages I could teach, until the late afternoon, or until Ben texted me to come back, whichever came first.

It felt nice, in Ben's clean clothes, to become reacquainted with *Moby-Dick*. It was the first novel I'd ever read that didn't care for resolutions. It validated for me the experience of confusion, of exploring something as stupid and vast as a white whale, as an ocean. Or, at least, it made me feel okay about the philosophy major I'd settled on after failing all my classes in chemistry, first, and then economics. Equipping teenagers to sniff out the nonsense of society, I told myself, that was the logic behind this new curriculum. I wanted my students to understand the doomed nature of Ahab's hunt for Moby Dick, the profound calm of Ishmael's aimless wandering, the difference between having "purpose," like Ahab, and finding "meaning," like Ishmael. I thought my students should learn the best ways to be lost.

The morning I finally took the Muni back to my Inner Sunset apartment, my regular coffee shop was booked for a networking mixer targeted at single coders. I was pissed off by the mixer because stickers reading QUEERS HATE TECHIES were pasted all over the bathroom. The pointless stickers had previously made me laugh because every "radicalized" gay guy I knew worked for Apple as a UX designer, but now, seeing this mixer, I became furious at the management for leaving them up without committing to their politics, or, hell, even just the aesthetic. In terms of San Francisco subcultures, the coffee shop was trying to have its cake and eat it, too, and I texted my sister that the place was dead to me. Then, for good measure, I sent her a picture of Ben, dubbed "the first Cambodian guy to fuck me."

By the time I reached my apartment, my sister had thoroughly interrogated me about Ben—about the minutiae of his life that couldn't be gathered from a straight statistical analysis of his LinkedIn, Facebook, and Instagram accounts. I told her what I knew, that Ben was a recent online MBA grad and a late bloomer who'd started living as openly gay in his late thirties. He had moved to San Francisco to network with venture capitalists, after taking care of his mom until she died of a diabetes-related stroke, which was part of why he'd been such a closet case. These days he was living off life insurance money, freelance database coding gigs, and renting out his dead mom's house on Airbnb.

My sister texted me: he sounds like a guy mom would arrange-marry to me.

I texted back: yeah he's low key infuriating but his apartment has working Wifi.

She responded: lol, still using sex for free shit. Glad to know you haven't changed.

My sister never commented on the fact that Ben was Cambodian, or that he was almost twice my age, though she was probably used to my flings with older men—my daddy phase hit hard in college, when I'd loathed everyone our age even more than I did now. Still, I felt a pang of resentment toward her, for not acknowledging the strangeness, the idiotic sadness, of my finding a Cambodian dude to fuck me a decade too late, long after I'd stopped fantasizing about the perfect boyfriend who would just "get" me.

I texted: I hate everyone, quit your job and move back.

She answered: stop being dramatic, you're the Frank Chin Endowed Teaching Fellow for Diversity. Also, fucking shit, I love my new job.

Back in my own apartment, I lay in my bed, surrounded by stacks of dusty books from college. All these classic stories and groundbreaking theories I was too lazy to throw out or even organize. The next big earthquake—fuck, even a door slammed too hard—would've buried me in a mountain of recorded thought no one gave a shit about anymore. I stared at the ceiling while my sister texted me about the eccentric new boss who'd convinced everyone on her marketing team to do a juice cleanse, about the unmatched congeniality of her coworkers, the shocking number of employees who also happened to be women of color, how every other Thursday the company rented out an entire bar for happy hour, even though their office kitchen was stocked with craft beer on tap. It had been totally worth the semipermanent dislocation, this dream job of hers.

I waited for her to ask me when I was applying to grad school, if I'd signed up for the GRE yet, as she'd done every week since we graduated from Stanford, but she only went on about her job. Sounds like you're having a great time, I texted, before falling asleep and waking up to another wasted day.

Several days later, after Ben learned that I was subsisting primarily on coffee shop bagels, he started cooking me dinner. "It's the least I can do," he said to me on his bed. When I told him I didn't need to be fed, he held me close, nuzzled my neck, let me feel how hard he was even though we'd just had sex. Where he got so much energy—in bed, in work, in life—remained a mystery to me. Could I actually be the thing exciting him, I thought, skeptical and semi-repulsed, even as a warm buzz settled in my chest. I inched even closer to him, and his arms tightened around me to the point of impracticality. I wanted his hot breath all over my entire body.

Dressed only in our underwear, Ben and I relocated to the kitchen. The modern style of the apartment, with its platinum surfaces and minimalist furnishings, struck me as clinical when populated by our bare bodies, like we were test subjects in some well-financed medical study.

"Isn't life great?" Ben said, chopping some chili peppers. "I mean, *look* at this view!" With the knife still in his hand, he pointed at the single window that stretched across an entire wall, the view ogling the Bay Bridge, the expanse of water it crossed, all the opportunity bursting from the iron seams of that wide span.

"Yeah, I think the view from my apartment is just *this* building," I said from the dining table.

Ben laughed. He was intent on finding the underbelly of positivity lurking beneath everything I said. "How do you *not* have a boyfriend?"

"Boys can't handle me," I said flippantly. He smiled in response, and part of me felt tender, too much so, my insides exposed to the air. I had the perverse desire to test the limits of his optimism.

We ate a traditional Cambodian meal that Ben had altered to be healthy. He squirted raw honey into the coconut milk instead of adding sugar, sheared the extraneous fat off the pork belly, and swapped the white rice for cauliflower smashed into bits. The dish tasted good.

The essential ingredients were there—the spices, the fermented fish, the lemongrass. But it looked disfigured, like it'd been extinct and was then genetically resurrected in a petri dish.

"I want to know everything about you," Ben said.

"I'll show you my LinkedIn page if you want," I said, chewing flavors mutated from my childhood.

"You like the prahok?" he asked. "One of my aspirations is to disrupt the Khmer food industry with organic modifications." Hearing a man with 4 percent body fat talk about health, in tech speak, using *disrupt* without sarcasm, all in his underwear, it made my head hurt. "I wanna curate a series of online video recipes that lay out well-balanced diets for Khmer folk," he continued. "See, my mom died from diabetes. And most Khmer folk have no idea white rice is unhealthy. It's basically sugar!"

"I'd pay twenty bucks for this," I said, taking another bite for emphasis. Commodifying his work seemed to please him. "So that's the app you're working on? Healthy Khmer food?"

"No, no," he said, as if brushing off an overzealous compliment. "That's more like the ten-year goal versus, say, the five-year goal." He said *goal* with the same intonation as my sister, with the complete confidence that donning a growth mindset was undeniably a virtue. My sister could go on and on about her life plan—MBA from Wharton, *Forbes* 30 under 30, three kids before she turned forty—to the point that my own meandering life had become a casualty of hers. Halfway through college, after I'd proved incapable of handling my own education, she started mapping both of our career goals on a shared Excel spreadsheet. She would be the CFO and CEO of her own marketing analytics firm; I would become an Ivy League professor in philosophy. Our whole lives we'd been geniuses, role models, twins destined for greatness. We were the only kids in our neighborhood, basically the only Cambodians in general, to make it as far as Stanford, and my sister was intent on maximizing this potential. She kept the two of us elevated in a stratosphere of legible success, with internships and research opportunities—anything to prevent us from falling to our old lives, to the poverty shackling almost 30 percent of Cambodian Americans, a statistic that she readily cited in all her job interviews, making sure to note that it was more than twice the national rate. As for the goals she projected for my future, it had been a while since I checked our spreadsheet, not since she moved to New York anyway, and the thought of it left me exhausted.

"So you wanna hear my pitch?" Ben asked. He'd finished eating and was holding his stomach with his hands, as if measuring how many calories he would need to burn during his next workout session.

"Sure," I said. "But if you ask me to sign an NDA, I swear to fucking god I'm leaving. In my underwear and everything."

"Ha. Ha. Don't worry, I trust you enough," he said, and I cringed without his noticing. "Okay, so you know what cruising is, right?"

I furrowed my eyebrows.

"I'll take that as a *yes*," he said in what sounded like

a rehearsed voice. "So one day while I was, you know, *looking*, it dawned on me: Why can't we take the idea of cruising—of seeking intimate connections that are marginalized by the public—and apply it to *other* aspects of our society, you know? And, specifically, to the lives of those hidden from the mainstream." He paused for dramatic effect, spreading his arms wide in a controlled movement. "How often do you walk through life wishing for a space you can immediately feel at ease in? Right? Imagine filtering through profiles of people who share similar identifying factors with you. People only a message away from becoming a new point of cultural connection. Imagine using the technology of Grindr, Scruff, Growlr, for building a new community, a new future. My app seeks to forge pathways between individuals and safe spaces through a cutting-edge algorithm and a network of thoroughly screened members. Think of it as a digital interface that allows people of color, people with disabilities, people identifying as LGBTQ, to cruise for safe spaces—spaces not specifically for sex, but for the *whole* of their lives."

He finished and stared at me. The whole time he was speaking I'd done my best to project that I was taking him, and his idea, seriously. And it wasn't even like I thought Ben's app was unfeasible. After my freshman-year roommate received a million in VC funding, for a fucking dog walking app, I stopped judging people's startup ideas in terms of their viability for success in the field. He just—and I tried, really I did, not to care—sounded like a clueless kid during his pitch, like he'd learned something new at school and was now obsessed with talking about it. Buzzwords rolled off his tongue as naturally as a robot trying to act human—*LGBTQ, people of color, safe space.*

"So what do you think?" he pressed. "Pretty awesome, right? Being able to find Khmer folk wherever you *are*, whenever you want?"

I forced a smile. "Sounds like a cool idea."

SOMETHING IN OUR CHEMISTRY—in the way I saw him—shifted after Ben explained his app to me. When he cooked extravagant meals, I felt guilty, because, honestly, it would've made zero difference to me if we ate frozen pizzas instead of his thoughtful culinary creations. He had this notion that I always wanted to eat Cambodian food, as if it provided some critical nourishment to my soul. "Doesn't it feel good to eat what we're supposed to be eating?" he'd ask, and I'd nod, wondering how long he was going to last as a worthwhile distraction.

And then our sex became more—how to say this?—more deliberate. Thrusting into me, he'd fix upon me intently with his eyes, with an unwavering sympathy, without breaking his gaze, and ask if he was hurting me, even when I was penetrated by all of two fingers. I would have preferred him to be rougher, of course. Sometimes, though, I was completely disoriented by how comfortable I felt in his presence, how easily shocks ran up and down my spine as he fucked me.

A few weeks passed and I realized my only social interactions now involved Ben. He spent his days having phone conversations with all kinds of different startup employees, reading articles about diversifying Silicon Valley with more brown faces, as if that brown-ness could make the whole tech industry any less absurd, grotesque, and frivolous. About six hours of his day he dedicated to vigorous typing as he stared into his laptop—the morning was for his freelance work; the afternoon for his "safe space" app. For the life of me, I couldn't understand how he always broke into a sweat while coding.

On the weekends, Ben met with another gay Southeast Asian man dedicated to fitness and tech. Vinny was helping with the development of Ben's app. He was Vietnamese. Our first encounter, I asked if his parents had hoped the alliteration of his name and his ethnicity would make it easier for him to assimilate. He laughed so hard that I regretted saying anything at all. Though Ben concluded that we—the three of us—would get along from then on out. "This is gonna be fun," he said. Several times I watched Ben and Vinny code as I planned lessons about Ahab's inexorable hunt and Ishmael's never-ending musings. Waiting for Ben to stop working and slide his hand up my thigh, I wondered if the only thing that distinguished me from Vinny, that kept Ben's hands sliding up *my* thighs, was the fact that I was Cambodian. How easily could I be replaced by a different gay man who also happened to be Cambodian? Who could say? I listened to Ben and Vinny debate about memory issues and algorithms and recursion, observed their comfort in massaging each other's shoulders, and didn't care to know the answer to my question.

What I did know was that Ben's "safe space" app unsettled me. I was offended by it, really, how it struck me as something I should want, something masquerading as objectively good, a solution to all our problems. It reminded me of the established curriculum for my Human Development class. It evoked for me the lee shore in *Moby-Dick*, these supposed safe spaces in which we'd be forever bound, or even the white whale himself, that failed promise of closure. Ben wanted technology to offer people a sense of fulfillment, to rush them to shore, secure everyone to land, and I wanted to be indefinite, free to fuck off and be lost.

Even so, Ben's genuine enthusiasm impressed me. He seemed not to care if he made money, only that his vision be fully realized. And he was so hyper focused that I felt especially productive around him. Or was my strengthening drive to teach *Moby-Dick* just a product of how stupid I thought Ben's app was? I was doing meaningful work, right? Changing the lives of the younger generation? Who knew? But in ways both tender and ugly, Ben allowed me, for once, to feel good about myself. Was that what drew Ishmael to Ahab? That he saw clearly how futile Ahab's mission was, how there was no world in which he could actually kill Moby Dick? Did he watch Ahab scream into the unconquerable face of the white whale so that his own life might have meaning?

At the end of June, a month after Ben and I first hooked up, my sister texted me: it sounds like this relationship is pretty fucking serious.

I responded: if it is idk how it happened.

She texted back: sorry I haven't been able to skype. shit's been crazy.

It's ok, I texted. I'll find another Cambodian twin who also went to Stanford.

She texted: lol. tell Ben I want to meet him.

I never asked Ben how serious he thought we were, as I felt apathetic about asserting any expectations onto our dynamic, but he did want to meet my sister. When he found out my twin had also attended Stanford, I almost thought he was suffering the rupture of a brain aneurysm. "Jesus, man, this is just so *great*," he said, recovering from the news, caressing my ass like a prized object. "Your family is breaking new ground for Khmer folk, you know? Now the younger Cambos are gonna know it's freaking possible to get into a school like Stanford." I didn't feel like explaining to him that Stanford had allowed me to *escape* my hometown, my neighborhood, my Cambodian life. There was no point.

"Maybe you *should* meet my sister," I told him.

Flattered, he interlaced his fingers into mine. Then he climbed on top of me, pushed my face deeper into the mattress, whispered something about how he couldn't help himself when he was around me. His dick rubbing against my lower back, he slipped his hands under my stomach, grabbing for my inner thighs, and spread my legs open, for once with neither concern nor apology. I surrendered to his body, and for a brief moment, I thought, Why not? Maybe I could go on like this forever. I felt safe when I was pinned under him. Ben made me feel safe.

"Can I run some ideas by you?" he asked the next morning, before launching into a ten-minute monologue about the pros and cons of the color teal as a method to optimize user engagement. "On one hand," he started, wide-eyed, serious, "it's calming and unique because it's not just a regular blue or green, and that's symbolic of safe spaces, right? They're supposed to be these special and unique, calming communities. On the *other*, do you think a more unique color, like, sacrifices the security of using a simple color everyone's accustomed to? There's a *safety* in familiar colors, right? And what am I doing if not trying to make people feel safe?"

"I wouldn't exactly call teal unique," I said, curtly, looking down at my book.

"Oh," he said. "Yeah . . . maybe not. So what color should we use?"

"Honestly I don't think it matters," I said, not caring that he'd sounded hurt. "Anyway, you should ask your partner," I added, with some spite, though he took this suggestion at face value. For the next hour, he proceeded to consult with Vinny on the phone. And I pretended to read *Moby-Dick*.

ON THE FOURTH OF JULY, Ben and I went to a picnic in Dolores Park, another Stanford affair, only this time hosted by a gay softball team. Ben was the one who had wanted to make an appearance. He kept calling it a "networking opportunity."

Dolores Park was packed and unreasonably warm for San Francisco. It seemed like the entire city was drinking beer and smoking pot on the grass—desperate hipster trash, elitist Marina snobs, vapid gay cliques, and so on. "Do you also wish Dolores Park would fall into the ocean,"

Ben asked, nudging me in the ribs, "or is it just the bridge you hate?" We stepped through a cloud of smoke created by a group of teens in expensive-looking tie-dye shirts. He gripped my hand and dragged me into the dead-hot center of Bay Area gentrification.

"I just wish it was less crowded," I said. "If we keep bumping into sweaty shirtless guys, we're gonna get ringworms."

Ben laughed and then immediately integrated himself with my Stanford peers. They played drinking games, threw footballs around, dished about the latest gossip among VC firms. He tried to get me involved, but I told him I was too tired, that I was bored by all the talk of the future. I could see he was disappointed and I expected him to get mad, to snap on me for belittling his passion. The fact that he didn't felt like an intrinsic flaw in our relationship.

A group of guys arrived with a beer pong table, and not long after that, Vinny popped up out of nowhere, forcing me into a hug. "Sup guys," he said at large, so good-natured it vexed me.

"You invited Vinny?" I whispered to Ben, almost hissing.

"Why not?" he responded. "He's gonna help me network."

These are my friends, I wanted to say, though it struck me as false. Instead, claiming I needed to clear my head, I split off from them. For the first time in a month, I felt that Ben and I were untethered, and I walked around the park, sipping from a cup of straight vodka, until the idea of casual conversation stopped feeling alien. I thought of my sister, how she always knew exactly what she wanted at any given moment, down to a disturbing power to order off menus perfectly, and how I'd always been swept into her hunger for life. I thought about what I wanted to do now—if I wanted to eat or leave the park, if I wanted to apply to grad school in the fall, if I wanted to find Ben in the crowd.

Nothing sounded appealing, and I had the vague desire to slip through the cracks of what everyone else was doing. Then, not paying attention, I bumped into someone, literally, painfully, and fell over onto the grass. A burly hand picked me up, and I realized the man apologizing for knocking me over was the guy from the last party—the one who'd witnessed himself get blocked, by me, on Grindr.

"Fuck, I'm sorry." He brushed the grass off of my shoulders, and I felt my muscles contract at his touch. "I'm such a klutz—spilling water over you, it's not cool at all."

I shrugged. "It's vodka."

"Wait, you're Annie's twin bro," he said. "Anthony, right?"

"That's me," I answered.

"Jake," he said, smiling, forcing me into a handshake. "Damn, I like hardcore *miss* Annie. She was a blast, you know?"

"Yeah, she's a fucking asshole for leaving," I said, and he laughed.

"I guess it must be nice in some ways, though," he said. "Now you can be seen as, like, individuals, and not just twins or whatever."

"You could see it like that," I responded.

"Look, I feel bad—you're drenched." He patted my side to test the dampness. I felt nervous, animated, and then guilty at finding him so attractive. I couldn't help but feel drawn to his casual manners, the way he made the very act of being relaxed somehow noteworthy, as if answers simply manifested in his mouth while speaking, plain and perfect. He seemed like the type of person who harbored no desire to prove anything, to *be* anything but himself. I looked around the crowd, tried locating Ben among the other bodies.

"What're you gonna do about it?" I asked. "My shirt."

"I live around the block. We could, uhm . . . put your clothes in the wash."

"Let's go," I found myself saying, feeding off his easy energy.

Where'd you go, Ben texted me, sometime after Jake took off my clothes and swallowed me whole. Later, I came too early, his dick still sliding in and out of my asshole. No longer intensely aroused, the bottom half of me went numb from the continued friction. It wasn't bad, the sex. It was almost nice to know I could find relief so quickly.

After we finished, Jake left to check on my laundry. I texted Ben: I went to my apartment cause I felt sick.

He texted: one of your friends is hooking me up with a VC connection!

I texted: that's great.

I saw several messages from my sister and ignored them.

DESPITE MYSELF, WE CONTINUED ON, like before, all through those remaining weeks of summer. And, despite myself, I kept sleeping with Jake, covertly and without permission. Ben and I even took a day hike through the Muir Woods at the end of July. I'd been telling him that I was taking long, solitary walks, that I needed fresh air to mull over *Moby-Dick* passages, but really I was going over to Jake's. Eventually Ben grew to think I'd developed a passion for scenic strolls, then declared to me that I *needed* to witness the glorious redwoods. I wasn't against seeing the trees, but it was just that—it all happened so fast, his planning, the departure, the drive. I barely had time to process any of it. Out of nowhere, he was buying us hiking shoes so our feet wouldn't blister. He packed enough healthy Cambodian food to feed a whole village.

We spent the first hour of the hike in near silence. With his DSLR camera, Ben took high-resolution photos of every flourish of nature. Panting from the exertion, I was in a daze of bemused fascination at his endless curiosity with bark. At one point, a few butterflies stormed out of a bush, and Ben gasped in astonishment as he furiously snapped photos, his DSLR glued to his face. I had to admit, they were pretty cool.

Once the butterflies cleared the area, he reviewed the shots he'd taken on the camera's mini HD screen, clicking the little buttons rapidly while squinting his eyes. Then his gaze lingered on a single photo. Rotating the camera, he examined the image at different angles. After that, he looked up and asked me, point blank, "Do you want kids?"

"No," I answered, a bit thrown, "not at all, actually."

"Really? How can you be so certain?"

"Why are people always so skeptical about this?" I responded. "Fucking shit, I *work* with kids. I'm around them all the time."

"Yeah, but it's different, isn't it, when it's your own blood?" He took a drink of the warm veggie stock in his industrial-grade thermos. Perfect, he'd claimed, for replenishing electrolytes. "Don't you think we need to give the world more Khmer folk?" he asked, and as he handed me his thermos, I suspected, faintly, that Ben seriously believed he could change my mind on things. Perhaps he even thought my desires were definite enough, pointed and graspable enough, to be overturned with the right levels of persistence. Maybe they were? "That's part of my motivation," he added. "Plus, I love kids."

"How noble of you," I said, declining the veggie stock. He slipped the thermos back into his bag, and I hoped he wouldn't take my refusal personally. I just didn't want to swallow something that hot in this heat. "Shouldn't you have started making kids like yesterday?" I asked, hands in my pockets. "You're an old man, a daddy, after all."

"Probably," he said, and pulled me close. I couldn't stop laughing as he nibbled at my ear. I would've let him do that for hours, but the camera hanging from his neck was pressed between us, and I started to worry that it would break. For the rest of the hike, I reflected on the differences between Ben and Jake in bed, how Ben's touch felt warm, never-ending, so different from the crashing rush I inevitably had, later that night, with Jake.

A week later, we were working at my regular coffee shop. Ben was pushing himself to finish his "safe space" app, having successfully networked his way into a pitch meeting with a big VC firm. Nearing the end of his mission, he started to wax existential, the way so many of my Stanford classmates had done a week before graduating.

"I spent so much of my life not making much of anything," he suddenly said over his laptop, the screen reflecting off his reading glasses. He'd spent the past two hours coding, occasionally conferring with Vinny through a Bluetooth headpiece, never once looking up.

"Because you were in the closet for so long?" I joked, closing my copy of *Moby-Dick*. I'd been lesson-planning the chapter "A Squeeze of the Hand," drafting summaries of how Ishmael reaches into a tub of sperm oil and squeezes, accidentally but with elation, the hands of his crew members. I was trying to figure out a way to prevent my students from devolving into vulgar laughter, but it seemed like a lost cause, to think they could appreciate the tragic beauty of that brief, fleeting moment, of finding unexpected kinship through this opaque liquid, without someone cracking a cum joke.

Ignoring me, Ben leaned forward, his whole face now catching the blue light. "Anthony, I'm *this* close to achieving my goals, isn't that wild? Of course, this is making me realize a lotta freaking things. For example . . . we don't have the privilege of wasting time—not anymore—not with the stuff we've survived. Man, I wish, I really do, that I had someone in my life that told me how important it was for me—for *us*—to work hard."

"That's why you're making a safe space app?"

"It's why I'm with you." He reached over his laptop,

over the table, and grabbed my hands. "It means something for us to be together. You know? I hope you realize that."

Impulsively, I withdrew from his grasp. He looked hurt but didn't say anything, and before I could stop myself and pause, before I could even begin to understand why I wanted to yell at him—for being weak, for making *me* feel weak—I was leaving the table and heading for the bathroom, a knot of dread vibrating in my gut. Then I sat down on a toilet and thought of calling my sister, but had no desire to explain my feelings, nor did I care to hear about her life, so I stared at the posters pasted all over the stalls. The stickers saying QUEERS HATE TECHIES had been replaced with advertisements for a Google-sponsored event headlined by drag performers. I wondered if it was possible to resist something as immense as Google, if only for the sake of being uncertain.

I did eventually talk to my sister—about Ben, about Jake, about everything—that night. She listened intently over the phone, providing the appropriate intermittent comments. She took no moral high ground. She wasn't frustrated that I had no idea if I wanted to stay with Ben, that I kept joking about my standing in front of a luxury salon that specialized in grooming pure-bred dogs, which occupied the storefront next to Ben's apartment. "The city's fucking doomed," I repeated. "We're suffocating it with rich puppies."

"Just tell him the truth," she said, "but if you really need it, I'll buy you a ticket to visit New York."

By the weekend, after Ben had pitched his "safe space" app, I felt normal again. We were eating a late breakfast at his apartment—brown rice and quinoa congee, pickled mustard greens sautéed with ground turkey, hard-boiled tea eggs, but with the yolks thrown out to preserve our cholesterol levels. "By the way, I invited Vinny over for dinner," Ben said, staring into his bowl. For days, he'd been anxious about the results of his pitch meeting. "I promised him a home-cooked meal," he continued. "To celebrate, you know, finishing the app."

"That's fine," I said, even though a wave of discontent was lapping its way over me. Suddenly I wanted to hurt Ben, to provoke him into finally snapping on me the way I surely deserved. Then my sister's advice came back to me. "I've been fucking a guy since Fourth of July," I said, mushy rice dripping out of my mouth. I had no end goal in mind for this confession.

Ben dropped his spoon. Eyebrows pushed together, he stared at me as if trying to figure out if I was joking.

"I thought I should tell you," I added, deciding right then to omit the fact of Jake's whiteness. In his expression, I saw Ben register the reality of my words. He crossed his arms, leaning against the back of his chair. "I guess," he said, "we never did have a serious discussion about, you know, *us*."

I waited for him to keep talking, even as I felt terrible for not saying anything, for keeping him suspended in my confession. After a moment, I started eating again, though I could no longer taste the food. I began to regret the past few weeks, all the moments of intimacy Ben and I had shared—intimacy that extended beyond the confines of sex itself. This felt, in retrospect, like the cruelest thing I'd done to Ben, letting him think that nothing was wrong, that I was willing to overlook any problems we may have had.

"We can be open if you want," he finally said, and clasped his hands together on the table, as if offering me a stock option package. "I just . . . if you *want* to have see other guys, I can be flexible with that. But I believe we should . . . work a little harder at this. Staying together."

Bitterness pulsed through me. "Stop that."

"Stop what?"

"Making it seem like we *have* to be together, like it's our fucking duty."

"What're you talking about?" He made a face as if he'd changed his mind about something. "What do you even want from me, Anthony?"

I looked at him angrily, offended, only to realize how reasonable the question was.

"I just think we want different things," I said, ashamed that I had nothing concrete to offer. "I guess *I* want to live in a world where every action doesn't *need* to get us somewhere. And you . . . you want to be impactful, always."

"What about the book you're teaching," he said, the defiance in his voice sliding into desperation. "I mean, look, we both have ambitions. We both care about things." He threw his arms out in exasperation. "Why are we even talking about this? What does it have to do with you fucking a—"

"I can't be with a Cambodian guy just to be with a Cambodian guy."

Slowly, Ben's faced dropped at the words I spit out, the words that rushed out of me in single steam of sounds. He looked down at his stomach, shaking his head. For the first time in weeks, I noticed how much older he was than me—the fatigue deepening the circles around his eyes, the laugh lines accenting his mouth. I had started the exact conversation I wanted to avoid.

"I'm sorry," I continued. "It's not about you, specifically, or even Cambodian people . . . it's, like, a moral thing."

He sighed and turned away from me, grimacing in the direction of the window. "We don't have it like that, do we? None of us can afford to be *moral*."

"Maybe moral isn't the right word for it."

"I don't think you realize how much we owe each other," he said, his voice now diminishing to a whisper, as though his power source were about to die. Standing up, he started to gather our half-empty plates. "Are you done?"

I nodded, handing him my bowl. "I do realize— I mean, I *know* our history," I said, but he was already walking to the kitchen sink, and this last excuse of mine could only fall against his back.

That afternoon we stayed in bed, not quite knowing what to do, where to go, if we should keep talking about our relationship or just give it a rest. After a couple of hours, we started kissing, our hands reaching into each other's pants, but we progressed no further than that. It felt impossible to leave our current state of dissonance.

We were still in bed when Ben's phone went off in the early evening. He left the room and I could hear him mutter choppy sentences. Ten minutes later, he returned looking pale faced, giddy yet terrified.

"I just . . . I just got five hundred thousand in VC funding."

"Holy shit," I said in disbelief. "That's great, right?"

"It's more than I ever imagined."

"We should, like . . . *do* something."

He stuttered incomprehensibly, his brain undergoing some sort of information overload. "Yeah, sure, we should!" he finally got out, before he shut his eyes, centered himself back into his body. "Shit," he said suddenly. "Vinny's coming over." He looked at his phone, then at me, then back at his phone, and so on. "I'll cancel."

"No, don't." I smiled. "This is a big deal. For Vinny, too! We should have fun."

Vinny arrived an hour later, and we told him the news, which prompted him to holler so loudly I was sure Ben's neighbors would file a noise complaint. In all the excitement, one thing led to another, and the three of us found ourselves on the bed, buzzed from white wine and talk of the future.

"You guys are gonna revolutionize safe spaces," I said, genuinely, hot from the alcohol, and both of them laughed. Then I kissed Ben while stroking Vinny's thigh. And then I surprised myself by kissing Vinny. When I unlocked my mouth from Vinny's, I glanced over at Ben, who seemed at once confused and enthralled. "It's okay," I assured him, biting his ear softly and pulling Vinny closer to us.

Soon each of us was devouring another part of someone else. My heart was beating so fast I swore it was the sole audible thing in the room. We took turns in each position, in each role, to the point that we became interchangeable, mere parts of an improved system of fucking. I experienced such intense moments of pleasure I could barely breathe, and the only thing preventing me from passing out, from gasping for air, was looking at Ben, our eyes locking every few moments, even as we were both intertwined with Vinny's perfect, sculpted body.

For the duration of our three-way, I saw the possibility of existing in a dynamic in which every pleasure received, every favor granted, every dick sucked, every bottom filled and every top gratified, could energize you to give back more than what you had in the first place. I saw clearly Ben's ideal vision of the world, a way of being that could sustain communities, protect safe spaces, and ensure that political progress kept happening. I felt euphoric, high, blood rushing to my head. I felt unbearably hopeful.

Then we started to unravel, our mouths tired from sucking, our asses by now chafed and sore. Our dicks ached, our wrists gave out. We came. We finished. We detached ourselves from our positions, collapsed onto the bed, and returned to our bodies as three different men, each of us exhausted from all this pleasure.

"That was intense," Ben said to the ceiling.

"Hell yeah," Vinny responded, and sprang up from between us, his hands touching both of our thighs. "Ben, let's hire Anthony to work for the startup."

Ben laughed. "Be more specific."

"A safe space tech company led by an all–Southeast Asian team? I mean, how awesome would that be? We'd be profiled by *Forbes, Business Insider*, maybe freaking *GQ*. Think about it . . . our headline could read 'From Refugees to Silicon Valley: The American Dream.'"

"What would I even do?" I asked.

"I don't know, man," Vinny answered. "You can write the instructions and copy for the interface, or, shoot, be the head of HR."

"I'll need to consider *all* the qualified candidates," Ben said, flicking my ears.

Vinny jumped to his feet and slapped his stomach. "We can talk salaries over food. There's a new sushi bar on Valencia."

"Sounds good," Ben said.

He sat up and motioned for us to leave. But I shook my head.

"Anthony," he said, softly. "Come."

"Don't worry about me, I'll be here." I rose and rested my head on Ben's shoulder. "I just need . . . to think," I whispered into his neck.

Disappointed, depleted—I could tell—he wrapped his arm around me. He kissed my forehead, leaving his lips connected to my skin, and we lingered in this position, in silence, as Vinny went to the bathroom. Ben's breathing remained steady, deep, strong. I closed my eyes, listening to its rhythm. I felt it resounding through his chest, and also into mine.

AFTER THE TWO OF THEM had showered and set off to the Mission, I drifted, naked and covered in cum, to the living room. Utterly alone but at peace, I looked out of the window, taking in the lights of the Bay Bridge, until every ounce of my former impressions had fallen away, or had maybe faded, or dissolved, into the depths of my mind. That fight between me and Ben appeared so distant now, as if it had occurred ages ago, before we had even met.

Then I put on my clothes, gathered my copy of *Moby-Dick*, my keys, my wallet, and made my way to the Embarcadero Station. The process of catching the N train struck me as surprisingly seamless, despite my phone having died in my pocket. I had forgotten how easy it was to return home.

Summer break was about to end, and it was senselessly cold, as San Francisco always got in August. In a couple of weeks, I would begin my second year as a teacher. My workdays would resume. Watching the hilly streets of Victorians pass me by, I thought of my lesson for the first day of school. Even though I still planned on teaching *Moby-Dick*, I would pose the same question I'd started last semester with: *What's the point of this class?* I remembered my old students' answers, their tentative convictions, their stabs of belief that all knowledge might be reduced to dumb platitudes. *We're learning how to be citizens*, they tried. *Everyone needs to be socially engaged. Everything is political.*

The train came to my stop, so I stepped off and started walking. A dense fog from the ocean had crawled through the neighborhood, pulled in by the valley heat of my childhood and Ben's prior life. I couldn't see far ahead, but I knew where I was going, and I was reminded of Ishmael "working" on the masthead of the *Pequod*, Ishmael dozing to the cadence of his dazed reflections, diffused into the clear sky, the total opposite of my current waking moment. As I waded through the fog, I wondered, then, at the impossibility of my existence. Here I was! Living in a district that echoed a dead San Francisco. Gay, Cambodian, and not even twenty-six, carrying in my body the aftermath of war, genocide, colonialism. And yet, my task was to teach kids a decade younger, existing across an oceanic difference, what it meant to be human. How absurd, I admitted. How fucking hilarious. I was actually excited.

SOMALY SEREY, SEREY SOMALY

Right after I shot out of my mother's womb, Somaly latched on to my body with such spite, no wonder I still dream that I am, and will never stop being, her. That's what the Mas and Gongs have told me at least, that I was a sickly baby, so thin my bones poked through sparse layers of fat. Then, as a toddler, I burned through pounds of food and never gained weight. Whenever I had three plates of rice or more, I was summoning Somaly, chanting secrets known exclusively by the dead.

The ritual required plain rice. Adding a drop of anything ruined the grains' white purity, scared her off from this world. Rice was sacred, after all, the only food Somaly stomached following the brutal murder of her father, Battambang's very own Rice Factory King. The leaders of the concentration camp slit her father's liver right from the gut, only days before the fall of Pol Pot, and then feasted on it for good luck. They believed it was steeped with the flavor of his lost fortune, that if they drowned their rice with his bile, stained every speck reddish brown—the color of blood mixing with earth—they might survive the Vietnamese invasion. This was how the Mas and Gongs have explained Somaly's aversion for tainted rice. Not that her father wasn't doomed from the start, according to Somaly, as only I know, having carried her spirit all these years.

Maybe this is why I am the only nurse in the Alzheimer's and dementia unit who doesn't refer to our patients' recreational hour as "herding the dying cows" or "midafternoon of the walking dead" or "playtime for the rusty shit machines." Because, unlike Nurse Anna or Nurse Kelly or even Nurse Jenny, my friend, I know something about disorientation. I understand how it feels to live with a past that defies logic.

ROOM 39 UNLEASHES A STREAM of shit right as I'm carrying her to the bathroom. She's screaming about her late husband, dead now over a decade, how she needs to crush gout medicine into his scrambled eggs. "Do you want Mike's feet to get swollen?" Room 39 cries in my arms, the shit seeping through her nightgown and onto my scrubs. So there's diarrhea on me, but I try not to hold it against her. His gout must've been real intense if he couldn't wait a moment longer, not even for his wife to squat on the toilet.

"Someone should pull the plug on Room 39," Jenny says to me in the staff locker room.

"That's dark," I say, wearing only my bra and underwear. Our thirty-minute break is almost over and I'm still washing my scrubs, rubbing a Tide to Go pen into the brown stains. It's the fifth one I've uncapped in the past month. "That would put us out of our jobs, you know. I'm not trying to work at McDonald's."

"Which is the only reason I am not—at this very moment—smothering my patients in their sleep," Jenny says with a smirk. We're both young, just out of nursing school, and the kind of idiots who agree to work in the Alzheimer's and dementia unit, with the worst patients of Saint Joseph's Elderly Care, the ones whose minds are mushed into pulp. Jenny's always talking about leaving this dump, moving up the ranks of nursedom, and working at Kaiser Permanente, a nurse's dream job, apparently. Kaiser's on the nice side of town, where the sidewalk trees are pruned by the city and decorated during Christmas, where you can buy something to eat that doesn't involve a drive-through.

"Whew, that smells nasty," Jenny continues. "Is she on Exelon? I swear it makes their shit smell worse, you know? Like they're shitting *after* eating a pile of their own shit."

"It's fine," I say. "No difference between this and changing a baby's diaper."

"Baby shit's pure, Serey," she says, nasally, pinching her nose shut. "It's, like, digested mashed-up carrots and breast milk. What *we* clean up is all jacked up with drugs. Like mutant shit, you know? Chemically enhanced."

"Like the X-men of shit," I respond.

"X-men of shit is too generous," Jenny now says, her words echoey. "Our patients are, straight up, sacks of rotten meat."

I try rubbing harder and harder. "That's pretty harsh."

"*You* go into room twenty-nine and tell me something isn't rotting. I'll trade room twenty-nine for room thirty any day."

"*You* told me to take rooms thirty to thirty-five," I snap, recalling Jenny's spiel about the extra shifts being my chance to impress management.

Jenny sighs and crosses her arms. "Serey, it's just so unfair. None of my patients have rooms with windows."

"Goddamn it," I say, and throw my scrubs into the sink. "The stains won't come out."

"Use my extra pair," Jenny says. "Don't fret."

"Thanks." I close my eyes and lean against the lockers. I am already exhausted, but I have another four-hour shift.

Before I can even rest my feet, I'm back in the hallway, rushing because the time has come to change Room 34's sheets. It's time to bathe her and administer the medication prescribed by her doctor. Which, I suspect, only makes the chemistry of her brain even murkier. I care more about this assignment because Room 34 is Ma Eng, my dead grandmother's second cousin. Though she has a warped sense of our relationship, and not just because of her dementia. Of course, the dementia doesn't help.

The Mas and Gongs in my neighborhood think of me as Somaly's reincarnation. When I was born, Ma Eng saw in my infant face her dead niece, Somaly, and with the amniotic fluid still coating my skin, my Pous and Mings all agreed with her, after which the monks, too, agreed, so unceasing was Ma Eng's vision. The neighborhood threw a celebration to honor Somaly's spirit, her peaceful transition back into life. It was supposed to end at that, with a blessing from the monks. Her reincarnation was thought of as a good omen for my future. Never was I supposed to *live* as her, and it came as a familiar shock when Ma Eng was first admitted here, a year ago, and started calling me Somaly.

I knock on the door of Room 34 and hesitate the required beat—a courtesy enforced by management, despite our patients never being lucid enough to recognize a knock—before walking in to find Ma Eng sleeping, and also sleep-chanting in Khmer. She jolts when I wake her up, then takes me in with her sunken eyes. Her pupils are dilated and darting, searching for something she can recognize.

You've gotten fat, Somaly, she says to me in Khmer. I look down at my body to realize that Jenny's scrubs are several sizes too big. Then Ma Eng pinches my ear, almost twisting it off. She has a surprising amount of strength for a woman with osteoporosis. *You're not stealing food from the Communists, are you? You'll get us killed!*

Ming, I need to give you a bath, I say through the pain, stumbling over my Khmer words, remembering to call her *Ming*. Whenever I assert that I am not her niece, Somaly, that I am actually just myself, Serey, that she is my Ma and I am her grandniece, whom she has known for twenty-three years, the entirety of my current life, Ma Eng gets mad and slaps me across the face. She tells me to stop being childish, even when I concede that I am merely a reincarnation. For a while now, I have played along with her delusions. *And I'm not stealing food*, I add, prying her fingers off my ear.

Yes, if they're going to execute me, she says, *I will at least be clean. The Communists shot your father with dirt still on his face. It must have been humiliating for him.*

No one's going to execute you, I say.

After I help her out of the bed, we walk over to her private bathroom. My back slouched over, I am supporting her with my arms wrapped around her waist. She is heavy and light, obese and emaciated, that elderly mix of mature flesh, weakened organs, and brittle bones, which I have always found awkward to hold up. Imagine carrying a hot air balloon as it's deflating, is how I describe it.

Last month, Ma Eng smacked Nurse Anna right in the face, and continued to smack her all over, forcing Nurse Anna into a crouched position on the floor. Nurse Anna was already pissed at Ma Eng for being a difficult patient, and only got more pissed when I translated the Khmer that she wailed and wailed during the beatdown. *Short and squat*, she repeated, *short and squat*. Nurse Anna kept sounding off about Room 34 having *assaulted* her. Management didn't want the union to intervene, so they transferred Nurse Anna to a corridor placement far away from Ma Eng. They also reduced her workload, and then asked me to cover the rooms unassigned from Nurse Anna's work reduction, including all aspects of Room 34's caretaking—the morning, afternoon, *and* evening shifts. Previously I was responsible for Ma Eng only in the mornings, but management could no longer risk assigning a non-Khmer-speaking nurse to Room 34. I would have these extra duties, they told me, until they hired another Cambodian nurse part time. I asked them if they wanted referrals to

Cambodian nurses I knew. They told me they would reach out when the funds became available.

Ma Eng's fat slips right over her bones after I undress her in the shower. I finally ask her who is short and squat in her life. *The whore who killed our family*, she says, and as I wash Ma Eng's sagging breasts, something clicks in my head.

I remember sitting in a living room surrounded by parents and grandparents. I was dressed in an oversize T-shirt, pajama pants decorated with monkeys, and a golden chain attached to a jade pendant. The grandparents had fed me plate after plate of white rice. *Tell us something about Somaly*, they chanted, drunk off Heinekens, as my stomach expanded with rice, making me sluggish and faint. Finally, as I dozed off, my mouth started moving, hissing words that never, really, belonged to me. A Ma heard *slut*. Someone else heard *whore*. A Gong grabbed me and sat me on his knee.

It all makes sense, he said, patting me on the head. *You did good, oun*. He turned to the crowd. He said that he now knew why Somaly's spirit was so restless inside my body; she sought revenge on her father's mistress. Before the Khmer Rouge took over, Somaly's mother, Ma Sor, he explained, had refused to let her husband's whore flee with the family. But Gong Sor, that hopeless old dog, he just couldn't leave his mistress behind. So no one fled and everyone suffered! A real tragedy.

That's nonsense, Ma Eng said, before asserting that the spirit of her niece, Somaly, wanted simply to be reunited with her daughter, Maly. She walked up to the Gong and picked me up. *Now let this child go to sleep*, Ma Eng said, handing me over to my mother, unaware of the nightmares that would plague my night.

Now it's time to wash Ma Eng's private parts. Following our patient protocols, I announce to her the next area my hand is headed. Jenny never thoroughly cleans her patients' genitalia, I know, almost to spite Nurse Anna's purism. "It's not like they're having sex," she jokes. I'm hardly the best nurse, but I work hard for Ma Eng. Inside room 34, I switch into overdrive, working with meticulous focus, even when I swear my limbs are getting pulled down extra hard by gravity.

Dragging my washcloth down her stomach, I wince at the idea that Ma Eng might think I'm attacking her. But, of course, she wouldn't, would she?—because I'm Somaly. My hand reaches its destination. Ma Eng stares right into my face. *If a Communist touches you here*, she says gravely, *don't fight. Fighting him off would be choosing death.* Afterward, when I am spraying her with the showerhead, I wish I could say that Ma Eng hasn't told me this already, so many times over.

Mom's sleeping on the couch, to the dinging and wooping of *Family Feud,* when I finally get home. On the kitchen table, some stir-fried tofu has congealed in a plastic bowl—probably left there for my dinner—but I dish out only cold rice so Mom can have tofu for tomorrow's lunch, so we can spend a little less on groceries, so Dad won't need yet another graveyard shift. Mom thinks I'm saving for my own house, where I'd raise the ten grandchildren she expects to pop out of me. She doesn't know I never want kids, that I put away most of my paychecks. Dementia runs on both sides of our family, Mom suffers from carpal tunnel because of her Amazon packaging center job, and Dad has diabetes. I refuse to watch their minds and bodies deteriorate into nothing. Mom would hate to know I intend to stick her in a nursing home, especially after hearing my stories about work, how nurses pin patients down, shove pills into their mouths, and then massage their gullets like ducks for the table. But that's why I save money. It'll be nice, her and Dad's place. All the rooms will have windows and the staff will actually care about their patients. They will give my parents proper baths.

Sitting at the kitchen table, I stare at my plate of plain rice. Since becoming Ma Eng's full-time nurse, I've had nightmares of Somaly, nightmares I haven't experienced since I was a kid. Most mornings I now wake up gasping for air. I know these nightmares aren't real, that they're only dreams, that they aren't based on fact or anyone's actual life. Still, I feel as though I'm being drowned by the past, by Somaly's memories, her torrent of unresolved emotions, which burrow deeper inside my body with my every restless night.

The dreams are horrible—Somaly working in the rice fields, pregnant and starving, her unborn child already lacking the nourishment it'll need; Somaly's water breaking in the darkest hour of the night and Ma Eng covering her mouth so the screams of labor won't carry over to the ears of the Khmer Rouge soldiers, then Somaly muffling her newborn's mouth so that nobody will catch the crying, cooing into its ears, *Sorry, sorry, sorry*. Some dreams *I'm*

Somaly, and pregnant with her daughter, Maly, my cousin and Ma Eng's other grandniece. It never makes sense, as Maly wasn't born until the late eighties. But the dreams strike me like real life, as I desperately try to protect the hungry fetus kicking the walls of my womb, this baby abandoned with me, this doomed daughter whose weight feels both too heavy to easily bear and too light to be any kind of healthy, or secure, or whole. I suffer the consequences of the indispensable rage that Somaly harbored toward her then husband—who actually did flee the country without his wife, even as she was pregnant with what would've been Maly's older sibling, had Somaly not miscarried. This rage surges through my veins, fueling my will to survive my hellish and haunted subconscious, and then, when I am awake and working, it continues to flare up in me, inducing migraines that color my sight with resentment. I don't blame Ma Eng for the return of these dreams, but I can't possibly endure them for much longer.

In other dreams, I'm watching Somaly as if I'm her reflection. On rare occasions—when I eat too much rice, maybe—Somaly and I will have a conversation at her old apartment on Greensboro Way, over a dinner of, yes, heaps of white rice. Usually these occasions involve Somaly telling my future, as if reading from a fortune cookie. But one dream, in particular, stays with me.

The dream unfolds: Somaly and I are sitting at a dinner table. She wears a white sampot covered in jewels perfectly matching her necklace. She's almost akin to an apsara in a painting—aggressively elegant, like at any second, she'll bend her hands backward to her wrists, and sway. I watch her raise the rice to her mouth, grain by grain, pinching each speck between her index finger and thumb. After a while, she stops and studies me, without focusing her eyes, as though I were a large expanse of nothing. *My daughter*, she finally says, *will inherit the golden chain hugging my neck*. I don't say it's the same necklace I wore as a kid, the one I was given to celebrate our connection.

It's been in my family for generations, she explains. *Maly's grandfather refused to let the Communists take his wealth. And that's why he died. Because everyone knew the Rice Factory King buried things. My father wanted too much. He wanted his wife and his mistress, his wealth. He died because he wanted, wanted, wanted. Let this chain remind Maly of that.*

I wake up right as Somaly removes the necklace and hands it over to me. In every reoccurring version of this same dream, I never find out what Somaly says next.

From the other room, I hear the opening credits to *Deal or No Deal*. I splash soy sauce onto my rice, as I'm too exhausted for dreams of Somaly. I know it won't work, but it's worth a try.

Sometimes in the morning, Ma Eng remembers that Somaly is dead. The sight of me shocks her into tears. She starts praying for me to bless her and her grandnephews and grandnieces, of whom I am one. Then she asks what I—or rather the ghost of Somaly—*want* from the living world, why I've appeared before her mortal eyes. In these moments, I see my resemblance to Somaly, to that woman in the few surviving photos. My reflection, in the wardrobe's mirror, zeroes in on my cheekbones, my dark hair both wavy and straight, how my eyebrows settle into an expression of blankness. Whenever Ma Eng sees me as dead, a ghost, I plead for her to take her medication without a fight. By the time the afternoon comes, Ma Eng will have reverted to hallucinations of war and genocide. Communists lurk behind the curtain. The plants by the window sprawl into "rice fields." Ma Eng waters those plants like she'll get beaten to death if she doesn't.

This morning, I don't know which I'd prefer—for Ma Eng to think I am Somaly as living or dead. A woman enslaved by Communists or a ghost haunting her Ming. But when I get to work, it doesn't matter. Right after I knock on Room 34's door, a man's voice answers, "Come in, goddamn it. Come *in*!"

I rush into the room to find Ma Eng's grandnephew, Ves, struggling to pull her up by the wrists, up from the floor. "Hurry and help me!" he shouts.

"*Stop*," I say, "you'll yank her arm from its socket!" Crouching, I grab on to Ma Eng, wrapping around her waist, and lift her to the bed, where she coils instantly into a fetal position. She doesn't look good. Her eyelids flutter. Her mouth stretches wider and wider, sounding out only silence.

"I glanced at my texts for a second and she fell to the ground," Ves says, pacing back and forth, hands on his head. Ignoring him, I raise Ma Eng's nightgown to examine the damage. I gently prod her flesh, and her entire body spasms. The wrinkles on her face become the ripples of agony, the echoes of her silent screaming. A pang of relief digs into my gut—uncontrollable and selfish and rotten—and I have to lean against the bed frame, my face nearly touching Ma Eng's. The thought of her dying spins violently in my head.

"What should we do?" Ves asks.

"We need to call 911," I say, then whisper, *Ming, I'm sorry*. I find myself rubbing Ma Eng's monkish buzzed head, which gives her the appearance of a giant ancient baby.

Ma Eng spends the following week in the hospital. Family members grace room 34 with belated senses of respect and pity: other Mas and Gongs who also barely recognize their own family; estranged Mings and Pous trying to recover their karma; annoyed teenagers who couldn't care less about their zombie of a Ma. They bring new blankets and pillows and packaged desserts Ma Eng shouldn't be eating. On the coffee table next to the window, they set up framed photos of her deceased husband and children who never made it to America. They burn incense to rid the premises of evil spirits. All this because the hospital doctors have informed us that Ma Eng's too old and broken to be cleared for an operation. Her hip has already been replaced, and new prosthetic implants won't fix much of anything. Ma Eng is returning to Saint Joseph's, to live out her last remaining days.

All week my nightmares as Somaly stay unbearable. Every night, I flee through the mine-encrusted forest. We are traveling as a group, a family, but half of us are dead. I clutch an infant Maly. My grip bruises her flesh and she cries and yells, but there's no other way to lock her in my arms as I am running as fast as I can to reach a border, any border, where we think we will find safety, where we will soon find only Thai soldiers at the Thai borders, with their rifles aimed at us, their voices screaming in a language not our own, which maybe Ma Eng understands because Ma Eng is also screaming, for us to stop, to turn back, to give up, as there's no hope, and yet I swear I see hope, so I keep running, Somaly keeps running, Maly pressed up against our chest, right up until we reach a bullet that was fired. And finally I am dead, so I wake up and go to work.

All week I think about Ma Eng dying. I think about joking with my coworkers and being myself, nothing more. I think about returning home from work at a reasonable time, for once, and seeing Dad before he leaves for his own shifts. I wonder how it'll feel to be rid of Somaly, to have complete ownership of my life, to move through the world without half my energy drained by memories not even mine, and then I fall asleep. I dream as Somaly dying, Somaly being ripped away from her infant.

All week I anticipate the inevitable—a confrontation with Maly, who will visit Ma Eng on her deathbed. Maly, the newborn in my nightmares. Maly, who has resented me since I was a kid, into and past her thirties. She has never understood that I have no desire to embody her mother's legacy, that I'd do anything to stop dreaming as Somaly.

Two days before Ma Eng's return, I have the same dream of Somaly and her necklace, except this time I wake up screaming. The parts I don't remember must truly be scary. It's a couple of hours before I need to start my day, so I decide to make breakfast, which I don't usually have time for. While I'm stirring instant oatmeal in a pot, Mom enters the kitchen and startles when she sees me.

"Don't do that to me!" she yells, sinking into a chair at the table.

"Want some?" I point at the pot, then at the coffee maker.

"I'm too tired to eat, it'll make me nauseous." She props her chin on her hand, as though her head will roll off her shoulders without the extra support. So I pour a cup of coffee and hand it to her. "Every night," she says, her eyes struggling to stay open, "your Ba wakes me up when he gets home. He's so inconsiderate, he can't open the door without banging around. Every night at four—*bang, bang, bang.*"

"Mai, you should eat," I say, taking a seat with my bowl. I spoon out some oatmeal and wave it in her face. She laughs, batting my hand away, before I find myself asking, "Do we have jewelry from the old days?"

She motions for me to wait, leaves the room, and returns with a small wooden box. Then she pours the contents onto the table—stones, earrings, tiny Buddhas, dust now flying everywhere—and suddenly I see it: Somaly's necklace. Picking it up, I feel its weight in my left hand. I use my right to drag the chain against the skin of my palm. It's thinner than in my dreams, less substantial. Slowly I fasten the chain around my neck, with hesitation, with unease.

"Ma Eng gave that to you when all those croaks thought you were some walking ghost." The tone of Mom's voice is the verbal equivalent of an eye roll. "But it still looks nice on you," she adds, and sips her coffee.

All day at work, I wonder if Maly thinks she deserves this necklace over me. That it's yet another thing, in the aftermath of her mother's suicide, ripped from her grasp. Is that the reason she started to hate me? Why she refused my existence the second I stopped crawling, once I was big enough to walk on my own? Maybe if I return this neck-lace to its rightful heir, I start to believe, my nightmares will cease and I'll be able to rest.

The morning Ma Eng comes back to Saint Joseph's, she embraces me for a long time as I am trying to change her nightgown. A bruise has settled across her left hip and reaches and fades onto her lower back. The green and pur-ple colors eat away at her flesh, and as we hug, I keep my hands hovering over her body. I can almost feel the radiat-ing heat of her pain. We rock back and forth, because Ma Eng can't stay upright without doing so.

I had a chance to escape, she whispers into my ear, *but I couldn't leave you with the Communists.*

I love you, I say, wondering if she'll recognize it—Somaly's necklace dangling over my scrubs.

When I finally dress Ma Eng and place her on the bed, I hear screaming outside in the hall. Ma Eng whacks me on the head. *Shut that girl up before someone worse notices her.* I step out of room 34 and see Maly a couple of doors down, a baby propped on her hip, a kid holding on to her legs. She's yelling at Jenny, who beams a look of complete indifference.

"There's a margin of risk and error that accompanies el-derly care," Jenny says flatly, reciting a line from the clip-board hanging in our staff locker room. "There's nothing else to say. You have our deepest gratitude for choosing our facilities."

"Everyone here's fucking horrible at their jobs!" Maly screams. "She's about to *die*!" The baby on her hip starts crying. "Look what you've done," Maly hisses through her teeth, before walking off to soothe her kid, down the hall to where I'm standing.

Dread floods my body, and I bolt back into room 34. The last thing I want is to feel the frustration, the frivolous torment, of being around a person who can't see past her own suffering. Ma Eng's already asleep on the bed, and I realize how stupid it is to hide in this room, but it's too late. Maly walks in with her baby. I haven't seen her in years, and I remember what I've heard—that she moved to the next town over, after she divorced her first husband and remarried.

She looks the same, despite the faint wrinkles around her mouth and eyes. Her cheekbones jut out, and I almost think they might cut her baby. She stares at me as though demons are squatting on my face. I try to meet her gaze, but I can only look at her forehead, which is shiny, broad, and wrinkle-free, despite the violent contortions of her eyebrows.

Ma Eng rolls onto her broken hip, and the pain startles her awake. She groans loudly, Maly rushing to her side. *Ma, are you okay?* she asks in Khmer, then glares at me. "How did you let this happen?"

I want to explain that, until I'd heard her yelling, I was in the process of strapping Ma Eng onto the bed, but there's no time for words. Quickly I rotate Ma Eng to her back, place pillows at her sides, and wrap the bed's belt around her waist. Her groaning gets louder, so I decide to hook

Ma Eng up to an IV of painkillers. I prepare the syringe to inject into her arm, while Maly stands over me, staring me down with a protective focus.

"What're you *doing* to her?" Maly says. "It was under your watch she broke her hip, right?"

"Bong," I begin, pausing to emphasize that I'm calling her *Bong* out of respect, "let me do my job." Without waiting for a response, I wipe Ma Eng's arm with a disinfectant wipe for the shot, and right as I'm piercing her skin with the needle, Maly's other kid walks into the room.

"Gross!" she yells before asking, "What's wrong with Ma?"

"Go outside and wait for mommy," Maly says, masking her frustration with tenderness.

Maly and I wait in silence, on opposite sides of bed, as Ma Eng's groaning diminishes into a whimpering. The air in the room swells with awkwardness. Once Ma Eng falls asleep, Maly bitterly says, "Can you leave me alone with my great-aunt?" and for a brief moment, I want to scream, *I'm the one who takes care of her.*

Outside room 34, I find Jenny and Maly's kid in the small waiting area across the door. They are drawing colorful flowers on a bunch of the medical pamphlets.

"I've met you before," Maly's kid says, looking up at me, her tone rising into uncertainty, a question. "Everyone calls me Sammy. Don't call me Sam."

"Yeah? Well, I'm your Ming," I say, kneeling down, already regretful that I've claimed that kinship. "Your drawings are pretty."

"I know, I'm *five*," she says rudely, and Jenny laughs.

"Maybe you should check on your mom," I say.

Sammy considers this, then gathers her drawings. She doesn't say goodbye before she goes into room 34.

Jenny and I retreat to the recreation room for coffee, because Jenny's on "herding the dying cows" duty, and because I won't risk another interaction with Maly. Sunlight glares off the tile floors in a distracting blaze. It's almost like the view from the window *doesn't* feature an overgrown patch of unincorporated land, which was, according to the rumors, where a local gang buried dead bodies for years. Rooms 39 through 43 are watching *Jeopardy!* on the TV, shouting all the wrong answers. Room 32, a Chinese man with huge bifocals, speed-walks across the room, back and forth, still training for a marathon he ran decades ago.

"It's like, I *get* it," Jenny says, a mug of black coffee in her hands. "Her relative's dying. But she doesn't have to be an asshole about it." She looks past me while speaking, at Room 37 and Room 38 and their game of checkers. Room 37 throws tantrums when he loses, and also when he wins, and so, Jenny has to monitor him closely. "Aren't you tired of people blaming us for their shitty decisions?" she continues. "*We* were not the ones who ditched their relatives."

"I'm just worried about my great-aunt," I say, and Somaly's rage begins to bang on my skull.

Jenny turns to look at me. "Fuck, I forgot."

"It's fine. She's old." I focus on Room 32, on his endless training. "And Maly," I add, "she has legitimate reasons."

"Serey, be real." Jenny places a hand on my shoulder, splashing coffee onto my scrubs. "It's not *okay* to come in here screaming."

"Yeah, I guess it isn't," I say, before I feel a total exhaustion, and just that.

The next week several visitors come to room 34, but Maly stays by Ma Eng's side more than any of them. From the hallway, I hear Maly recite stories from her childhood. How Ma Eng got so mad at her for sneaking out at night. How Ma Eng hated her high school boyfriends, complained about them constantly, while still always cooking them elaborate meals to bring home. How grateful she feels that Ma Eng raised her when no one else would.

Every night this week I dream I die in Somaly's body. My nightmares have rendered my sleep useless. My body aches, my shifts drag into endless tedium, my migraines pound at my head. I need the nightmares to stop, and I don't know what to do, other than to give Somaly's necklace to her daughter. This is what Somaly wants, I tell myself, almost delirious. Let Maly bear the burden of her mother.

Each day I start my shift with the intention of giving Maly the necklace. Each day I fail. When she addresses me, I can barely look her in the eyes. I don't want to give Maly the satisfaction. Don't want her to think I'm apologizing for my existence, that I'm submitting to her perspective, her conviction that I've wrongfully held on to the memory of her mother, that I'm an interloper of her inheritance. Out of spite, I find myself wanting to keep the necklace. And I know that, deep down, I don't care to act this stubborn, as stubborn as Maly herself, but sometimes I can't help it. Sometimes I wish I could refuse her version of our history the way she does mine, that this would be enough.

Some afternoons Maly's second husband will bring Sammy and their baby to visit Ma Eng. If Ves happens to be here, he'll accompany them to get ice cream across the street. "I don't know why Maly is *so* insistent on, like, having her kids witness Ma Eng's death," he says to me one day. "It's depressing."

"Guess she wants them to have a chance to know Ma Eng," I say curtly, so strung out that Ves's sudden interest in me seems normal. I am organizing a tray of pill cups for each patient in the wing. I squint at the tray and try to focus. For the sake of my own sanity, I need to maintain a firm grip on this corner of my world. I have no energy to spare if chaos were to erupt at work, like the time Nurse Kelly gave Room 32 the pills intended for Room 38. The entire staff had to chase Room 32 around the parking lot—his marathon training really has been working.

"Yeah, well, it's a little late for that," Ves says, biting into his dollar ice cream cone. "Now they'll just remember Ma Eng as broken and dying." He closes his eyes, cracks his neck, and takes a breath. Then he reenters Ma Eng's room, where Maly and her family stand over Ma Eng, like they're trying to calculate, from the steadiness of her breath, the exact time of her future death.

After the minor medical emergency that occurred when a Ming sneaked a Big Mac into room 34 and fed it to Ma Eng—who has lost the ability to digest solid food, despite Big Macs being her favorite American meal—Ma Eng ceased to retain consciousness, not even the deranged sort, except for when I give her a bath. The Big Mac, most likely, had nothing to do with the regressive turn of Ma Eng's health, but Maly still yelled at the Ming for twenty minutes. Technically, according to management, I have no obligation to keep washing Room 34. She's officially entered in the computer system as "dead," as Nurse Anna likes to keep on top of our data entry. Still, I feel obligated to keep giving Ma Eng baths. It's the only time I can spend with her without Maly breathing down my neck.

Today Ma Eng is calm, subdued, collapsed into the shower chair. *I'm dying*, she says, as I lather her hair with shampoo. Words escape me so I keep silent. *I'm going to die in this hell*, she continues. I check to see if she's crying or expressing remorse, but her stony face seems carved into time, and I feel dumb for thinking that Ma Eng feels anything other than boundless detachment.

I rinse the soap out of Ma Eng's hair, white suds trailing down her bruised back. *You're going to survive this*, I say. *You'll go to America and live another fifty years and only then will you die, surrounded by those who love you.*

I want you to kill me, Ma Eng says. *My kids are dead. I don't need to live like this.*

I'm not sure if she's speaking in the past or the present. Underneath my scrubs, Somaly's necklace feels cold against my bare chest.

Is there anything you want before you die? I ask.

I want to eat some of your father's rice. I want to taste something pure.

Let's get you some rice then.

I pat Ma Eng dry with a towel and dress her in a fresh nightgown, careful not to bring her any more pain. I figure that's why she's okay with death in the first place, to end the pain. Her arm around my shoulders, we slowly walk into the bedroom, where Maly and her daughter Sammy are waiting for us.

Now is the time, I think. Give Maly her mother's necklace before Ma Eng willfully kills herself, before she refuses to breathe like Room 35 did last month. Do it before Maly has to face the death of another mother.

From the other side of the hospital bed, Maly helps me lay Ma Eng down. Her black sweater adds to the severity of her features. Behind her mother, Sammy is drawing on pieces of paper at the coffee table. She's oblivious to the photographs of Ma Eng's dead husband and children.

A boulder of guilt clogs my throat. Guilt for meeting Maly's resentment with my own. Guilt for resisting the very thing that could help us both gain closure. I stare at Maly, our dying great-aunt stretched out between us. I can feel the pressure of tears swelling behind my eyes, but I am still too stubborn and proud to let go in front of Maly.

"What are you looking at?" Maly says to me, taking a step back from the bed. She places her hand on Sammy's indifferent head.

I try to tell her about the necklace, but my throat is still blocked by my guilt, and I can only manage to say, "Do you want some rice?"

Maly responds with a skeptical look. She crosses her arms as if guarding herself from my foolishness.

"Ma Eng does," I add. "White rice."

Just then a loud dinging goes off from inside her purse. "I have to take this," she says, checking her phone and then brushing past me. Behind her she slams the door, creating a slight draft through the room. It washes over me in a dull chill, our final chance of reconciliation disintegrating into the air.

Sammy replaces her mom at Ma Eng's side, carrying a stack of drawings. "Ma, I made you these," she says, and Ma Eng doesn't respond. "Maaaaaaaa," Sammy continues, yanking at the bedsheets.

"Don't pull," I say calmly, though I feel like yelling at her. I want to tear her drawings into scraps and banish her from the room. *Can't you see Ma is suffering?* I think of screaming, but instead I say, "Ma Eng needs to sleep."

She ignores me, and keeps yanking the bedsheets, which leads to Ma Eng's head slamming against Sammy's. Startled, she takes a few steps back, but Ma Eng stays frozen, eyes still shut, as though she has just died. Her mouth is wide open, a black hole sucking all its surroundings into the afterlife. I check her pulse, and even though the doctors have never cared to be optimistic with their diagnoses, even though my nursing career and management work and work to desensitize my soul, even though I just suspected her of dying a moment before, I am shocked to feel nothing within Ma Eng's wrist, only absence.

"She's dead," I whisper to myself, and the tears finally emerge and pour out of me. I feel endlessly sad, like a chunk of me has eroded away. I can barely breathe, I am crying so hard, but Sammy doesn't even notice. "Ma," I hear her saying, "this drawing is a dragon in her garden."

I half expect Ma Eng to yell, *Go back to work before*

the Communists come. Pretend the rice fields are your goddamn garden. But that's not what happens, of course. Sammy and her stupid drawings have no effect on Ma Eng's corpse. Now she's showing Ma Eng a purple dragon eating a rainbow.

I shut my eyes, the darkness comforting in its blankness, and when I open them again, the sight of Somaly's ghost appears before me. I'm not surprised to see her; I've lived with her so long. She stands behind Sammy, dressed the way she always does in my dreams, her dress a vision of white, pure white, and we lock eyes for what feels an eternity. Finally, she places her hand on Sammy's shoulder.

Staring at Somaly, I find myself clutching the necklace in my hand, and I know what I need to do. Undoing its clasp at the back of my neck, I walk over to Sammy's side of the bed and kneel down. "Let's give Ma some space," I say, as Somaly stares us down.

"But I have more drawings." Sammy holds up a portrait of Ma Eng riding the purple dragon. She fires a stubborn look, but it dissolves as I dangle the gold chain in front of her face, the jade pendant twirling, a planet, an entire world of its own, rotating on its axis.

"I have something for you," I say, and loop the chain around her neck. "It belonged to your other Ma."

"Thank you," she says, incredulous, before hugging me out of obligation.

Her hair sticking to my wet cheeks, I look out the window, straight through Somaly's transparent figure, at the burial ground for all those gang victims. It seems fitting that no matter where I look, I am facing what the dead have touched. "If your mom asks," I say, as she releases me from her embrace, "Ma Eng gave it to you."

Then I grab Sammy's shoulders and peer into her eyes. Maybe I am gripping her too hard, but I can't stop, I am trying to see if she knows Ma Eng is dead, if she can sense Somaly's ghost hovering above us, ready to inflict her with nightmares of our family's past. She's not fazed at all, and I wonder if she's just that comfortable around death, whether the force of my grasp does nothing to her new flesh. Maybe the younger you are, the more dying seems unexceptional. What's the difference between birth and death, anyway? Aren't they just the opening and closing of worlds?

"It looks nice on you," I say, pulling her into another hug.

Feeling the warmth of her little body, part of me wants to spare Sammy, to protect her from the history of her grandmother and her great-great aunt, from the ghosts of all our suffering. Part of me wants to throw the necklace into the Delta, let that heirloom be carried off by the murky, polluted water, right through California, through the Pacific, so that no one but me has to live this burden. Part of me wonders if the new generation should be allowed some freedom from the dreams of the dead. But I'm also tired and don't see any other path. I need the dreams to stop. For once, I will preserve the self I want.

GENERATIONAL DIFFERENCES

1989

Cleveland Elementary, Stockton

By now you've read the story of my life. You asked me to document my memories, and I've written down what you and my grandkids need to know. I was hesitant at first, I won't lie. Why would anyone want to relive *that*? But you were persistent, kept saying, "We can't let your history become lost in time," among other intimations that I'm too decrepit to avoid my own mortality, especially now that your Ba has died. So I relented. For months I culled my memory for gruesome details, the shrapnel of the past you want stowed away for future generations, but mostly for yourself, I suspect. And if you're reading this last section, you're now probably exhausted, defeated from those earlier pages about my time in the camps, my witnessing of all those deaths. My life isn't easy to digest. But forgive me for being your mother, because I am writing this section about you, my only son. Even if you already know the story, I want to explain one more thing, properly. A memory that has gnawed at me for years. This, you should also keep.

I remember with clear eyes, even in my old age, the first time *you* encountered tragedy. It was in August 2000, and we had just moved into our first real home. It would take a lifetime for your Ba and I to pay off the mortgage, but we were still ridiculously grateful, so much so that I was anxious to set up the house, quickly and efficiently, before the school year started. Remaining in that transitory state for too long, I thought, would leave our family forever adrift and uncertain, vulnerable to outside forces.

Naturally, though, unpacking was taking longer than I'd wanted. It was your Ba's fault. He had ordered you—and only you—to sort through the boxes peppering the clean white carpets, all crammed with worthless junk. He needs to learn to work, he told me, when I insisted on doing everything myself. To prepare boys for what the world will give them, that's what your Ba called nuanced parenting; in those days, he wanted desperately to be a good father. Our son's only nine years old, I told him, to no effect, and of course, a week later, you hadn't accomplished much of anything. Even when I scolded you to stop dilly-dallying, you bided your time by flipping through the family albums. I believe that was how you came across the photo of Michael Jackson visiting my ESL students.

"Mom, what's in this photo?" you asked, coming up from behind me in the kitchen. I was busy right then, chopping lemongrass and garlic to freeze in the plastic containers that reeked of kroeung, the knife heavy in my overworked hands, the grassy citrus burrowing deep into my nose and piercing my eyes. But you wouldn't stop bothering me for an answer.

"That's Michael Jackson," I said finally, my hands dotted with sticky yellow-green bits. "He's a musician that cared enough to visit us survivors."

Stepping back, you hesitated over your next words. "What do you mean, 'survivors'?"

"Nothing," I said, "I don't mean anything by it."

"Tell me what you mean!" you shouted, and kept shouting, your pleas clawing at my eardrums, your thirst for answers growing with each passing second.

I washed my hands and knelt down before you. Heat radiated off your trembling body. "What's wrong, oun?" I asked, placing my hand on your dampened forehead. You felt like a doughy space heater.

"Your hands stink like garlic and soap," you said, pushing my hands away. "That's worse than just garlic."

I smelled my fingers and laughed, because you were right.

"Why are you laughing?" you asked in a flurry. "I know what that word means. I'm not stupid."

"Sometimes I wish you *were*," I responded, rubbing my cold hands together. You were often hot, ready to burst, while my circulation had always been pathetic, as if the blood in my veins had exhausted itself long ago. It was part of our generational difference.

"Well, are you going to *tell* me?" You crossed your arms, straightened your back, which you often did to seem older, closer to the height of the other boys in your class. Something about the look in your eyes felt insurmountable and sad.

"Fine," I said, defeated, thinking about what your Ba would do. "If you really want to know, you can know."

We sat down at the kitchen table. Stacks of dishes and a sewing machine lay between us. I thought about that horrible day—the five kids shot dead, four of them Khmer, all around your age. Then the piercing gunshots and the heartbreaking screams, the chaos of three hundred bodies running in all directions, and then the thirty other kids wounded, decorated with bullet holes, experiencing pain no one should experience, let alone anyone *that* young, and then the blood pooling on the chalked-up concrete, the jungle gym and the monkey bars scarred by a massacre, and then, finally, the man dressed in army-green combat gear, who had shot sixty AK-47 loads into the playground before shooting himself in the head, all to defend his home, his dreams, against the threat of us, a horde of refugees, who had come here because we had no other dreams left. What other choice was there but to escape to this valley of dust and pollen and California smog? Where else was there to go in the aftermath of genocide? Then I asked myself, How am I supposed to tell you this? Where do I even start?

"Before you were born," I began, trying my hardest to look directly in your eyes, "a very sick man came to Cleveland Elementary . . . with a gun . . . and then he shot bullets into the playground." I took a deep breath, studied your face for a reaction, but you didn't give me one. "Some kids died," I continued, "many were injured. This was in 1989, so two years before you were born. That photo you're holding, it was taken because Michael Jackson came to pay his respects to the dead."

I finished speaking and we plunged into silence. I still don't know if it was good parenting to let you know about such events. But I can tell you it was intoxicating, strangely so, to unload a whole chunk of the past onto you, and this intoxication in turn made me feel ashamed, like I had gutted myself in front of my only son.

"What were you doing when it happened?" you finally asked. I could tell that your mind was spinning in circles, that you had a thousand other things to say but couldn't get them out.

"I was alone in my classroom," I said, "watching through the window."

"Mom, that's so *bad*!" you cried, lurching forward and slamming your hands onto the table. "You're never supposed to stand at a window during a shooting! I'm only in the third grade, and even *I* know that."

"*Control* yourself," I said, because I had no further explanation. Of course it was dumb. We lived in a city of gang violence, where campuses went into lockdown whenever a teenage boy dressed in red or blue walked down the street. There was no excuse for not forcing myself to move from the window, the view, to do anything but stand there and watch history bleed out over the playground. All this I knew very well, and I was annoyed to be reminded of that.

The photo was in your hands again, and you were staring at it intently. I remember wondering why exactly, in the first place, you were drawn to this image. Did it catch your eye because it was free of our unsmiling relatives? Was it the Khmer students in the background, the boredom and gloom stuck to their faces, the way their bodies tilted in those half-broken desks? Were you already resentful, as you would be later on in your life, that we'd moved away from the old neighborhood, from all those kids who looked exactly like you?

Or was it Michael Jackson himself? How his skin was simultaneously light and dark and see-through? How his jacket stuck out like a sore thumb in front of kids dressed in hand-me-downs, how it almost glowed, reducing the surrounding students' faces to a dull blue film? You have always been drawn to what couldn't be defined, especially what couldn't be defined by me. And if there was something I couldn't figure out, back then at least, it was Michael Jackson. Come to think of it, though, it was probably just my perm that you noticed in the photo. To this day, I can still feel the curly weight of that unnatural hair.

"Take me to your work," you demanded, and then started rambling. We had to investigate the premises of my classroom, you were saying, to make sure it was safe in case of future attacks. It was clear you had no idea what you'd hunt for once there, but I could also see a stubbornness in your face that would only fester if left unaddressed. I guess that's another part of our generational difference: you believe we deserve answers, that there is always some truth to be uncovered.

"Fine, let's go," I said, getting up to wash the residual garlic stench off my hands. I figured it was pointless to fight you on this, and I needed to prep my classroom, anyway. Before we left the house, I told you to seal the photo into its album, and then the album into the closet. At least one thing I wanted you to put away.

As I write this section, I can recall many instances when I have been worried about your attitude toward the world, about your acute sense of . . . awareness. But driving to Cleveland Elementary that afternoon might have been the first real occurrence of these worries. Other boys, you see, I can't imagine them being so disturbed by their mothers saying *survivors* in passing. A mere slip of the lips was enough to jar your imagination. A single word had sent your thoughts running wild in all directions.

I suppose I am to blame for how upset you got. I don't just mean my clumsy explanation of the photo. I raised you to care deeply, too much so. About words, for one thing. All those years spent working as a bilingual teacher's aide, undoing what Khmer children learned at home, perhaps it had made me paranoid. I thought I needed to ensure your fluency in English, in being American. The last thing I had wanted was for you to end up like your Ba—speaking broken English to angry customers, his life covered in the grease of cars belonging to men who were more American. So I read to you as much as I could, packed your room with dictionaries and encyclopedias, played movies in English constantly in the background, and spoke Khmer only in whispers, behind closed doors. No wonder mere words affected you so much. Even now, you still think language is the key to everything. And that's my fault—I thought the same thing.

Several cars were in the parking lot when we arrived at

Cleveland Elementary. It surprised me to see them there, a week before school would start up again. I knew other teachers needed to prep their classrooms, too, but you and I were just on a wholly different mission, and right then, the idea of talking to my coworkers made my face burn.

I turned the engine off and the radio cut into silence. Your light snoring filled the car's interior, along with the one-hundred-degree heat. You had fallen asleep during the thirty-minute drive, exhausted not from your own experiences, I suspect, but from mine. I reached back from the driver's seat and softly stroked your cheek. I didn't want to wake you, not yet.

After a few minutes, you yawned and stretched your arms out wide, as if trying to hold the world in your wingspan, or at least all of Cleveland Elementary. "I had a dream where I found Michael Jackson hiding in your classroom," you said, eyes barely open. "He was up to no good, so I scared him off with my karate moves." For a brief moment, as you punctuated your story with kicks in the air, our day seemed perfectly normal.

I looked at you sternly, pretending to be unamused. "Michael Jackson's a good person for coming to our school. Newspapers took notice of us after that. People gave us donations."

"Yeah, but why didn't he visit sooner, so that people could notice us *before*?" Defiance crept through your voice. "Then no one would've messed with us. We would've been important."

There was an air of truth to the sentiment, even if it sprang from your dream of combat with Michael Jackson;

still, I felt the responsibility to say, "Oun, that doesn't make sense."

"Come on!" you cried, now fully awake and unbuckling your seat. "I don't have all day!" So I followed you out of the car and through the parking lot. I allowed you to be our leader.

In my classroom, I sat at my desk, preparing worksheets of mildly useful English words. The stale dust of two months was settling into my lungs. You were on the floor, on your hands and knees, looking under the desks speckled with stale gum, under the crusty old rugs that were never properly vacuumed, which covered sticky floors never properly mopped. Every step in my classroom was a fight to get your shoes unstuck.

Using a system I didn't understand, you tested all the windows, tapping, knocking, and pressing your ears against the glass. After that, you thoroughly examined the cabinets for anything suspicious, opening each one quickly before you hopped back, assumed a fighting stance, and screamed, "Ah *hah*!" Then you thumbed through the books on the shelf, in case there were secret notes stuffed inside the pages, any clues as to the location of potential dangers. It would've been cute if I hadn't been so exhausted, my classroom a burning furnace, if this whole day hadn't been overtaken by a massacre I had tried to forget. A number of times I wanted to yell at you to be quiet, but I stopped myself. I wanted you to have closure. To forget these ugly feelings.

By the time you were flipping rugs over to examine the hidden patches of tile, I decided you were sufficiently engrossed in your antics to be left alone. And so, gathering a stack of papers I needed to copy and laminate, I told you I would be right back, and then left the room.

The sunlight pounded me in the face as I marched down the hall. I thought about how odd it was for California schools to be made up of detached buildings connected by outdoor halls. The sprawling landscape immediately outside made the school feel *too* integrated with the outer neighborhood, neither a real end to one nor a start to the other, all the borders just blurring together. Walking around, you felt that anything that happened at the school was happening in the streets was happening in people's very front yards. Maybe that was why, even before the shooting, I had never felt like I belonged on the campus.

When my copying was done, I stood outside my classroom and watched you from behind the windows. You were under the desks now, worming your way through a tight maze of tubular metal legs, your expression creased with lines of concentration. You were lost in your own world, and for a while, I admired your sense of purpose.

Then someone touched my shoulder, startling me from behind. I nearly dropped my copies. "Ravy!" this person exclaimed, and I turned around to see my younger coworker, Ruth, also carrying a bunch of papers. "I'm sorry. I didn't mean to scare you," she said. "How's your summer been?" Her blond hair appeared combative, as if forcing me to register its abundance. A broad smile widened across her face.

"It's been okay," I responded, briskly. After spending

two months away from school, I'd forgotten how to interact with someone like this, someone who wore flowery blouses and frilly skirts and had actually chosen, with every door open to her, to be a teacher. I gestured toward the windows. "I'm here with my son."

"How adorable!" She stepped closer and peered through the glass. "What's he *doing*?" she asked, her smile stretching to show more and more teeth.

It may have been her smile that disarmed me, or that I was too absorbed in my own thoughts, but right there, with both of us standing in that haunted playground, the truth spilled out of me, everything that had occurred between me and you. It was one of those moments when—after spending so much time in your own head—you forget that other people take up a different space from your own. Or perhaps I simply needed to confide in someone, anyone, about this unfortunate day.

"Oh, wow," she said, placing her hand on her chest. "That's so awful to have to *deal* with that—and at such a young age . . . and now he wants to protect you? It's just . . . heartbreaking. Really heartbreaking. I was only a kid then, but still, I remember exactly where I was when the shooting was announced on the news. My mom burst right into tears. You know, I still *think* about all those lost little lives." She looked up at the sky, at heaven, at a cosmic realm that was irrelevant to the parents of those children. No, the universe had already spit their children right back into the world that had destroyed them, reincarnated, reborn to live and die and live again, destined to an eternity of being exhausted, as everything, even the privilege of living, is exhausting when set on repeat. "All those beautiful little souls," she intoned.

Her gaze fixed on me now, and I could tell she wanted a response, like a student waiting for the teacher to identify an answer as right or wrong. It was a demand I received a lot, in fact, being the only Khmer teacher at a school teeming with Khmer youth. My expression was mined for validation a hundred times each day, and all the more so after the shooting.

So we stared at one another—Ruth's eyes searching for a sign of approval, with my own cutting straight into hers—until, from the corner of my sight, your head popped out of the classroom.

"Mom, can we *go* now?" you shouted, half your body still behind the door. "I think I'm ready." My coworker and I broke our gazes and focused our attention on you. The sun hit your face like a spotlight, made your skin look pale while also, somehow, exaggerating its brownness.

"Grab my purse and we can go," I yelled back, grateful for an excuse to end this interaction, to go home, to swap the overheating asphalt for the lingering scent of lemongrass and garlic. I turned toward my coworker, who was now, to my own disbelief, softly crying.

Completely thrown, I found myself taking a step back, even though I knew, logically, that there was nothing outright offensive about her behavior. If anything, she probably had a better heart in her than I did—why else would she be reacting this strongly, years after the shooting had taken place? Yet I felt insulted. I wanted her to stop filtering the world through her own tears. I almost slapped her for crying at the mere sight of you, for conflating you with the memories of dead children. But I only turned away. I felt cold, my hands frozen in the sauna of this late-August day, and, despite myself, as I scanned the playground, I started to laugh.

"How can you— What's so funny?" my coworker said, alarmed.

"It was the morning after Martin Luther King Jr. Day," I answered, not talking to her anymore, really. "We were supposed to teach the 'I Have a Dream' speech."

Then, before she could respond, you jumped through the classroom doorway and said, "Let's *go*!" as you pointed in the direction of the parking lot, waving my purse around. My coworker cried harder now, seeing you act like the genuine, impatient child you were, as she grappled with my total disregard for her tears. Unable to withstand her presence any longer, I left her there, without even saying goodbye.

Back in the car, you declared you felt better. We were safe now; what had happened had already happened, you muttered to yourself, as if humming a lullaby meant to soothe an infant to sleep, the expression on your face glazed over, coddled by the heat. Staring out of the car window, you seemed at peace, the liquor stores and fast food chains and patches of unused land whizzing by.

My attention began to drift then, as it often did while I drove, and I remembered how popular Michael Jackson songs had been when your Ba and I first came to California. They were the only American songs played at Khmer weddings, in between traditional songs salvaged from before the regime. "Man in the Mirror" was my favorite, but most Khmer people, including your Ba, loved "Thriller." Your Ba was so excited when I told him Michael Jackson would be visiting my very classroom. He kept reminding me to take photos. He didn't seem to care about anything else, had told me, the morning after the shooting, "Bad things happen all the time." Years later, he would refuse to watch the documentaries and news specials that accused Michael Jackson of atrocious crimes, and I would think of that same resigned condolence he had offered me.

I've never really told you about his visit, have I? It was in the afternoon, a bright winter day, the kind that made you think spring was around the corner, ready to slap February with blooming flowers and pollen. My students were reading chapter books in pairs, as neither they nor I had the energy for an actual lesson, before we heard thunderous choppers, the deafening drone of an engine, dust and debris being swept up and into the air. The more shell-shocked students burst into tears. I gathered my class and we headed outside, where the rest of the school awaited our famous visitor. When his helicopter landed on the concrete playground, countless security guards issued from the open doors, like solemn clowns from a tiny car, all of them intimidating in their sunglasses, their black suits imposing an air of restrained brutality. It made me furious to witness all this commotion, all this nonsense, on the very ground those children had died. Their blood was staining the pavement.

Michael Jackson was on campus, from his arrival to his

departure, for barely thirty minutes. "Hello, my dear little darlings, I'm so sad to have heard about your tragedy," he said to my kids, in my classroom, and I could not fathom how he had dared to call them *his* darlings. When I asked if he could answer student questions, he only offered, "Let's take a few pictures!"

A week after the visit, I got the photos developed and showed them to your Ba, who marveled at Michael Jackson's luxury brightness for about five minutes. Then, still mad, I threw the photos into the trash. All but the one you found, which I carefully placed into an album. As furious as I was, it felt wrong not to preserve at least one.

But I'm losing track of the story. By the time you learned about the shooting, I'd stopped feeling angry, stopped feeling much of anything, really, until you forced me to explain the whole affair.

"Man in the Mirror" had suddenly come to me as I drove back home from Cleveland Elementary. I found myself humming its tune, the chorus echoing in my head. *I even searched through the radio stations, in case the song happened to be playing.* Then I glanced at the rearview mirror and saw that you weren't okay at all. You were crying, almost choking from your tears and snot. "Mom!" you shouted in between heavy gasps, "answer me!" I had no idea you were trying to reach me. All the peace you had worked for at my school had fled the car.

One hand on the steering wheel, the other reaching back from the driver's seat, I recklessly tried to console you. I was handing you a bag of pretzels, a bottle of water, anything that might calm you down. The car swerved back and forth as I tried to stop those tears. You sounded like you were continuously reaching for air, a surface to emerge from. Your little spirit was shaken to the core.

"Look, a McDonald's!" I cried, but you were unmoved; still, it felt worth a try. Only after I'd pulled into the drive-through, bought an ice cream cone, and shoved it into your hands did you begin to calm down.

I parked the car behind the McDonald's, next to an abandoned gas station, and we bathed in the stench of used frying oil. From the rearview mirror, I watched your reflection as you devoured the melting mess, opaque white streaks dripping down your hands, the remedy to your crying already going to waste.

"Why were you ignoring me?" you asked, gravely.

"Was I?" I said. "Oh, oun, I'm so sorry—I'm sorry for ignoring you."

"But tell me *why*," you responded. "I was talking to you."

"All I can say is I'm sorry," I offered, as disappointment settled into your face.

You continued licking your ice cream in silence. Looking at your visibly sticky mouth, I thought about Michael Jackson again, the absurdity of his photo jolting our day into being, how the more he had tried to change, to reinvent himself into something completely new, the more he seemed horrifically burdened by what he used to be.

"I'll finish this later," you said, fitting the cone into the cup holder. I was too tired to tell you the ice cream would melt, that only a worthless puddle would be left. It was late, and we needed to get home. We had to finish unpacking.

Even now, so many decades later, I often return to that afternoon of ours, and then I look back on everything else that happened to us, and I think, how silly of me to see our pain as situated in time, confined to the past, contained within it. Don't take this the wrong way, but I should apologize to you, for refusing to be forthcoming into and through your adulthood; before your Ba's death, I was continually thrown, perhaps even upset, by your endless curiosity with the regime, the camps, the genocide. Every slight detail you would demand to know, as if understanding that part of my life would explain the entirety of yours. Through my frustration, my clenched teeth, I didn't have the words to say those years were never the sole explanation of anything; that I've always considered the genocide to be the source of all our problems and none of them. Writing this final section about Cleveland Elementary, your first tragedy—maybe that is my way of telling you.

As it happened, as the gunshots were fired, and our kids started crying and bleeding and dying, I stared out of my classroom window and finally understood the brother I never really knew. Why he had committed suicide years before Pol Pot, when no one saw strife on the horizon. How, for my brother, even as a teenager, a child, the weight of life was always too immense to bear.

Then, in a matter of minutes this time, it stopped. We counted the dead, the injured, those left over, and we grieved, as we had for the many lives before and since.

When you think about my history, I don't need you to see everything at once. I don't need you to recall the details of those tragedies that were dropped into my world.

Honestly, you don't even have to try. What is nuance in the face of all that we've experienced? But for me, your mother, just remember that, for better or worse, we can be described as survivors. Okay? Know that we've always kept on living. What else could we have done?

ACKNOWLEDGMENTS

There would be no book, no writing, no ability to tell a story, no sense at all of how the world can be, without my parents, Ravy and Sienghay So, who somehow clawed their way to a livable, beautiful life, who never thought to spare me from their stories, their history, who, instead, prepared me the best they could to seek growth, to not crumble under the pressure of everything bad and unjust. Thank you, Mom and Dad, for surviving, fighting, and creating a world out of nothing but your own wills, your imaginations. Thank you, Dad, for knowing how to tell a good joke, for working so hard all the time. Thank you, Mom, for being smarter, more philosophical, a better genius, than anyone I've ever read or encountered, including all those posturers I met at Stanford.

There would also be no book without Alex. Thank you for always wanting to talk and listen. Thank you for reading all my stories and telling me which ones were terrible.

Thank you for being hilarious, absurd, beautiful. Thank you for showing me that a queer Cambo from Stockton, California, could find a wealth of commonality with a queer half-Mexican kid from rural Illinois. I don't think I could've finished this book without knowing that. I love you. You wrote these stories with me.

My teachers all provided necessary support not only to the early drafts of this book but also to my development as a writer. Thank you, Dana Spiotta, for giving me the confidence to be critical of my work, for recommending the exact writers who helped me conceive of this book, and for being an inspiration—everyone should read *Stone Arabia*. Thank you, Jon Dee, for giving me the confidence to love my work, for teaching me how to read like a writer, for answering my manic emails, and for providing genius feedback on just so much of my writing. Thank you, Mary Karr, for giving me the confidence to believe in my work, for your insights on writing I still use for guidance, for volleying with me about literature, culture, the things that matter. Thank you, Chris Kennedy and Sarah Harwell, for our discussions about life, Will, death. Thank you, Arthur Flowers and George Saunders, for your critical eyes, and for being so transparent about what it takes to be a writer. Thank you, Mira Jacob, for critiquing several of these stories, and for teaching me how to locate the heat, the heart, of my writing. I am indebted to my Stanford teachers, too. Eavan Boland, Scott Hutchins, Blakey Vermuele, and Alexander Nemerov pointed me in the right direction. Allison Davis pulled my Levinthal application from a stack of privileged fucks and thought I had something true to say. I was so lost in college, and you helped save me.

My Syracuse family, thank you, especially Zeynep, who literally nursed me back to health once, who is an airtight vault of all my opinions that the world is not ready for yet. My Cambos—my cousins and Sam, my sister—thank you for making sure I got to college, for equipping me to navigate the system, for inspiring my characters. My best friends, Gaby and Sharon, thank you for never letting me be just a writer, for reminding me that I am more than that, for providing me a home when I needed it the most. My kindred spirit, Soo Ji, thank you for being my personal Princess Carolyn, for strategizing with me our livelihoods, and for gifting me the horror story of I—n B—ll, which inspired the opening of "Human Development."

I would be remiss if I didn't give shout-outs to those who pulled me out of the realm of the aspiring writer, to a place where I could sustainably thrive and have a career. The *n+1* team, especially Mark Krotov, took a chance on me, publishing "Superking Son Scores Again" and "The Monks," after I rolled into the offices with my cheap duffel bag one cold afternoon and talked nonsense for thirty minutes. *Granta* published "The Shop," the story I hold closest to my heart. *The New Yorker*, in particular Cressida Leyshon, published "Three Women of Chuck's Donuts" and gave me a master class in editing my work. *Zyzzyva* helped push "Generational Differences" to its final form by accepting to edit and publish, for Spring 2021, this story based off my mother's life. Sometimes, for absurd reasons pertaining to just staying alive, you need hard cash to write, to imagine worlds, and thus without the generous support of the PD Soros Fellowship for New Americans, and without Jolynn Parker and her guidance, this book would certainly be 30 percent worse, at least.

Finally, Helen Atsma fought for this book, in all its shades and tones, but still pressed on how it could be better, and for that I am so grateful. Rob McQuilkin read two stories of mine and knew that I could have a long career as a writer. He looked past what most readers saw in my work, and found its pulse, its soulful longing, the urgent questions it was trying to answer. He oversaw so many drafts, and was always open to my ideas, never once second-guessing my wild ambitions. And Will, dear god, I hope you're happy now, I really do. I feel so blessed I got the chance to know you when I could. This book is a love letter to you, to everyone I mentioned, to Stockton, to California, to my Khmer and Khmer American universe, and to the generations lost and living and upcoming.

Portions of this work were previously published in different form in the following publications:

"Three Women of Chuck's Donuts" originally appeared in the February 10, 2020, issue of *The New Yorker.*

"Superking Son Scores Again" originally appeared in Issue 31 of *n+1* and was the winner of the Joyce Carol Oates Award in Fiction.

"Maly, Maly, Maly" originally appeared in Issue 236 (Spring 2021) of *The Paris Review.*

"The Shop" was originally published online on January 13, 2020, in *Granta.*

"The Monks" was originally published online on July 13, 2018, in *n+1.*

"We Would've Been Princes!" was originally published in the Spring 2021 issue of *American Short Fiction.*

"Somaly Serey, Serey Somaly" was originally published in the Summer 2021 issue of *BOMB.*

"Generational Differences" was originally published in the Spring 2021 issue of *ZYZZYVA.*